Betrayal

ALSO BY VELVET

The Black Door
Seduction

Betrayal

A Black Door Novel

Velvet

ST. MARTIN'S GRIFFIN ≈ NEW YORK

Rom
Velvet

This is a work of fiction. All of the characters,
organizations, and events portrayed in this novel are either
products of the author's imagination or are
used fictitiously.

www.stmartins.com

Library of Congress Cataloging-in-Publication Data

Velvet.
    Betrayal : a black door novel / Velvet.—1st ed.
        p.   cm.
    ISBN-13: 978-0-312-37583-6
    ISBN-10: 0-312-37583-2
  1. United States. Supreme Court—Officials and employees—Fiction.
2. African Americans—Fiction.   3. Washington (D.C.)—Fiction.   I. Title
    PS3622.E555B48 2008
    813'.6—dc22   2008013015

10   9   8   7   6   5   4   3

To my partner in Creation—J. T. A.

We're going to make great movies together!

acknowledgments

Here we are once again at the end of another Black Door novel, and though my name is solely on the cover, *Betrayal* would not have been possible without the following people:

Sara Camilli, who's more than just an amazing agent, she's also a friend!

My editor, Monique Patterson, your comments are always right on point. I truly enjoy working with you and the rest of the St. Martin's Griffin team: Matthew Shear, John Murphy, Kia DuPree, and Katy Hershberger.

I'd also like to say thanks to the many publications, bookstores, book clubs, radio stations, and Web sites that have given me support, including Black Expressions, Urban Reviews, the National Book Club Conference, *Today's Black Woman*, Afrocentric Bookstore, Voices of America, Savionlife.com, and Ginger Lynn and Christy Canyon of Playboy Radio's *Night Calls*.

To my family, whom I love, love, love dearly, especially my Mom!

Without you guys, I wouldn't have made it this far. Thanks for propping me up when I couldn't stand on my own!

I have the most amazing friends in the world, some of whom I've known since we were hanging out back in the day, trying to be grown! And some of you are newly minted. All of you guys are the best! One call (or text) and you're there giving me your love, wisdom, and support. And I can't forget my writer dawgs: Ron Shipmon, Dywane Birch, Eric Jerome Dickey, and Risqué, who know exactly what life is like in the creative trenches!

And thank you to the readers who always want more, compelling me to explore the depths of my imagination!

Velvet

Betrayal

prologue

AS MUCH as Trey tried to remain professional, from time to time his libido got the best of him. As the owner of the Black Door, an erotic club catering to the sexual desires of women, he seemed to be hard on a regular basis. He had been a good boy lately, but tonight he was feeling extremely horny. He hadn't been laid in weeks. His girlfriend, Michele Richards, had relocated to Washington for professional reasons. In the beginning they saw each other every weekend; either he went to D.C. or she came to New York, but lately their passion had begun to wane. They were both busy with their respective careers, and unfortunately their love life suffered as a result. He tried to ignore the throbbing bulge in his jeans and concentrate on work, but was having a difficult time staying focused. Trey used every ounce of discipline he had to check the vendor invoices and write out the payments that he owed. He was signing his name to the bottom of the fifth check when the office phone rang.

"Trey Curtis speaking," he answered with an air of authority.

"Hey, sexy," whispered a seductive-sounding female voice on the other end.

Trey couldn't help but blush from the compliment. "Who's this?"

"Someone who's been wanting to fuck you for a long, long time."

His dick began to twitch as he listened to her confession. "Is that a fact?" he said nonchalantly.

"Yes, sexy, that's a fact. So . . . are you still drop-dead gorgeous?"

Trey chuckled at the overused line. "Well, I don't see any bodies lying on the ground, so I guess it's a matter of opinion," he said with a cocky assurance to his tone.

"Well, in my opinion, you're one of the finest men I've ever met, and I'd love to find out what makes you tick."

She still hadn't revealed her identity and now he was really intrigued. Obviously it was someone who knew him, but wanted to get to know him better. "Are you going to tell me your name now or after you find out what makes me tick?" he asked, toying with her.

"It's Lexi, Lexington Samuels. We met last year when I joined the club, and again at the grand opening of Hirschfield Multimedia Studios. I gave you my number that night; remember?"

Trey definitely remembered the beautiful Lexi. She was tall and lean with a nice rack. He flashed back to the night of the opening and remembered how Lexi's black, form-fitting dress hugged her slim hips and dipped low in the front, exposing just enough cleavage to entice any man. Her hair was cut close, and was highlighted to match her caramel complexion. "Yes, I remember." He smiled. Though she was supermodel gorgeous, he wasn't interested in pursuing her. His untimely affair with another member of the club was still fresh, and at the time his wounds had yet to heal.

"Well, since Muhammad didn't come to the mountain, the mountain has come to Muhammad," she said. "I'm downstairs."

"You're here at the Black Door?" he asked, slightly surprised. It had been a little over a year since his last indiscretion and thankfully his wounds had totally scabbed over. Hearing the sound of Lexi's sexy voice was piquing his interest. Besides, his girlfriend was safely away in another city, and what she didn't know wouldn't hurt.

"Yep. I'm calling from my cell phone. I got your office number from information. Why don't you come down and have a drink with me? I'm in the Leopard Lounge. I'll be the woman in the pink mask with silver rhinestones around the eyes."

"I don't think so," he said, trying to ignore his rising erection. He'd made a promise not to fuck around with the clients anymore, but the wicked voice in his left ear kept saying, *Why not? Michele will never know.*

"Aw, come on, sexy, don't be a spoilsport. It's just a drink, and if you're good, maybe I'll let you take me to one of the private booths in the back of the lounge so I can whisper nasty sexual positions in your ear." Lexi was a relentless temptress, saying all the right words, breaking down Trey's resolve. She had desired him from the first moment she laid eyes on him, and though it had taken her a year to have a conversation with him, she was still determined to win him over.

He looked at the invoices and checks on his desk and thought, *Fuck it, it's just a drink.* "Give me a few minutes and I'll be down."

After hanging up the phone, Trey crossed the office to his private bathroom. He changed from a white oxford shirt into his signature black wife beater, and kept on his bulge-hugging jeans. He opened one of the bureau drawers to his left, took out his black leather, onyx embellished mask and strapped it on. He abandoned the paperwork on his desk and headed out of the office.

The second floor of the Black Door was bathed in soothing indigo lighting. Trey strutted down the long hallway like a panther en route to slay his prey. As he made his way toward the Leopard Lounge, he caught sight of a statuesque woman wearing a red negligee and a familiar looking red mask. He squinted his eyes against the dim lighting, trying to get a better view. *No, it can't be her,* he thought.

The last time he'd seen that red patent-leather mask was when it concealed the face of Ariel Vaughn, his father's then fiancée, as he fucked her into another realm of ecstasy. At the time he had no clue that he was coveting his father's woman. Life could be cruel; just when he thought he had found "the one," she turned out to be someone else's "one." Trey had put Ariel out of his mind, not because he wanted to, but because he had to. She was now married to his father, and strictly off limits. He knew that "man law" totally forbade him from

looking at her lustfully anymore, but deep down inside, he still desired her, and he felt like a Judas every time those thoughts entered
his head.

The woman in red retreated into another chamber of the club,
and out of an animalistic instinct, he followed closely behind. When
he was within touching distance, he reached out and gently put his
hand on her shoulder. The moment she turned around to face him,
his heart caught in his throat. He opened his mouth to speak, but was
speechless. . . .

1

JUSTICE PRESTON Hendricks sat behind the masculine mahogany desk in his home office, perusing the mail. This task was normally left to his personal assistant, Michele Richards, but she was out of the office at the moment, so Preston decided to do the honors himself, since he had no other pressing matters to attend to. He picked up an invitation from the two-tiered in-box, and looked at the writing. Written in gold calligraphy across the front of the envelope was *Justice and Mrs. Preston Hendricks.* He touched the lettering and smiled as he read his name, not once but twice. He never tired of seeing and saying his official title. Preston had worked tirelessly throughout his career—from lowly associate, to respected law partner, to federal appeals judge—to achieve his lifelong dream of sitting on the Supreme Court. The dream began for him as a young man growing up in the turbulent civil rights era, watching helplessly on television as countless men, women, and children in the South were brutalized on a regular basis as they tried to demand the same rights as their Caucasian counterparts. It infuriated Preston as he read about the struggles of his people, who were being persecuted in order to have the right to vote, to attend integrated schools, to dine where they pleased, and to sip water out of a fountain that wasn't designated *colored*. He made a promise some forty years ago that one day he'd be in a position to affect the laws that governed not only his people, but the entire U. S. of A. However, that promise was nearly broken when Preston suffered a mild stroke during the prenomination process. The stroke threatened to ruin his chances of sitting on the Supreme Court, but with the help of his friend, Senator Oglesby, who used his considerable clout in the media as well as politics to keep Preston's medical records from becoming a negative sticking point, his vision was now a reality. Besides, his doctors assured him (and the senator), that aside from the short-term memory loss he was currently experiencing, he was as healthy as a thoroughbred. Preston had lost track of the last seventy-two hours prior to the stroke, but the doctor told him not to worry, that eventually his memory would return. Preston attributed the stroke to all the hard work he had been doing trying to secure the nomination. Now that he was confirmed, his schedule was considerably lighter. He didn't have to split his time between working as a judge in New York and flying off to Washington for an impromptu meeting with the senator. Though he kept his town house in Manhattan, he and his wife took up permanent residence in the nation's capital.

He reached for the silver-plated letter opener to his right, slid the blade into the top of the envelope, and sliced it open. He took out the invitation, read it, and then discarded it in his wastebasket. When Preston and his wife Ariel first arrived in Washington as newlyweds, Senator Oglesby and his wife, Angelica—who were well connected— made sure that the Hendrickses were included on every major guest list in town. And they attended functions almost every evening during their inaugural months. Now that their social standing was well established, Preston didn't feel the need to attend every party that they were invited to.

"I thought going through and disposing of the mail was my job," Michele said, walking into his office the moment the invitation landed in the trash.

Michele Richards had been working as Preston's personal assistant

for over a year, and was extremely loyal and efficient. He had hired
her to coordinate his Washington agenda before he won the nomination, and she had done a stellar job. Now that he was a justice, he was
grateful to have such a dedicated person on his team. He only wished
that Ariel shared his enthusiasm about Michele. From the first day
the two women met on a trip from New York to Washington, Ariel
had her doubts about the brazen young assistant. Michele's personality was extremely outgoing and friendly, and she often referred to
Preston by his first name instead of addressing him by his official
title, only fueling Ariel's suspicions. Initially, Ariel thought that
Michele had the hots for Preston, which he thought was totally absurd, since he was old enough to be the young woman's father. But
the age difference didn't stop Ariel's paranoia, so to quell her suspicions, he encouraged his son Trey to date Michele. Only then did
Ariel ease up on her accusations, but Preston could sense that his
wife still had an eyebrow raised when it came to Michele, because
whenever he mentioned his assistant's name, she would cringe slightly.

"Well, if you were here to do your job, I wouldn't have to do it for
you," he teased, looking up at her. Preston and Michele shared a
comfortable working relationship and joked easily with each other—
to the chagrin of his wife.

Michele took off her coat and folded it across the arm of the sofa
that was near the door. She wore a royal blue knit dress that clung to
her body like a second skin. Her midsection was cinched with a wide,
black leather belt, making her small waist seem even smaller. She was
fond of sheer, unconstructed bras that didn't restrict the movement of
her breasts, or repress her nipples. Since she was a full C cup, she
didn't need padded push-up bras for enhancement like some women.
As she made her way toward Preston's desk, her boobs bounced freely
with each step. Her raven hair was swept back in a long ponytail. Her
makeup was minimal, with just a touch of blush, mascara, and a
dusty rose lip gloss that complemented her copper-colored skin. If it
wasn't for the imprint of her thimble-sized nipples against the snug
knit fabric and the tight belt, her appearance would have been considered politically correct instead of enticingly provocative.

Michele reached into the trash, retrieved the invitation, and quickly read it. "You're *not* going to the cocktail party for Bill and Hillary?" she asked with a quizzical expression on her face.

"I would love to, but I have a previous engagement the same night, so I'll have to decline," he said, writing on a piece of paper in front of him.

"Where's the response card? It'll look bad if you don't at least send back the RSVP. You know, D.C. is all about protocol, and you don't want to be known as the justice who never responds," she said, talking to him as if she were the boss.

"The RSVP card is right here. I didn't throw it away," he said, putting his pen down and holding up the card. "I had no intention of not responding. Thank you very much," he said sarcastically.

Michele stepped closer and took the card out of his hand. "I'll make sure this goes into the outgoing mail today."

"Good. Can you also send an arrangement of flowers to Mrs. Oglesby? I spoke with Senator Oglesby earlier today, and he reminded me about the birthday dinner he's hosting at their home tomorrow night."

Robert Oglesby and Preston's friendship dated back to their college days at Georgetown Law, and they had remained close ever since. Even though there had been a few bumps in the road as of late, they were friends nonetheless.

"Sure, and I'll have the card signed *Happy Birthday, Love Preston and Ariel.*"

Before Preston could issue another task, the telephone rang. Michele reached over and picked up the receiver. "Justice Hendricks's office. Michele speaking. How may I assist you?"

"Well, hello, Michele. It's Laird Forester. How are you?" asked the man on the other end of the line.

"I'm fine, Congressman Forester, and yourself?" she asked out of politeness.

"Great, now that I'm speaking to you," he said, in a come-hither voice.

Michele ignored his tone, and said, "Hold on. I'll see if Justice

Hendricks is available." She depressed the hold button and asked Preston, "Do you want to speak to him?"

"Yes, but before you go, can you take the mail out of my in-box and sort through everything?"

"Sure, no problem," she said, scooping up the contents of the box.

Once Michele had left the room and closed the door behind her, Preston picked up the phone. "Hey there, Laird, what do you know good?"

"I know you have a good-looking assistant. I saw her today at lunch, and couldn't help but notice how delectable her knockers looked in that tight outfit. She must have been cold, because her nipples were firm and poking against the dress. I don't know how you work with her and not get a hard-on. If my assistant was as hot as yours, I'd have her taking dictation on her knees, if you know what I mean." He chuckled.

Laird Forester was a seasoned congressman, and a well-known figure on the Hill. Though he was in his mid-sixties, he was well preserved. He jogged five miles every morning and steered away from eating red meat. He didn't smoke and only drank socially. He still had a full head of blond hair, and even though the color came straight out of a bottle, it was the same shade of his youthful locks. The hair complemented his ice blue eyes. In his heyday, he had been called the "golden boy" and was on the radar of every woman in Washington. Laird did his fair share of sleeping around, but eventually got married, since it was expected of a politician. But marriage didn't stop him from keeping a mistress on the side. He exercised, ate well, and didn't abuse his body with toxins. His only vice was sex. He fucked—with the help of Viagra—like a teenager in heat.

"Come on, Laird, don't talk about my assistant like that. I realize that some of her outfits are inappropriate, which I intend to talk to her about, but she's still a professional and should be treated as such," he said sternly. Preston had been so preoccupied with his own agenda for the last few months that he hadn't addressed Michele's lack of discretion.

"Oh, come on, Preston, don't get so defensive. You know as well as I do that she's one hell of a sex kitten."

Laird had first spotted Michele at B. Smith's, one of Washington's premier restaurants, and was captivated by her curvaceous body. That night, she wore an emerald green silk blouse, which clung to her breasts like plastic wrap, and a pair of black slacks that hugged her round ass suggestively. Even though it was just pants and a blouse, she made the simple outfit look provocative and sexy. Laird had played it cool and didn't approach her that night, even though watching her from across the room made him salivate with lust. He was determined to find out who she was, so he used his resources and learned that she worked for Justice Hendricks. He knew Preston in passing, but didn't know him personally. Laird wasted no time befriending the new justice. Even though he had ulterior motives, he genuinely liked Preston and valued their new friendship.

"I don't view her in those terms. Besides, she is dating my son."

"Oh, I didn't know that. How long have they been dating?" he asked, eager to learn more about his future mistress.

"For over a year. It must be serious because Trey usually loves them and leaves them."

"I remember those days. Back in my youth, I had a girl for every day of the week. Oh yes, those were the good ole days," he said, with a lilt in his voice. "Now if I'm lucky, I have a new girl every few months, but I still fuck her brains out as often as I can. And once I've used and abused her body, I'm on to fresher meat." He chuckled slyly.

"Laird, you're such a hound dog," Preston said, shaking his head in disgust. He enjoyed sex, but it wasn't the first thought on his mind in the morning or the last thought on his mind in the evening.

"I'll take that as a compliment," he said, roaring with laughter.

"Well, I'm sure you didn't call to talk about your sexual exploits," Preston said, ready to change the subject. "Did you?"

Actually, Laird had called to hear Michele's sweet voice, but he wasn't about to tell Preston that. If Preston knew he was sizing up Michele as his next victim, he'd probably distance himself and stop taking his phone calls. "No, I didn't. I called to see if you're going to the Oglesbys' tomorrow night. My wife wants to know if you and Ariel will be there. She seems to have developed a fondness for your wife," he said, now sounding like the committed husband.

"Yes, we'll be there."

"Okay, see you guys tomorrow night. I've got to run into a meeting now," he said, ending the conversation.

Once Preston hung up, he scribbled a note on his calendar to talk to Michele about her attire. As much as he tried to ignore her appearance, he had to admit that most of her outfits were too sexy for the office, and needed to be toned down. He hated being the domineering boss and instituting a dress code, but now that his colleagues were taking notice of her alluring outfits, he realized that it was time to ask Michele to alter her appearance, since it was bringing negative attention to her. Now that he was a justice he had to maintain a respectful image, and Michele was a part of that image.

2

MICHELE METHODICALLY picked through the mail from Preston's in-box, taking out all the envelopes that appeared to be invitations and spreading them across her desk. Once they were arranged according to postmark, she sliced each one open with the tip of her razor-sharp letter opener, and read the contents. She was looking for the invitation to the Congressional Black Caucus annual awards dinner. The dinner honoring some of black America's Who's Who was the highlight of the caucus's four-day conference, and the hottest ticket in town. Michele could have easily bought a ticket since it was a fund-raiser, but she didn't want to be grouped with the masses. The gala was huge, with over three thousand in attendance. She knew that if she wasn't seated in the VIP area, she'd never get a chance to rub shoulders with some of the politically conscious entertainers who flew in from Hollywood every year to attend.

Preston, as the newly appointed justice, definitely qualified for special treatment, and Michele, being his assistant, wanted the same privileges. She knew that the invitation would be addressed to Preston and his wife, but somehow she'd figure out a way to ride in on their coattails. However, first she had to make sure that they were indeed going. Lately, Preston had been declining invitations right and left. Even if he said no to this dinner, Michele planned to mark the response card yes, and go in his place. This was one event that she didn't plan on missing. She'd worked too hard over the years to tweak her sexy image, and now that her body was perfect, she finally felt like an A-lister and wanted to be treated as such.

As a child, Michele had been the overweight ugly duckling of the family who lived in the shadow of her younger sister, Janet, a former beauty queen. Janet was taller, thinner, prettier, more stylish, and Michele always felt inferior to her sister. With diet and rigorous exercise, Michele finally lost weight, but it wasn't until she had moved away from the family and gone to college that she finally began to feel like her own person. Without the judgmental eyes of her parents comparing her to Janet, she was free to wear exactly what she wanted, and she wanted to stand out from the crowd and be the center of attention for once in her life. Luckily, Michele had inherited her mother's full C cup, which now she didn't have to hide underneath oversized sweatshirts. Throughout her four years of college, she hardly ever wore a bra, just T-shirts two sizes too small, which stretched across her chest like thin pieces of gauze. She loved the attention her breasts got. Every time she entered class, the entire male student body (and even some of the girls), would stare at her boobs. Even the professors had a hard time taking their eyes off of her threadbare T-shirts and nearly nude breasts, especially Professor Garret, her political science teacher.

One day after class, Michele had been summoned to the professor's office regarding her term paper. Walking into the office, Michele was nervous. She had gotten an *A* on the paper and was confused as to why the professor wanted to see her.

"Have a seat, Michele," the professor said, pointing to a worn-out brown leather couch.

Michele did as instructed. "Is there a problem with my paper?" she asked, sitting on the edge of the sofa.

"Yes and no," Professor Garret said, still standing. "It's almost too perfect. Where did you get your information on appellate courts?"

"My father is an appeals judge in New York, and helped me with most of the research," she said nervously.

The professor nodded. "Oh, I see."

Michele breathed a sigh of relief. "Is there anything else you needed, Professor?" she asked, ready to leave so that she wouldn't be late for her next class.

"Just one more thing. Where did you get that T-shirt? I had one just like it in college," the professor said, easing down on the couch next to her.

Since she had a wardrobe of various T-shirts, Michele looked down to remind herself which shirt she was wearing. "I got this one in Greenwich Village a few years ago."

The professor reached out and touched the picture on the front of her top. "Is that Malcolm or Martin?"

Michele was stunned. She couldn't believe that the professor was touching her chest. "Uh, uh . . ." she stammered, not knowing what to say.

Professor Garret ran her hand back and forth over Michele's nipples. "Hmm, I've been wanting to do this since the first day you walked into class with your boobs jiggling underneath your shirt," she said, licking her lips.

"Uh, I think I should go," Michele said, sounding like a timid child unsure of what to do.

"Wait a minute." She held on to Michele's arm with one hand. "I know it's inappropriate for a professor to come on to a student, but we're both consenting adults." She continued to rub Michele's boobs. "Have you ever been with a woman before?"

"No," Michele said quickly.

"Why not?"

" 'Cause I like men," she said, point-blank.

"I like men too. As a matter of fact, I'm engaged, but sometimes men can be a little rough and insensitive. Women know just how to touch other women. Doesn't this feel good?" she asked, now gently massaging both of Michele's breasts.

Michele didn't want to admit that it did indeed feel good. She had never even thought about sleeping with another woman. She had a boyfriend and enjoyed making love to him. Suddenly she felt conflicted. She wanted to get up and run, but was paralyzed by Professor Garret's touch.

"I take it that your silence means yes." When Michele still didn't say anything, Professor Garret slowly lifted Michele's top. She let out a slight whistle. "Girl, you got the prettiest boobs that I've ever seen," she said, looking at Michele's espresso-colored nipples and perfectly round youthful breasts that sat straight out at attention. She leaned over and slowly licked the smooth skin in between Michele's breasts. She then cupped her left boob and began sucking on her nipple like a thirsty kitten.

Michele's mind was screaming *stop*, but her body was responding *yes*. She slumped back on the sofa and let Professor Garret feast on her rack. She closed her eyes and gave in to the exhilarating sensation. The professor's mouth was soft and gentle, unlike her boyfriend's frenzied sucks.

Professor Garret then took her right hand and unbuttoned Michele's jeans. This girl was beyond delicious and she wanted to suck her young student's delicate flower. "Come on, honey, let me make you cum," she whispered.

Hearing the professor's voice bought Michele back to reality, and the reality was that her *female* professor was sucking her titties and getting ready to suck her clit. As nice as it felt, Michele pulled herself away. She wasn't gay or bisexual. She was all woman, and didn't want another chick sexing her up. Suddenly she felt ashamed and embarrassed that she let the professor go as far as she did. "Look, I'm not gay!" she blurted out.

"Neither am I," Professor Garret said, still holding on to Michele's tit. "I just thought that we could have a little fun, that's all," she said, smiling slyly.

Michele jumped up from the sofa and pulled her top down. "Professor Garret, I'm sorry, but I'm not gay," she repeated.

"You may not be gay, but you're a little tease. You strut into class with those too-tight T-shirts, knowing damn well that everyone can see your boobs through the thin cotton. Obviously, you wanted to be noticed, and now that I'm paying you some attention, you're scared," she said angrily.

"I'm sorry if I led you on, but I'm not into women. I promise I won't tell anyone what happened. Just let me go," she said, nearly pleading.

"I don't care if you do tell, because it'll be my word against yours. And I promise you'll lose. I've been with the university for years and my record is unblemished." She stood up from the couch. "If I were you, I'd start wearing a bra and stop parading around campus like a hooker. The next professor you entice might just take your pussy." She walked over to the door and snatched it open. "Now get the hell out of my office."

From that day on, Michele started wearing bras. She decided to compromise, and chose the thin mesh type instead of the padded ones. She never told anyone about the incident with Professor Garret, preferring to dismiss the lesbian encounter from her mind. The next day, she withdrew from the class, and never gave her experience with another woman a second thought.

MICHELE CONTINUED OPENING the mail until she found the invitation that she was looking for. Preston and Ariel were not only invited to the Congressional Black Caucus dinner, but also to the VIP cocktail reception preceding the dinner. She'd seen Preston toss one invitation away today, and wasn't about to chance him throwing away her opportunity to attend the caucus dinner. She marked yes on the response card without confirming the date with her boss. She then noted on her calendar to remind Preston about the affair. Even if he declined to go, she was assured a spot on the elite guest list. Well, it wouldn't exactly be her name on the list, but Michele didn't have a problem posing as Ariel for the night, as long as it got her into the party.

As Michele walked outside to the mailbox, she promised herself that one day soon she would be invited to these special events on her own merit. She was on the fringes of the in crowd, and knew that it was just a matter of time before she was embraced by the circle. All it took was allying herself with the right person, and she would be in with the mere snap of a finger. She still loved Trey, but he couldn't care less about attending some hoity-toity affair. He was happy in his world, and wasn't impressed by celebrities or politicians. Once, when Trey was visiting D.C., she invited him to a black-tie affair that her friend Fiona was having. He went, but didn't enjoy himself. All evening he kept whispering in her ear that everyone in the room was phony and only interested in talking about politics, real estate, the stock market, and how much money they made on each transaction. He began to get antsy, and started loosening his bow tie, which felt like a noose around his neck. He didn't like wearing a tux, and felt more comfortable in jeans and a T-shirt. Trey was down to earth, and didn't like pretentious people. Two hours into the party, he was ready to go, so he called a taxi and left her there in her glory. After that incident, Michele realized that if she was going to climb the social ladder, it would be alone, with no help from her boyfriend.

The phone rang, and she answered on the first ring. "Good afternoon, Justice Hendricks's office, Michele speaking. How may I assist you?"

"For starters, you can get your fine self up to New York, so I can tap that ass."

Michele blushed at his boldness. "Trey, you're so crazy."

"I'm not crazy, just horny." After the other night when he saw Lexi at the club, he realized that he needed to get laid soon, or else he was going to fuck someone other than his girlfriend. "Are you taking the train up this weekend?"

Michele wanted to see Trey as well, but there was a cocktail party she wanted to attend. "No, I won't be able to, I've got a lot of work to do," she lied. She didn't want to tell Trey about the party, since he would be full of criticism. "I'm horny too. Maybe I can come up one day during the week, and we can have a quickie."

"Now you're talking." Trey wasn't totally in love with Michele, but he was in love with the pussy.

"Okay, sweetie, I'll let you know which day will work for me," she said, before hanging up.

Michele and Trey had the best sex life, but the sheets were beginning to cool off, and now she realized that she wanted more out of life than just a good, hard dick. She wanted status. Something Trey couldn't care less about. *If only I could convince him that being a part of the in crowd isn't a bad thing, we'd be the perfect couple.* Michele knew it was a long shot, but it was a comforting thought nonetheless.

ARIEL RENEÉ Vaughn Hendricks should have been hard at work, but she was hardly working. She was a partner with Yates Gilcrest, one of the country's premier law firms. During the early years, Ariel worked herself ragged trying to make partner, and once that position was secure, she kept up the pace to maintain her reputation as a workhorse. After generating millions of dollars in billing for the firm, Ariel began to slow down, and felt entitled to a slacker day once in a while, and today was one of those days.

She had relocated to the firm's Washington office after she and Preston were married, but was finding it difficult to adjust to the slower pace of D.C. Having grown up in upper Manhattan, near the Bronx, she was a New Yorker through and through and thrived on the frenzied tempo of the city. She was not only homesick for the concrete jungle, she also missed her pseudo-family and best friend. Though Ariel wasn't raised in a traditional two-parent household, she longed for her foster mom Mrs. Grant's fried chicken, collard greens, macaroni and cheese, and warm hugs.

Mrs. Grant wasn't thrilled that her oldest foster child had moved out of the city, but she was delighted that Ariel had finally married her longtime boyfriend; maybe now she would find the happiness that had eluded her during childhood. Mrs. Grant had watched Ariel pine away for her birth mother, praying nightly that her mother would come and take her to her real home. But the woman never materialized, leaving the young girl feeling unwanted and insecure. As much as Mrs. Grant showered Ariel with love and affection, she could tell by the way the child would sulk around the house that she still felt a sense of abandonment. Now that she was married, Mrs. Grant hoped that Ariel and Preston would have children, so that Ariel would finally have a family of her own. Something she never had as a child.

Ariel picked up the phone and dialed her foster mother's number, but the line was busy. She shook her head out of frustration. For the life of her, she couldn't understand why Mrs. Grant never subscribed to call-waiting. Ariel sent her a sizable check every month, so she knew money wasn't the issue. Knowing how old-fashioned Mrs. Grant was, she assumed that the woman wanted to stay in the dark ages, and not be bothered with clicking over every time another call came through.

Ariel felt like chatting instead of working, so she dialed her best friend Meri. Meri Renick was a wealthy widow in her late forties who spent oodles of money trying to reclaim her youth. She had her face, boobs, and butt lifted. Then there was a tummy tuck, waist sculpturing, and liposuction to suck that stubborn fat from around her kneecaps. Once she was satisfied with her newly enhanced body, she spent another bundle entertaining men nearly half her age. Meri was a highly sexual being, and didn't mind paying for a firm dick, attached to a fine young stud.

"Daarling, how's life on the Hill?" Meri asked, greeting Ariel.

"It's *not* New York." She sighed. "I miss strolling down Madison Avenue and browsing in those scrumptious designer boutiques, and I miss our girlie lunches at your penthouse," she whined.

"I'm sure D.C. has some of the same stores. And you can always catch the Acela to New York anytime you want to enjoy Jacqués's double-whipped garlic mashed potatoes and homemade cheesecake,"

Meri said calmly, referring to her personal chef, who always made Ariel's favorite dishes. She could hear the disappointment in her friend's voice and didn't want to add to her stress by saying how much she missed having Ariel in town. Meri didn't have many girl-friends and cherished the time that they spent together.

"You're right. Georgetown does have some great shops, but like I said, it's not New York. Actually . . ." She hesitated a second. "I'm thinking about working in the Manhattan office next week. One of the partners has asked me to assist him on a case, and I need a dose of the city."

"You think that's wise?" Meri asked knowingly.

Ariel knew exactly what Meri was referring to, and had a ready answer. "It's been over a year. I think the coast is more than clear," she said, without skipping a beat.

"Suppose you run into *him* while you're alone?"

"It's highly unlikely that I'll bump into Trey."

Ariel and her stepson Preston III, aka Trey, had a sketchy past. Unbeknownst to her at the time, Trey was the owner of the Black Door, a private erotic club for women, where members and servers wore identity-concealing masks.

During one of her bouts with insecurity before she and Preston were engaged, Ariel had gone to the club disguised as Meri, a card-carrying member. Ariel's intention was to relieve some built-up sexual tension by enjoying a little eye candy. Preston had been preoccupied with his impending nomination and had put their love life on the back burner. Meri convinced her that going to the club just to look around was harmless. Ariel planned to watch the handsome studs who worked as servers, and nothing more, but when she spotted the hot muscular man in a black wife beater and tight jeans, she couldn't help but fantasize about him once she left the club. She wondered how his hands would feel around her waist, and how his tongue would feel inside of her mouth. This wondering prompted her to re-turn to the Black Door and seek him out. When she finally found her intended target on her second trip to the Black Door, they fucked like professionals. During their third tryst, Trey's mask fell off mid-stride.

Ariel took one look at his handsome face and to her horror, realized that she had been fucking Preston's only son. After that surreal night, which turned from pleasure to sheer disbelief, she never stepped foot inside of the Black Door again, but their affair didn't end there.

They fucked one last time at Trey's apartment, and the morning after, when Ariel was in the shower, the doorbell rang. To Trey's surprise, it was his father. He naturally assumed that his dad had found out about the affair, but Preston was there for a different reason. Senator Oglesby's investigator had questions regarding Trey's livelihood and Preston needed answers to satisfy the senator.

When Ariel stepped out of the bathroom and overheard Preston say that the nomination was *the* most important thing in his life, she was furious and felt totally rejected. She knew fucking Trey was wrong, but she wanted to hurt Preston like he had hurt her by being so neglectful. Trey tried to tell her that morning that they should end the affair, but she didn't want to hear those words at the time, and feel forsaken twice in the same day.

Trey called her a few days later to talk, and she invited him over to her apartment for dinner. When he got there, Ariel opened the door wearing a sexy, tissue-thin, black negligee. She wanted to start with dessert, but he had other plans. Trey told her that a relationship between them was impossible. She knew he was right but wasn't ready to let go yet. Preston had chosen his nomination over her, and now Trey was choosing to end their short-lived love affair. His decision made Ariel feel, once again, like the unwanted foster kid, whose mother abandoned her. The rejection was hard to swallow. To soothe her bruised ego, she tried one last attempt at seduction.

As Trey opened the door to leave, Ariel sauntered up to him with her boobs practically hanging out of the negligee, and planted a juicy, wet kiss on his full lips. She pressed her body into his and didn't stop grinding until she felt his manhood spring to life. Though Trey had no intention of fucking her again, he couldn't stop himself from tasting her luscious breasts—he was a man, after all. Before their final tryst proceeded any further, Michele, Trey's girlfriend, burst through the open door and caught him mid-suck. She had cleverly disguised herself as a delivery guy and snuck past the doorman. Once upstairs she shouted a few choice words before running away in shock. Trey wasted no time rushing after her, leaving Ariel standing in the doorway with nothing but her exposed boobs and wounded ego.

That was the last time Ariel had seen Trey behind closed doors. Of course she saw him *and* Michele at her wedding and reception. Apparently, they had made up and Trey brought her as his date, and all evening they were locked arm in arm, appearing to be the cozy couple.

"Why do you think it's highly unlikely that you'll see Trey while you're in New York?" Meri asked.

"Because I'm not planning on going back to the Black Door, and it's not like we socialize in the same circles. So, I think it's safe. And even if I did run into him, we're definitely not picking up where we left off. Trey made his choice perfectly clear when he chased after Michele that day, and left me standing in the doorway looking and feeling like a complete fool. Anyway, I've gotten over what happened between us, and so has Trey. He's come down to Washington a few times to see Michele, and trust me, there's no more chemistry between us," Ariel said, but failed to admit that she did feel a small tug at her heart when she saw his face. She preferred not to verbalize her feelings and give them life. Instead, she hid them deep inside, hoping that they would die once and for all.

"Well," Meri sighed, "it sounds like you've made up your mind."

"Yes, I have. I need to get out of this town for a while. Besides, I'm married to Trey's father, and wouldn't dare cross that line."

"You mean cross that line *again*," Meri said.

"Don't remind me. I prefer to forget about my past with Trey. Had I known he was Preston's son when we first met at the Black Door, I would have never slept with him. But I can't change what happened between us. All I can do is move on," she said, sounding spent.

"And how's that going?"

"How's what going?"

"How's it going with Preston? Has he shown any signs of regaining his memory?" Meri wanted to know.

The day Preston found out that his son owned the Black Door, he was extremely upset, since Trey's occupation threatened to ruin his chances of securing the nomination to the Supreme Court. Preston was in need of solace, so he rushed over to Ariel's apartment. He expected her to be comforting, but she was a drunken mess. Ariel tried to drown the pain of Trey's rejection in a few bottles of champagne, and when Preston entered her apartment, she was in rare form. The moment he mentioned Trey's name, she blurted out that she had fucked him at the Black Door. Ariel assumed that Michele had gone running to Preston with the truth about her and Trey and wasn't in the mood to defend herself, so she blatantly confessed.

Hearing the devastating news of Ariel's unforgivable betrayal coupled with Trey's deception was too much for Preston to bear in one day, and he collapsed on her living room floor from a mild stroke.

The stroke short-circuited his short-term memory, and when he recovered, he had no recollection of Ariel and Trey's affair. Ariel used his condition to her advantage and scheduled the wedding before his memory returned. She realized that marrying Preston was in her best interest. After all, he loved her unconditionally and she'd always been able to count on his love and unwavering support—a trait Trey never exhibited. It was only during the prenomination phase when Preston began to ignore her; before that, he was the perfect, doting boyfriend. Marrying Trey was totally out of the question, so Ariel married the next best thing. It wasn't like she didn't love Preston. The love they shared had grown more into a comforting type of love over the years, not the lustful desire that she felt for Trey. Ariel was smart enough to realize that what she and Preston shared would last a lifetime, so she walked down the aisle, said the vows, and committed herself to Preston for the rest of their lives.

"No, he hasn't shown any signs of regaining his memory, but the doctor said that eventually his memory is bound to return." She sighed.

"Have you given any thought to what you're going to do once that day comes?"

"That's all I've been able to think about, and I've found the perfect answer."

"And what's that?"

"I'm going to have a baby!" she said, with excitement in her voice.

"A baby?" Meri asked alarmingly. "Do you honestly think that Preston would want to have a child at his age?"

"Preston's only in his fifties and men have children well into their seventies. I mean, look at Larry King, he has two young boys. And Tony Randall had his first child in his seventies," she said, justifying her choice.

"Okay, point taken. But how is having a baby going to help you when Preston's memory returns?" Meri said, asking the two-hundred-million-dollar question.

"When that day comes, I think he'll be hard-pressed to kick me *and* his baby out on the street. I'm hoping he'll have forgiveness in his heart for the mother of his child, and pretend like my affair with Trey never happened." Ariel knew this was a long shot, but she was up against the clock, and desperate times called for desperate measures.

"Yes, Preston's too much of a gentleman to toss you both out," Meri said, trying to ease her friend's fears, even though she knew that was a real possibility.

Ariel sighed. "I surely hope you're right, but if he asked me to leave, I'd totally understand. It would take a big person to forgive a betrayal like that. I mean, how many women sleep with their prospective stepsons?"

"Daarling, don't beat yourself up too much. It's more common than you think," Meri said, trying to make light of the impossible situation.

"Thanks for the support, Meri. I really appreciate it. I'll give you a call once I finalize my New York plans," Ariel said, before hanging up.

After her conversation with Meri, Ariel sat at her desk, unable to concentrate on anything but Preston and his absentee memory. It was inevitable that one day in the very near future her husband would remember the dreaded morning of her confession. Ariel bowed her head and said a little prayer. "Lord, please help me to conceive a child soon. Also let Preston have compassion and forgiveness once he learns the truth about me and Trey."

"HOW MUCH longer are you going to be, honey?" Preston called out to Ariel from the bottom of the winding staircase. They were going to Angelica Oglesby's birthday party. Preston had been dressed and ready for nearly twenty minutes, but his wife, in true female fashion, was running nearly a half hour behind schedule.

"I'll be down in a few!" she yelled back.

Preston knew that *a few* could mean anything from five minutes to another thirty. "Okay," he said, practically to himself, barely loud enough for her to hear. He turned around and picked up the evening edition of the *Washington Post* from the Parsons table near the front door, and went into his office to wait for his wife to grace him with her presence.

"I thought the party started at seven o'clock," Michele said, looking at her watch. She was standing in front of Preston's desk, putting mail into his in-box.

"It does," he said, slightly annoyed, as he walked behind the desk and plopped down in the chair.

"You realize that it's a quarter after seven, and the senator's house is at least a fifteen-minute drive," she said, making a point of Ariel's tardiness. *If I were going, we would've left thirty minutes ago*, she thought. It irked Michele that Ariel seemed to care nothing about schmoozing with the bigwigs and their wives. Michele was trying desperately to get a foothold into the social scene, while Ariel took her lofty status for granted.

"Don't remind me," Preston said, flipping through the newspaper.

"Should I go out and tell the driver that you'll be another twenty minutes? Ariel should have started dressing earlier. She knows you hate to be late," she said, sounding just as irritated as Preston.

"Excuse me!" Ariel said, breezing into the room, holding a beautifully wrapped box decorated with a huge, ivory organza bow. She wore a magenta-colored cocktail dress with a moderate neckline and a triple strand of cultured pearls. Her shoulder-length hair was evenly cut and tucked behind her left ear. She gave Michele the evil eye. Ariel really wanted to give the girl a piece of her mind, but she refrained. She didn't want to get into an argument before going to the party, so she held her tongue.

Michele painted her face with a phony smile. "Hi, Ariel."

Ariel eyed Michele's blouse, which was so tight that the buttons across her chest were screaming *Help*. They were stressed to their limit and appeared as if they were ready to pop at any second. The way Michele dressed repulsed Ariel, and she wanted to reprimand her right then and there, but that wasn't her job. *I have to talk to Preston about this girl, and her inappropriate attire*, Ariel thought. "Hello, Michele," she said drily.

Preston glanced at his wife's sour expression. The aversion that she felt for Michele was registered all over her face. Preston quickly rose, walked toward Ariel, and relieved her of the gift. "Come on, honey; let's go. We're running late," he said, ushering her out of the room before snide comments began flying between the two women.

Once they were settled in the backseat of the Town Car, Ariel wasted no time verbally thrashing Preston's slutty assistant. "That girl has no shame," she said, shaking her head in disgust.

Preston had heard that line so many times from Ariel that it didn't faze him anymore. He wasn't in the mood to hear about Michele's poor taste in clothes, so he just nodded his head, hoping that she would drop the subject.

"Did you hear what I said?" Ariel asked, raising her voice slightly.

"Yes, I heard you, honey, and I'm going to talk to Michele about her office attire," he said, turning his face to the window and focusing on the passing scenery, praying that his wife would take the hint that he didn't want to get into another disagreement about Michele.

Shortly after Preston had hired Michele, Ariel became paranoid and began thinking that Michele was trying to seduce her man. Ariel's suspicions were solely based on Michele's provocative wardrobe, and how she paraded around the office in see-through blouses and skintight slacks. Preston did his best to assure Ariel that nothing was going on between them, but she wouldn't relent, and they argued on and off about Michele. The arguments didn't end until Preston's son Trey began dating the overly sexy assistant.

"When do you plan on talking to her?" she huffed.

He exhaled loudly. "Tomorrow."

"Well, it's about time. You should've had that conversation with her months ago. That girl has no shame," she repeated.

"You already said that. What do you want me to do? Fire her?" he asked, totally fed up.

Ariel's expression suddenly changed. That's the last thing she wanted. She, Trey, and Michele had made a pact to keep the truth of *the affair* hidden from Preston for as long as possible. The day after Michele found Trey feasting on Ariel's boobs, he whisked Michele away to the Cayman Islands for a romantic weekend. Trey used their relationship as leverage for her to keep quiet. Michele loved him so much that she agreed not to assist Preston in recalling the last forty-eight hours prior to his stroke. Part of the agreement hinged on Michele working for a Supreme Court justice. Ariel knew that the girl was a social climber and wouldn't do anything to jeopardize her position. She wanted to say, *Yes! Fire her immediately.* But she couldn't. If Michele lost her job, Ariel was certain that Michele would retaliate by telling Preston the ugly truth about her and Trey. "Of course not. I just want you to talk to her about proper business attire. Tell her that tight, see-through blouses are *not* on the list."

"Don't worry. I will," he said drily, ready to end the conversation.

They rode the rest of the way in silence. They were both preoccupied with their individual thoughts. Ariel was thinking about the impossible predicament she was in. Each new day brought with it the possibility of Preston's memory returning. And that thought scared her to death. She felt as if she were living in a house of cards, and with any slight movement, the entire structure would come crashing down without warning. And Preston was thinking about how he was going to broach the subject of Michele's inappropriate wardrobe to her without sounding like an old prude.

"We're here, Justice Hendricks," the driver said, breaking the uncomfortable silence between them. He got out, hurried around to the passenger side, and opened the door.

The Oglesbys lived right outside of D.C., in Arlington, Virginia. The neighborhood reeked of old money. The mansions on their block were valued in the seven figures, many with six-figure renovated coach houses in the back, which served as temporary housing for out-of-town guests. The luxury cars in the driveways punctuated the residents' wealth.

"Thanks, José," Preston said, before reaching inside and taking Ariel by the hand.

They walked up the winding redbrick walkway toward the front door, and Preston couldn't help but marvel at the opulence of the Oglesby home. He had been there a few times before, and with each visit, the historic-looking colonial house seemed grander. The landscaping of the front yard was precise, with perfectly shaped evergreens adorning the sides of the handsome door, and perennials strategically planted in all the right places. Preston rang the bell.

"Good evening, and welcome to Oglesby manor," said the uniformed butler, opening the door and waving them inside with a white-gloved hand.

The moment they stepped inside the marble foyer, Angelica approached them with warm hugs and air kisses. She wore a black, floor-length Michael Kors evening gown with her signature multi-carat diamond necklace—an exquisite anniversary gift from her husband.

"I'm so glad you two could make it tonight."

"Of course we'd be here to celebrate your birthday," Ariel said, giving her a tight hug in return. She genuinely liked Angelica. They had so much in common. They were both married to politicians, and they each harbored secrets from their husbands. "Happy birthday." She handed Angelica the gift. "This is for you."

"Thank you; what beautiful wrapping," she said, admiring the silver foil and organza ribbon. "Ted, can you put this with the other gifts?" she asked the butler.

"Yes, ma'am." He nodded, took the package out of her hands, and scurried away.

"Come on in. Robert's in there drinking and holding court." She chuckled and led the way into the living area where guests were sipping cocktails and noshing on gourmet hors d'oeuvres.

Ariel saw a few familiar faces, but really wasn't in the mood for idle chitchat. Most of the political wives didn't work a regular nine-to-five. They were consumed with their husbands' careers, and their jobs entailed planning elaborate dinners and swanky cocktail parties to keep their social status intact. Ariel didn't feel as if she had anything in common with these spa-pampered, event-planning women. She had a high-powered career of her own, and aside from their housewarming gathering, she hadn't planned a single soiree.

"I was just asking Laird if you guys were coming tonight," Leona Forester said, standing next to her husband. She leaned in and gave Ariel a friendly hug.

Ariel returned the hug. She admired Leona. Unlike most of the stay-at-home wives, Leona came from old money and was a politician in her own right. She came from a political family, much like Speaker of the House Nancy Pelosi. She entered law school the same time that her youngest son entered high school. Leona rose through the political ranks by running for alderwoman, then state representative, with plans on running for senator. Leona was a no-nonsense–type person who said exactly what was on her mind. She didn't have catty, gossipy ways like some of the wives, and Ariel appreciated that. "To be honest, I couldn't decide what to wear," Ariel whispered in Leona's ear.

"I know what you mean. If I wear this black cocktail dress one more time, Laird is going to cut it off of my back. He keeps trying to get me to throw it out. He thinks this dress is too old-fashioned, with the high neckline and boxy shape." Leona looked down at herself and chuckled. "Well, I guess he's right," she said, smoothing the front of the frock.

"Anytime you want to go shopping, let me know and I'll gladly tag along." Ariel smiled.

"Thanks, but no thanks. Shopping isn't my cup of tea. More than likely, I'll just turn on the computer and order a dress online; it's less time-consuming," she said matter-of-factly.

"Honey, you should take Ariel up on her offer," Laird said, after overhearing their conversation. He then leaned in and kissed Ariel on the cheek. "You look stunning," he said, quickly glancing down at her chest to sneak a peek of cleavage, but the neckline was too high for him to get any cheap thrills.

Ariel blushed from the slightly embarrassing comment. "Thanks."

"So, what's your take on Washington bloggers?" Leona asked Preston, gladly changing the topic.

"I haven't actually read any of the political blogs."

"Well, let me tell you, some of them can be quite vicious. During the Page scandal, there was a new discovery nearly every hour. How they can gather accurate information so fast is baffling," Leona said.

"The tips are probably coming from a leak within. I wouldn't be surprised if some of these bloggers actually work on the Hill," Preston commented.

"I'm sure you're right. Well, one thing is for sure, and that's we all better keep our noses clean unless we want to be crucified on the Web," Leona remarked.

Preston agreed, but Ariel didn't say a word. All she could think about was the day Preston regained his memory, and the possible scandal that it could cause. If one of those sleazy bloggers got wind of her affair, it could ruin Preston's reputation, and possibly force him into an early retirement.

Leona held up her empty glass. "I could use a refill. Where's the server?"

Ariel turned around to look for the waiter, but instead of seeing a white-gloved servant carrying a silver tray full of champagne, she saw an unwelcome figure gliding across the room. Coming toward them was Michele in her too-tight skirt and blouse. She wasn't invited to the party, and Ariel was shocked to see her there.

"Good evening." Michele smiled.

Everyone spoke except Ariel. Ariel was still in awe of Michele's boldness, and couldn't believe that she had the nerve to crash Angelica's birthday party. .

"Michele, what are you doing here? Is everything okay?" Preston asked, with concern in his voice.

"Excuse me for barging in, but this was messengered over from the chief justice," she said, handing Preston a large manila envelope. "I thought it might be important, so I drove it over, just in case it's something that can't wait until morning."

Preston took the envelope out of her hand. "Thanks, Michele."

Michele glanced at Ariel, and saw the daggers that she was shooting with her eyes. She could tell that Ariel wanted to toss her out of the party, but Michele also knew that Ariel couldn't say a word. Their secret pact to keep the truth from Preston was like money in the bank. Michele could cash in her bargaining chip anytime she felt like it, and tell Preston the truth. Ariel was aware of the power that Michele possessed, so she kept her mouth shut.

Now that Michele's job was done, Ariel wanted her to leave, but she just stood there as if waiting for someone to offer her a drink. Ariel thought that Preston would dismiss his assistant, but he didn't. Ariel was so mad that she could feel the vein in the middle of her forehead begin to pulsate. The vein was a dead giveaway that she was pissed, since it only sprouted out when she was angry.

The server approached them. "Would you care for a cocktail?" he asked Michele, since she was the only person in their group who didn't have a glass in hand.

"Thank you, don't mind if I do," she said, and reached for a flute of champagne. "Wow, this house looks even better inside," she commented, looking around the well-appointed living room.

"Yes, the view is indeed much better inside," Laird said, slyly glancing at Michele's boobs, but quickly averting his eyes so that his wife wouldn't catch him in the act.

"Will you please excuse me? I need to find the powder room." Ariel excused herself, and quickly walked away. She couldn't take another moment of standing in Michele's presence. The girl had crashed the party, and Ariel hated like hell that she was powerless to knock that brazen wench off of her perch. And what made matters worse, was that Michele knew that she had the upper hand. Ariel swore that the first order of business once Preston regained his memory, and the truth was out, would be to have Michele fired. She was almost tempted to tell Preston everything, just to get rid of the girl, but she knew that would be like cutting off her nose to spite her face. Ariel had to remain calm, and not let Michele push her buttons, which was easier said than done.

Once inside the powder room, she stood in front of the mirror, took a few deep breaths, and waited for the vein in the middle of her forehead to retreat. Once it was gone, and she felt calmer, Ariel swallowed the last of her champagne, put on a phony smile, and returned to the party, ready to endure an unpleasant evening with Michele.

When she returned to the group, another couple had joined them, and they were chatting with Michele like old friends. Ariel stood there for a few seconds before introductions were made.

"Oh, Ariel, I'd like you to meet my good friend Fiona and her husband Thompson Barelli. Thompson was recently appointed lead counsel for the Treasury," Michele said proudly, as if she served in the lofty position.

"Nice to meet you both." Ariel quickly sized them up. Thompson was tall with light skin—almost white. He was handsome in a Harry Belafonte type of way. Fiona was petite with a rich mocha complexion.

Her dark hair was cut short with precision, each layer lying in its place. She had a cute pug nose, and resembled a young Eartha Kitt. Fiona wore an ivory Chanel suit, with a small diamond broach on the lapel and a pair of matching studs. Her appearance was conservative, and tasteful. Ariel glanced at Michele's whorish getup, and couldn't believe the two women were friends. They were complete opposites. "So, how do you know Michele?"

"We've known each other since college. We were the only two black girls in fencing class, and immediately gravitated to each other, and . . ."

"And, we've been best friends ever since," Michele said, completing the sentence.

"Oh," Ariel said, still not getting the connection.

"Nice to meet you, Ariel, I'm sure we'll be seeing each other around." She then turned to Michele. "Can I talk to you for a minute?"

"Sure," Michele said, looping her arm into her friend's and walking off to the side.

Once they were out of earshot, Fiona said, "Girl, if looks could kill, you'd be dead."

"What do you mean?"

"I saw the way Ariel was eyeballing you."

"That bitch is just jealous, because I got a body, and ain't afraid to show it off," Michele said, sucking her teeth.

"Girl, you have always been bold with your outfits. Remember those tight T-shirts you used to wear back in the day? You had every boy, and even some of the professors drooling. But . . ." she trailed off her sentence, trying to find the right words. "Now, don't take this the wrong way, but you should probably tone down your look now that you're in Washington with these tight-ass politicians."

Michele's expression changed. Her smile instantly faded. "What do you mean? Tone down my look?"

"Don't get offended." Fiona rubbed her arm. "It's just that nobody will take you seriously walking around with your boobs on display."

"Look," she raised her voice slightly, "I can't help it if my nipples stay hard," she said, rolling her eyes.

"Calm down, Michele. You know I love you, and I'm only saying this out of concern. You told me that you want to be included on the A-list. Well, first you have to dress the part. How do you think I snagged Thompson? I dress like his little trophy wife in public, but in the bedroom, I let it all hang out. Look, you can do what you want. It's just a word to the wise, that's all."

Michele didn't like being reprimanded about her style of dress. It reminded her of the professor who had tried to seduce her, and when she refused the teacher, the woman told her to stop wearing those provocative shirts. Hell, she couldn't help it if she was blessed with natural assets. Michele weighed Fiona's words, and had to admit that she made a good point. She desperately wanted to be included in the in crowd, and if changing her wardrobe was a criterion, then she would consider it. But, if she chose to wear more conservative clothes, it would be her decision. Nobody was going to force her to conform.

"SO, WHAT did you think of Michele's friends?" Ariel asked. She and Preston were home from the party, getting ready for bed. She was still baffled about the connection between Fiona—someone so poised and refined—and Michele, the total opposite.

"I've seen Thompson on the Hill, but I've never had the opportunity to talk to him until tonight. He appears to be a stand-up type of guy," Preston said, removing his tie.

Ariel didn't give two cents about Thompson. She was more interested in his wife. "What about Fiona? She doesn't really seem like someone who would be friends with Michele. Does she?"

"Well, I really hadn't given it much thought."

Ariel was sitting at the vanity table taking off her makeup. She twisted her mouth in a frustrated gesture. Her back was to him, so he didn't see her face. At times men could be so clueless when it came to women. On the other hand, if they were sizing up another man for a networking opportunity, they were completely in tune. "What I mean is that Michele is so . . . how should I say? Rough around the edges. And Fiona seems as though she spent her formative years in charm school," Ariel said, wiping mascara from her lashes with a cotton ball.

Preston hunched his shoulders. "I guess," he said, sounding as if he couldn't care less.

Ariel realized that she wasn't going to get much feedback from Preston, so she decided to drop the subject. Besides, she had more pressing matters on her mind. She needed to put her pregnancy plan into motion sooner rather than later. She finished removing her makeup, and then went into the bathroom to take a quick shower. Ten minutes later, she reemerged wearing only a terry cloth towel. She sauntered over to the bed where Preston was laying on his back with his hands underneath his head and his eyes closed. He wasn't snoring, so she didn't know if he was asleep or just resting his eyes. She sat on the edge of the bed, and ran her hand over his chest. He wore a pair of cotton pajamas, so she couldn't feel his bare chest. She leaned in and whispered in his ear, "The champagne from the party tonight has me feeling a little frisky. What about you?"

"Actually, it's making me sleepy," he said, with his eyes still closed.

Ariel could tell from his relaxed position that he was ready to call it a night, but she had other plans. She began unbuttoning his pajama top. "Not too sleepy for a little roll in the sack with your wife?"

"Honey, I would love nothing more, but I'm exhausted," he said, yawning.

Tonight, Ariel wasn't taking *no* for an answer. Once his shirt was completely unbuttoned, she kissed his right nipple. She knew one of Preston's tender spots were his breasts, so she went to work sucking and licking until his tiny nodule of a nipple firmed up. She then ran her hand down to his crotch. His member was only semierect. Ariel unsnapped the closure of his pajama pants, and flipped out his cock. She quickly covered it with her mouth, before he could object. Ariel took in his entire shaft, and began sucking as if her life depended on it. In a sense it did.

"Oh honey, that feels so good," Preston moaned.

While still sucking him, Ariel took one hand and unfastened the knot in her towel, and let it fall to the floor. She started to straddle him. Ariel wanted to ride the soul pole, but he stopped her before she was in jockey position.

"Do you have your diaphragm in?" he asked.

"Of course. I put it in while I was in the bathroom," she lied. Ariel hadn't given the birth control device any thought. That was the last thing on her mind. While she was taking a shower, she had counted back to the first day of her last period, and realized that at this very moment she could be ovulating. There was a fifty-fifty chance that tonight their love child—her saving grace—would be conceived, so she aggressively straddled him, and didn't stop until her pussy was on top of his rising erection.

Preston gripped his shaft, and guided it into her ready orifice. Once inside, he held on to her hips and began fucking her with abandon.

"Cum for me, honey," Ariel panted. She wanted his seed inside of her.

Out of nowhere, Preston began to feel disconnected from his wife. He couldn't pinpoint it, but there was something in his subconscious that made him want to withdraw. He suddenly stopped fucking her back, and rolled them both over to their sides.

"Why'd you stop?" Ariel asked, totally frustrated. She wanted his baby more than anything in the world, but he wasn't cooperating, and she didn't know why.

"I'm tired," he said, in a deadpan tone.

"Oh honey, come on. We were almost there. Don't you want me?" She leaned in and licked his ear, trying to entice him.

Preston couldn't shake the feeling that something wasn't right. He trusted his wife and knew that she would never cheat on him, but still there was that lingering doubt in the back of his mind that made him question her fidelity. "I do want you. Just give me a minute. I think the champagne has gone to my head," he said, trying to explain his unexpected change of heart.

As he spooned her, Ariel could feel his dick going limp. It went from a full-blown hard-on, to a semierect cock, to a wet noodle. *Damn,* she said to herself. As much as she wanted to make a baby, tonight obviously wasn't the night. She lay beside him, but didn't go directly to sleep. All she could think about was her ovulation date the

following month. Now that she had a game plan, she had to put it
into action. She realized that her entire future depended on whether
or not she got pregnant. And if she had to rape Preston in the middle
of the night, she would. Ariel was determined to have his baby!

6

"DO YOU think that Thompson can get me into the black-tie reception?" Michele asked. She and Fiona were having breakfast at the Four Seasons. Though she had a backup plan to get into the Congressional Black Caucus affair, she would feel more secure if her name were actually on the list.

"I don't know. I'll ask him. Sometimes he can be such a tight-ass, and not want to ask for favors," Fiona said, taking a sip of coffee.

"Well, let me know as soon as possible, since the party is day after tomorrow."

"Don't worry. I'm sure he'll come through. So . . ." She looked over her cup. "What are you going to wear?" Fiona knew that was a touchy subject, so she was treading lightly.

"I don't know yet. It's between the red Cavalli that I just bought, or the pink Michael Kors," she said, taking a bite of her egg white omelet.

Fiona wanted to cringe. Both colors were much too loud to be discreet. She loved her friend dearly, and didn't want to offend her, but Michele needed a "dress for success" lesson or two. Obviously, their talk at Angelica's party had gone into one ear and out of the other. "Don't you have a black gown?" she asked, trying to be subtle.

"No. Those are the only two evening gowns I have. I'm leaning toward the red one, it's really hot."

Fiona's suggestion sailed right over Michele's head—either she purposefully refused to take the hint, or she really didn't understand that red and pink were colors befitting a creative black-tie affair, which this wasn't. "Oh," was all Fiona said. She didn't want to browbeat Michele about her overtly sexy wardrobe. Michele was a grown woman, and if she chose to display her assets for the world to see, then that was her choice, so Fiona just let it drop. "How's that fine man of yours?" she asked, changing the subject.

"He's good. As a matter of fact, I'm taking the train to New York today to see him. We're a little past due," she said, winking. "If you know what I mean."

A broad smiled spread across Fiona's face. "Chile, I know exactly what you mean. Last night after the party, I showed Thompson what a freak in the sheets I can be. I rocked his world so tough, that he overslept this morning."

"I know that's right. Way to handle your business, girl."

"I've got to handle it, to make sure no other woman creeps in. I truly believe that if you're satisfying your man in bed on a regular basis the way he likes it, then he'll be hard-pressed to stray." Fiona may have been prim and proper in public, but she was a straight-up whore in bed. She granted her husband's every request, from anal sex, to oral, to golden showers. She was determined to remain the first wife, and if being fucked in the ass and peeing on her husband would assure her position, then she wasn't opposed to the freak-fest.

"I heard that."

"So, when is Trey going to make an honest woman out of you? You guys have been dating long enough to take the relationship to the next level," Fiona asked, point-blank.

"I don't know, and the way Trey has been acting lately, I really don't care," Michele said cavalierly.

"What do you mean by that?"

"Well, you saw how he was at your last party. He was so uncomfortable, like being at a black-tie affair was the last place on earth he wanted to be. Don't get me wrong, I care about Trey, and may even love him, but I'm starting to wonder if he's the one for me. When I first met him, he was all that I could think about. He's handsome, successful, and can lay some serious pipe, but..." Her words trailed off, as if she were thinking.

"But what?"

"I want someone who desires to be in the limelight as much as I do, and Trey could give a rat's ass about schmoozing with the movers and shakers. I'm beginning to think that we jumped into a relationship too soon, before we got to know each other. I like the political scene here in Washington, but Trey has no desire to move to D.C. Even though we're in a committed relationship, how long do you think it's going to last living in two different cities? Besides, I don't have a ring on my finger, and until I do, as far as I'm concerned I'm a free agent."

"I guess you have a point. But what if he feels the same way, and cheats on you? How would you feel?" Fiona asked, throwing the question back at Michele.

"And who's to say that he's not already cheating? I'm here in Washington, and he's in New York, so who knows what he's doing." She shrugged her shoulders. "I'm a realist, and I know that if a man gets a whiff of some other pussy, then chances are that he's going to do more than sniff. I don't disillusion myself and think that Trey is being a Boy Scout. Truth be told, if I found the right man here, who was well connected, I'd give Trey his walking papers; that's why you have to get me into that VIP party tomorrow night."

"Isn't that a little harsh? I can't believe you'd drop Trey just like that. I remember when you met him, you were in la-la land, and thought the sun rose and set on him."

Michele took another bite of her omelet. "It's not being harsh. It's called being real. If he was really into me, he would have proposed months ago. I'm just reading the writing on the wall. Trey seems satisfied with the way things are. We see each other maybe twice a month, sometimes not even that much, and I'm beginning to think that he likes this arrangement just the way it is. Well, I want more. I want to be married." She put her fork down. "And not only married, but married to a man who's going places. Not that Trey isn't successful, but he's content with running his club, and staying in New York. Even if he agreed to spend two weeks out of the month in D.C. and schmooze once in a while, I could deal with that."

Fiona was taken aback. This was the first time she had heard Michele's true feelings. "Wow, sounds like you've given this a lot of thought."

"That's all I've been able to think about. I'm not getting any younger, and I don't plan on wasting my prime years in a one-sided relationship. When I see him today, I'm going to ask him point-blank where we stand. We've been together over a year, and I think it's time we've had that conversation. And you know how men are, if a woman doesn't broach the subject of taking the relationship to the next level, then chances are it'll never happen."

"Well, I guess you have a point. Why waste your time if he's not serious? Three months after I started dating Thompson, I told him straight-out that I wanted to be married and have a family. I took my chances, knowing that he could have said, 'Okay, see ya,' but he didn't. You're right. Most men will avoid marriage for as long as possible, as if it's a one-way ticket to Alcatraz."

They clicked coffee cups, and laughed. Even though the comment was humorous, it rang true nonetheless. Once breakfast was over, Fiona dropped Michele off at the train station. The Acela from Washington to New York was express, with few stops in between. Michele thought that she would have a chance to delve deep into her novel, but by the time they pulled into Penn Station, she had only gotten through ten chapters. She caught a taxi up to Trey's apartment. During the ride, she silently rehearsed her lines. Michele wanted to know exactly where their relationship was going, and if it was stalled, then that was all right too.

Once the taxi pulled in front of his building, she paid the driver and got out. The doorman was expecting her, so she went straight up to his apartment. Michele's plan was to have a conversation before they hopped into bed, but the moment she walked in the door, Trey engulfed her in a bear hug and gave her kisses on the neck.

"Hey you," he said, kissing her forehead.

"Hey yourself," she said, taking a half step back. She wanted to say "Wait, let's talk," but Trey was shirtless and his muscular pecs and smooth chest made her mouth water. He looked like he was sculpted out of chocolate and she wanted to take a bite. *The conversation can wait,* she thought. Michele ran her hand up and down his chest, stopping at his right nipple. She circled it with her index finger, before planting her mouth on the small black button. She sucked ever so gently, and then trailed her tongue to the other side.

"I thought sucking breasts was my job," Trey breathed.

"Yes, it is. I just wanted to remind you how I like mine sucked."

"It's been a long time, but it hasn't been that long." Trey started unbuttoning her blouse, and didn't stop until her bra was exposed. He unhooked the front clasp, causing her boobs to fall out. He licked his lips. Michele had the best "girls" in town, and he missed them dearly. Trey immediately went to work with his tongue. He sucked and licked and stroked her rack until she started moaning. He then picked her up and carried her off to the bedroom.

Trey laid Michele on the bed, and took off her shoes, panties, and skirt. Once she was stripped down, he unloosened his buckle and dropped his jeans. He hadn't bothered to put on briefs, so his cock sprang out before his jeans could hit the floor. "Spread them legs, 'cause I wanna get all up in there this afternoon," he said, stroking his dick. He and Michele hadn't had sex in quite awhile and he was anxious for some much-needed penetration.

Michele cocked her legs wide open, and began sliding her middle finger in and out of her moistness. "Come and get this wet pussy."

Trey leaned on her knees, pushing them down toward the bed. As he was about to enter her, he heard a phone ringing in the distance. Trey ignored the sound. He didn't care who was calling. The only thing he cared about at the moment was gliding his dick into a warm, wet place.

Michele raised her head off the bed. "Wait a minute. I think that's my phone."

"Whoever it is can wait. We got more important things to do," he said, easing in closer.

The phone stopped, but started ringing again. *That might be Fiona calling about the ticket to the VIP party.* "Hold on, Trey." She moved from underneath him. "I need to answer it."

Trey pulled her back toward him. "Let whoever it is leave a message. Mr. Happy ain't gonna be too happy if he has to wait much longer."

"It'll only take a minute," she said, getting out of the bed.

Michele went into the living room, dug her cell phone out of her purse, and checked her voice mail. It was Fiona calling with an urgent message to call back as soon as possible. Michele immediately dialed her number. "Hey girl, what's up?" she asked.

"I know you're with Trey, and I wouldn't have called if it wasn't important. Thompson has a ticket on hold for you at his office—"

"Oh, that's great!" Michele squealed before Fiona had a chance to finish her sentence.

"But there's a catch. You have to pick it up before the end of the day otherwise he's giving it to his assistant. I tried to get him to hold it solely for you, but he said that his assistant has been begging him for a ticket for months. Besides, he thinks that Preston can get you into the party. He said that being a justice, Preston has more clout than he does, and wonders why you didn't ask him in the first place."

Michele knew that she could never ask Preston for such favors. He would think that she was social climbing at his expense. "Okay, I'll be there. Talk to you later," she said, and hung up. Michele retrieved her bra from the floor, and put it back on.

"Whoa . . . what are you doing?" Trey asked as he watched Michele come back into the room and pick her clothes off the floor. "And why do you have on your bra?"

"Sorry, honey, but I've got to go back to D.C."

A shocked expression registered on his face. "What? Why?"

Michele started to tell a lie, but decided to tell him the truth, hoping that he would understand. "Fiona's husband has a VIP ticket for the CBC cocktail party, and if I don't pick it up from his office this afternoon, he's giving it away to his assistant," she said, zipping up her skirt.

"What kind of party?"

"The Congressional Black Caucus's party. It's going to be the hottest event in town. I heard that Denzel and his wife are coming, as well as Don Cheadle, Danny Glover—"

Trey cut her off. "Are you telling me that you'd rather go to some party with a bunch of celebrities who don't even know your name, than stay here with me and make love?" he asked, sounding upset.

"Well . . . it's not that I don't want to stay with you, but this is an opportunity of a lifetime, and—"

He interrupted again. "Fine. Go." Trey was pissed. He knew from the last black-tie party that he attended with Michele that she loved schmoozing with the rich and powerful, but he didn't think that she would leave him with blue balls, just to get her hands on some party ticket. His dick was still hard, so he softened his tone, and tried to persuade her to stay. "Come here, baby. Can't you at least give me some head?"

Michele looked at his swollen cock standing at attention, and had to admit that it did look enticing. She glanced at her watch. "I would love to Trey, but if I don't leave right now, I'm going to miss the next train," she said, heading toward the door.

"Well, at least give Mr. Happy a good-bye kiss," he suggested, still trying to get his way.

"I wish I could, but I've got to run." With that said, she blew him a kiss, and was gone like the wind.

"Ain't that a bitch!" Trey shouted into the empty apartment. His dick was still throbbing, so he did the next best thing—got out the K-Y and gave himself a good old-fashioned hand job.

7

MICHELE WAS so proud of herself. She had used her sly, fox-like ways to slip into Angelica Oglesby's birthday party. Initially, she hadn't planned on crashing, but when she was sorting through Preston's mail, she noticed a package from the chief justice. The package wasn't marked urgent, but it looked as if it could've been important, which wasn't unusual, since Preston received mail from the chief on a regular basis. As Michele looked the package over, a bright idea occurred to her.

She had spruced up her hair, refreshed her makeup, and hopped in the car with the package in hand. On the way to Arlington, she perfected her lines, over and over until the lie rolled off her tongue like the truth. And when she told Preston that the package had been hand delivered, and looked important, he believed her without asking any questions. From the expression on Ariel's face, Michele knew that the Mrs. was less than pleased that she had shown up uninvited. Fortunately for Michele, Ariel couldn't force her to leave. Ariel wouldn't dare say anything that could jeopardize their pact.

Michele had successfully crashed one party under false pretenses. Now it was time to crash another. She had hoped to get the ticket from Thompson, but missed the train by a hair. When she arrived at his office, the doors were locked. His assistant had no doubt gone home a happy woman, with the VIP ticket in hand. This event was the talk of the town, and Michele wasn't going to miss it, so she had no choice but to put plan B in action. Though she enjoyed schmoozing with the senior politicians and their wives, the Congressional Black Caucus Awards dinner was sure to be chock-full of celebrities as well as younger politicians, closer to her age. And she couldn't wait to rub elbows with the likes of Isaiah Washington, Blair Underwood, and the Obamas of the Hill. Michele was looking for the perfect sponsor, and this event was sure to be filled with a bevy of A-listers to choose from. There was only one thing standing between her and the party, and that was Preston. She had marked the event on his calendar, but he hadn't mentioned whether or not he was going to attend. Since the party was this evening, she decided she had better ask him before the end of the day, so that she could put her plan in effect.

Michele left her office area, which was right outside of Preston's, and knocked on his door.

"Come in," he said, through the closed door.

"Ah, just the person I wanted to see. Have a seat," Preston said, the moment she walked in.

Preston's invitation to sit down threw her for a loop. They hadn't planned a meeting, and usually the only time that she sat across from him was when she was briefing him about his schedule, or some other work-related issue. "Did we have a meeting on the calendar for this afternoon?" she asked, pulling out one of the chairs in front of his desk.

"No, we didn't, but there's something I need to talk to you about," he said, sounding mysterious.

Michele began to panic. Her first thought was that Preston had found out that she had lied about the chief's package being hand delivered. She quickly thought of a cover story, just in case he questioned her. "Oh," she said, sounding surprised. "What did you want to talk to me about?"

"Well . . ." He hesitated for a second as if trying to collect his thoughts. "It's about your wardrobe."

She wrinkled her forehead. "My wardrobe?" she asked. That was the last thing she expected him to say. "What about my wardrobe?" she asked defensively.

"Well . . ." He hesitated again. "Your clothes are a little too sexy," he said, making the understatement of the year. When in actuality he wanted to say, "They're waaay too sexy."

Michele dropped her jaw in shock. She couldn't believe Preston was talking about her clothes. "What do you mean?"

He took a deep breath and exhaled. Preston knew that this conversation was long overdue, and should have been addressed before he won the nomination, but during that time he had been too preoccupied with his own agenda to focus on much of anything else. "I hate to bring this up, but I've received a few comments from people saying that your blouses are too sheer, and your dresses and skirts are too tight for an office environment."

Michele sat there and listened while he basically insulted her. She knew those comments didn't come from "people," but probably from Ariel. *Wait until I have a talk with the Mrs. and tell her not to fuck with me. Once I remind her that her secret is safe only as long as I keep my mouth shut, she'll back the hell off,* Michele thought. "Oh really, and what people are those?" she asked with attitude, challenging him.

"Uh, uh . . ." he stammered. "I don't want to name names. Let's just say that Washington is a tad more conservative than New York. As a suggestion, maybe you could start wearing cotton blouses instead of silk ones, and suits instead of slinky dresses," he offered.

Michele suddenly remembered her brief conversation with Fiona at Angelica's party regarding her clothes. *Well, maybe they're both right.* "I'll take that under advisement," she responded.

"Okay, okay, that's all I'm asking," he said quickly, as if ready to end this unpleasant exchange. "Now, what did you come in to talk about?" he asked, switching gears.

Having been blindsided by this unexpected conversation, Michele had completely forgotten about the CBC VIP reception and dinner. She thought for a few seconds, trying to remember why she came into his office in the first place. "I just wanted to remind you that the Congressional Black Caucus dinner is tonight," she said.

"Thanks for reminding me, but unfortunately, we won't be able to attend. Ariel's upstairs in bed, she's feeling a bit under the weather. I think she's coming down with the flu, and I'm just plain old tired. So we're going to stay in tonight." Preston had been to the caucus event numerous times before, and now that he was a justice, he didn't have to mingle at every political affair on the calendar. His position was a lifelong appointment, without term limits, so he didn't have to lobby for votes at these highly visible functions. Besides, he wanted to give his wife some TLC, something he had been too busy to do a few months ago.

That's exactly what Michele wanted to hear. Now she'd have no problem impersonating Ariel. "Okay, well, I just came in to remind you about the affair. If you don't have anything else for me to do, I'm going to call it a day and head home."

"No, there's nothing else I need today." Preston was feeling guilty about reprimanding Michele and readily agreed to her taking off early to try and make amends. "Have a good evening, and I'll see you tomorrow," he said, smiling.

"You too," she said, and exited his office.

Back at her desk, Michele picked up the phone to call Fiona, and tell her about Preston's ambush. Instead of a dial tone, she heard Ariel's voice. Ariel had obviously called out on the business line instead of the home line.

"I'm telling you, Meri, this chick is bolder than bold. You should have seen the way she waltzed into Angelica's party, as if she were invited."

"Why didn't you simply ask her to leave?"

"Trust me, I wanted to, but since we have that stupid pact to keep the truth from Preston, I didn't want to make any waves. Believe me when I tell you, that once Preston has total recall, I'm going to insist that he fire that hussy posthaste."

"Why don't you have him do it now? Make up an excuse. Anything. Maybe say that you saw her copying confidential files."

"Now that's not a bad idea." Ariel thought for a moment. "No, I can't do that. If I do, it'll be my word against hers, which will start another brouhaha, and that's the last thing I need. No, I'll wait it out. But you can take this to the bank, once the truth is out her ass is history!"

Michele was livid. She had heard enough, and gently hung up the phone. She had the mind to march right up the stairs, barge into the master bedroom and give Ariel an earful. The only thing stopping her was time. She had to get ready for the party of the year, so her tongue-lashing would have to wait for a more opportune time. She quickly retrieved her belongings and huffed out of the town house. She could hardly wait to have a conversation with Ariel, to make it clear once and for all who held the winning cards.

Michele drove home in record time and practically ran into the bedroom. She had laid her outfit on the bed in the morning before she left for work, and she wasted no time showering and changing into the fire-engine red Roberto Cavalli gown, with the deep-cut halter back that stopped just above the crack of her butt. The smooth silk fabric flowed over her skin, making her feel sensuous. Michele knew that she should have worn pasties to hide her nipples, but she wanted them to protrude through the thin material. Her boobs were her best asset, and she wanted to show off her rack tonight more than ever. Since there would be potential sponsors at the VIP reception, and an equal amount of competition, she wanted to draw as much attention to herself as possible. And the sexy red gown that showed off her body exquisitely was the perfect eye-catcher. She wasn't looking for a lover, just someone who had connections and would be willing to help her gain status. And if her body attracted the right person, then so be it. In the back of her mind she heard Fiona and Preston's voices, reprimanding her about her overly sexy wardrobe, but tonight she didn't care what they thought. She stared in the mirror and admired how luscious she looked. As she swung around to check out the rear view—which was just as enticing as the front since she wore no panties or thongs and you could clearly see the separation of her butt cheeks—the Austrian crystal bugle beads at the hem made a jingling sound.

"Not only are they going to see me coming, they're going to hear me as well." She winked at her reflection.

She fluffed out her long hair, applied her makeup flawlessly, and sprayed her neck, wrists, and cleavage with a heavy dose of Turquoise by Ralph Lauren. She took one last look in the mirror. Satisfied with her transformation, she grabbed her evening bag, Preston's invitation that she nabbed from work, and her car keys from the dresser, and headed out the door.

The line of cars approaching the convention center was nearly two blocks long. And the cars moved inch by inch, like a slow-moving parking lot.

"I should've called a limo service so the driver could have dropped me off in front of the door, instead of me having to park," Michele huffed. At the rate this line was moving, she'd be lucky to arrive in time for dinner, let alone the preceding VIP reception.

"I'll be damned if I miss that reception," she said, and swerved to the right and onto the curb. She drove straight to the front, nearly hitting the car in front of her as she cut back in line. The driver honked his horn, and gave her a menacing look as she passed, but she ignored him. Michele waited at the gate for the automatic machine to dispense the parking ticket, and once it did, she sped through the garage looking for a space. She found a small spot near the exit sign reserved for compact cars, but she parked her midsize car there anyway, hopped out, and headed to the elevator, as fast as her four-inch heels could take her.

Alone in the elevator, Michele took a few deep breaths to compose herself. Her heart was racing a mile a minute and she needed to calm down before the doors opened. "You're here now. Stop panting and relax," she told herself.

No sooner than she had closed her eyes and taken another deep breath, than the elevator doors opened. She arched her back and coolly stepped out into the convention center. She walked with the confidence of a lioness—strong and purposeful—but inside she was as nervous as a cat stuck high in a tree.

Michele followed the signs that pointed out the direction to the VIP reception. Her heart began to pound faster and faster as she neared the ballroom. In the distance, she could see a security guard checking off names on a clipboard. *Here we go*, she thought, and took out the invitation.

"Your name please?" she could hear the guard ask, as she stood in line and waited her turn to enter the party.

As Michele inched toward the entrance, her nerves eased up and were being replaced with excitement. She couldn't wait to mingle with the Who's Who of Washington's elite, as well as an A-list of celebrities. Michele was third in line, and only two people stood between her and the party of the year. *Ariel Vaughn Hendricks,* she said to herself, as a reminder not to say her own name when the guard asked. Since her name wouldn't be found on the select list, she had to keep saying Ariel's name over and over, so that she wouldn't flub up.

The couple in front of her was cleared by the guard, graciously waltzed into the party, and now it was her turn. "Your name please?" he asked.

Just as she was about to say Ariel Vaughn Hendricks, Leona Forester came out of the ballroom, and looked directly into Michele's face. "Hi, uh . . ." She thought for a second, trying to remember Michele's name. "Didn't we meet the other night at the Oglesbys'? Yes, that's right, you're Preston's assistant," she said, finally remembering.

Michele stood there with her mouth open. She hadn't expected to see any of the people from the birthday party since that crowd was an old-money, Republican group, and the CBC attendees were mostly new-money Democrats. "Yes, I work with Justice Hendricks," she said, with about as much gusto as a wet flea.

"What's your name again?" Leona asked.

"Michele Richards," she responded, in a low voice, hoping that the guard wouldn't hear her. But it was too late for that, because Leona was talking loud, drawing attention to them.

"Are Preston and Ariel coming tonight?" she asked, looking around as if she expected to see them strolling through the crowd.

"No, they're staying in this evening," she said sheepishly.

"Oh. Well, it was good seeing you again. I've got to run. I have another function to attend tonight," Leona said, and walked away.

"Your name please," the guard asked again, looking rather impatient.

She cleared her throat, and said loudly, "Michele Richards." She prayed that her tone would convince him that she belonged. It was too late now to impersonate Ariel since the guard had heard the entire exchange between her and Leona. Her underarms began to perspire.

He flipped the pages until he reached the *R*'s, and then scanned the list. "I'm sorry, but I don't have your name on the VIP list."

If only Thompson had given her the invitation, which automatically assured her a spot on the list, since the invitation list was crossed-matched with the door list, she wouldn't be standing there sweating.

"Can you check by my first name?" she asked, trying to buy some time, so that she could think of another way to get into the party. Michele had gone through too many changes—from stealing Preston's invitation, to buying a designer gown beyond her budget, to driving like a maniac—to give up so easily.

He turned back to the *M*'s, read the list, and then looked up at her. "I have a Michele McGee, and a Michele Roland, but no Michele Richards." He gave her an "I know you're lying" look, and then said, "Sorry, miss, but I'm going to have to ask you to step aside, since your first *or* last name isn't on the list. This reception is for VIPs only."

Michele thought about belaboring the point, but she knew that she didn't have a leg to stand on. Besides, she could hear people behind her whispering, and assumed that they were talking about her. She gave the guard a sympathetic look, hoping that he would show a little mercy, but he just turned his nose up, and began addressing the next couple in line.

Michele knew there was no hope in crashing this reception, so she slunk away in embarrassment, before the scene escalated. Her plan had been shot down midair, and she had no other recourse but to leave. She quickly dashed toward the exit, before the tears that were welling up in her eyes fell. Her heel caught in the hem of her dress, causing her to stumble forward. Her shoe tore a hole in the dress and a few of the tiny bugle beads sprang loose onto the carpeting as she made her escape.

Acceptance was within her grasp, but it kept eluding her, like a cruel joke. *This is the last time that I'm ass out!* she fumed as she rode back down to the parking garage.

THE BLACK Door was New York's destination of choice for women of means who wanted to spice up their sex lives. Trey had taken the oldest profession in the world and given it an extreme makeover. He designed the club with a multitude of themed chambers on the second level, while the first floor was demure with only two cozy parlors. One room was for the older matrons who merely wanted to sip port or sherry while enjoying the company of a handsome young man. The other parlor had an ornate champagne fountain in the center of the room, but instead of spewing gallons of bubbly, it spewed ice-cold Belvedere. The straight vodka served as liquid courage for those who needed a little encouragement to go behind the velvet drape and venture upstairs into the blue light district, where the serious players played.

The second level was decadence personified, with chambers to satisfy the kinkiest of appetites. There was the Voyeurism Room with a one-way mirror where members could fuck while on display. The 8mm Room played retro porno flicks for those who needed visual stimulation to jump-start the evening. In the Leopard Lounge, members could enjoy cocktails while being eaten out by a server in one of the private booths in the back. The Tantalizing Toy Room offered heat-sensitive gels, edible panties, fur-lined handcuffs, butt plugs, and vibrators to enhance enjoyment. And those were just a few of the chambers inside the Black Door.

Trey strolled through the club in all black with his black leather and onyx mask secured around the top portion of his face. He was on his way to the Leopard Lounge to meet Lexi. In their last encounter at the lounge, she had teased him with a mouthful of dirty talk, enticing him to want more. He hadn't fucked her that night because he was trying to be faithful to Michele. But he had to admit that Lexi had piqued his interest, so when she called him to say that she was once again downstairs, he abandoned the paperwork on his desk and made a beeline to the lounge to find out more about her.

Trey still had a case of blue balls from Michele's unexpected departure the other day, and masturbation wasn't doing the job. Even a blind man could see that their relationship had lost its sizzle. There was a time when Michele couldn't get enough of him; now all she seemed to care about was being seen at some hoity-toity affair. Obviously, they wanted different things out of life, and at the moment he wanted sex—whether it was with his so-called girlfriend or not.

When he saw Lexington at the grand opening of the Hirschfield Multimedia Studios, he promised himself that he wouldn't get involved with her, since she was a client, and dismissed her overt advances. The last member he'd fucked around with turned out to be his father's fiancée, which left him more than a little gun-shy. But a year had passed since then, and he was no longer squeamish. Besides, he knew Lexington's identity, unlike Ariel's when he first met her at the club, wearing her friend's mask. Lexi was no mystery woman, and wasn't involved with anyone he knew.

The lighting inside the Leopard Lounge was so dim that Trey could barely see. He squinted his eyes, trying to decipher the various masks worn by the women sitting at the bar. He was looking for Lexi's mask, which was pink with silver rhinestones around the eyes. He walked the length of the bar, but she wasn't there. Then he made his way to the rear of the lounge, where the private booths were located. It was even darker in the back and all he could make out were silhouettes of maneuvering bodies. Though it was hard to see, the sound effects were loud and clear. Moans and groans of pleasure tickled his ears and the scent of sex hung in the air like honeysuckle in the spring.

"Psst . . . I'm over here."

Trey walked toward the sound of the voice. As he got closer, he could see silver rhinestones glimmering slightly from the small votive candle that sat in the middle of the table. "Lexi, is that you?"

"In the flesh."

And that's exactly what he came for. He wanted to taste that little piece of flesh between her thighs before he plowed her with his rod. "Hey you." He slid into the booth and brushed the side of her cheek with a kiss. Before he could say another word, Lexi turned her lips to meet his and began kissing him passionately on the mouth. Her lips were so soft, and each sensuous kiss made his dick grow, until he had a rock-hard erection. He had at least planned on having a brief conversation before delving right into sex, but she had other plans, which suited him just fine.

Lexi scooted her body closer to his, and began running her hands underneath his T-shirt and up and down his torso, feeling his ripped abs. She then began fidgeting with his belt, trying to unbuckle it.

Trey put his hand on top of hers. "Wait; let me taste you first," he whispered in her ear. Though he was horny as hell, he wanted an appetizer. Eating a woman out, and hearing her moan with pleasure turned him on.

"Really? Those are the magic words that every woman wants to hear." She leaned in even closer and whispered back, "Go right ahead."

He began softly kneading the interior of her thigh with his large hand, and slowly worked his way up her leg, until his fingers were touching the silk fabric of her thong. He started rubbing his thumb against the soft material of the panty, until he felt the lips of her pussy spread apart. "Once I eat you out, I'm going to introduce you to my big dick." He took her hand and placed it on his cock. "Feel how long and hard it is."

Lexi gasped at its girth. "Mmm, is all that for me?"

"Um-hum, and I'm going to feed it to you inch-by-inch until you scream for me to stop."

"And what makes you think I'm going to want you to stop? If the dick is as good as it feels, I'm going to want it all night. Can you keep it hard for hours?" she asked in a challenging tone.

"As long as the pussy's wet, the dick'll be hard. Now shut up and lay back, because I'm tired of talking."

Lexi eased back on the leopard-print cushion, hiked up her skirt, and slid off her thong. She'd waited for this moment since the first day she'd laid eyes on him over twelve months ago, and she could hardly believe that Trey was between her legs getting ready to sample her goodies.

He took a deep breath and inhaled her essence. Every woman had their very own smell, and he loved the variation of the scents. He flicked his tongue out and teased the tip of her clit and kept licking until the tiny piece of pink flesh swelled to nearly double its size.

"Oh yeah, daddy, that's it. That's it! That's-s-s i-i-i-t-t!" she sang.

Trey continued sucking, nibbling, and licking, until Lexi was near orgasm, and then he stopped, pulled out his cock and entered her with ease. She was so wet that his dick slid into place as if it were driving into its very own personalized garage. He started humping and pumping until they were both sweaty and on the verge of cumming.

"Damn, baby, your pussy feels so good! It's so tight," he exclaimed.

"And—and—" she tried to talk, but was short of breath, "your dick is super—fucking—fantastic," she panted. He was humping her so hard that she wrapped her arms around him, dug her fingers into his back, and held on for the ride of her life.

Trey pumped and she pumped back just as hard, and before long they were both singing the same song, "I'M CUMMING!!!"

After they each achieved climax, Trey pulled up his pants, and Lexi pulled down her skirt. Once they recovered from the hedonistic encounter, they slumped back on the booth, glistening with sweat, and took a deep breath of satisfaction.

"Now that was some good dick!" she said, resting her hand on his thigh.

"And that was some damn good pussy. As much as I enjoyed your company," he removed her hand, and stood up, "I need to get back to work, but call me the next time you're in the club, and maybe we can hook up for round three."

"Don't worry. Now that I know what you're working with," she patted his package, "I'll be sure to ring your phone real soon."

Trey straightened his clothes, gave her a kiss on the cheek, and made his way back to the office. Once inside, he noticed that the message light on his phone was blinking. He walked over to the desk, picked up the receiver, and dialed the voice mail code.

"Hey, baby. I just called to say how sorry I am for walking out on you. Can you please forgive me?"

Trey grunted at her message, as if he didn't believe her apology. *I bet if she had an opportunity to go to another party, she'd leave me hanging again.* He erased her message, and didn't bother calling her back. Trey should have felt remorseful for fucking around on Michele, but he didn't. There was no telling who she had met at that black-tie affair. For all he knew she was giving up her goodies to some powerful politician. Their relationship seemed to be falling apart at the seams, and neither was committed enough to hold it together. Trey knew that if he really loved Michele he would have never fucked Lexi. And if Michele really cared for him, she would have never left him high and dry. If it wasn't for their secret pact, Trey would have called off this farce of a relationship long ago. But if he had any chance of salvaging the relationship with his father, he'd have to go along with the flow until the timing was right.

Trey didn't know if his father would have total recall of his affair with Ariel, or if his dad would only remember bits and pieces. In either event, Trey wanted the chance to explain why he slept with his father's woman. He didn't want the story coming from a third party— Michele. He and Ariel had not meant to hurt anyone. Explaining that fact was going to be a hard sell no matter what his dad remembered. Trey thought about confessing now, but now was not the right time. Preston was happy in his marriage, and had no clue that Ariel had cheated on him. If Trey went to his dad now, it would only make matters worse. Preston would be confused. Yes, it was better to wait until his memory returned, at least then he'd have a point of reference— not a good point, but a point nonetheless. Trey was burdened with a basketful of ifs. One if seemed contingent upon another, and another, and Trey longed for the day when he could empty the basket once and for all.

9

"OH BABY, you feel so good," Preston moaned in Ariel's ear, as he eased his erect member inside of her. The last time they attempted sex, he wimpered out, claiming that the champagne from Angelica's birthday party had his head spinning, when in actuality something in his subconscious caused him to stop. But this morning was a different story. He had woken up with a massive hard-on, and attacked his wife while she was still asleep. His subconscious was clear, with no thoughts of his wife cheating on him. Now all he wanted was some heated lovemaking, something that they hadn't shared in a long time. During his prenomination, all he could think about was sitting on the Supreme Court. Now that that was a reality, he wanted to resurrect their love life.

Ariel was taken aback. It had been awhile since Preston woke her up ready to make love. Though she wasn't ovulating, she wanted him nonetheless, and scooted her ass toward him, causing his dick to slide in even more. "Ohh, now that's what I call a 'wake-up call.'"

Preston turned her over. "Get on your knees."

Ariel complied, and before she could say *fuck me*, Preston was deep within her, riding her doggy-style, like a man half his age.

He pulled her hips to him for deeper penetration. His libido was on ten, so he grinded into her like a man in lust. Now with additional time on his hands, Preston could focus more attention on his wife, and this morning that's exactly what he did. He fucked her hard, until his cum squirted into her canal. He then slumped down on the bed in sheer exhaustion. Twenty minutes later, he felt refreshed, and got up to shower for work, leaving Ariel asleep.

When she woke up, Preston was long gone. Though her husband had rocked her morning, she still felt homesick and couldn't wait to get back to New York.

She tried shopping at the boutiques in Georgetown for new clothes, which usually made her feel better. She tried a spa day at the Four Seasons to rejuvenate her tired muscles, but nothing seemed to bring her out of her funk. Sex with Preston helped, but she knew the real antidote was a long overdue trip home. Days ago she had called the New York office and told her colleague that she would be more than happy to work with him for the next few weeks. After that, she called Amtrak and booked a business-class ticket on the Acela. Her next call was to Meri, regarding her plans to spend time in New York. Ariel decided not to call Mrs. Grant, because she wanted to surprise her foster mother, and if she told Mrs. Grant in advance the older woman would be full of questions as to why Ariel could be away from her husband for so long.

Though she was only going to New York for two weeks at the most, Ariel packed enough clothes to last a month. She still had her Manhattan condo, but was leasing it out to a couple of empty nesters from Connecticut, who had sold their house and moved into the city to begin the second part of their lives. Since her place was occupied, she was going to stay at the firm's corporate apartment, overlooking Central Park.

Ariel tugged her two oversized suitcases out of the bedroom into the hallway. She struggled with them until she reached the top of the landing. It was at times like this that she wished she still lived in a doorman building on the east side; then all she'd have to do was to call down and have the porter come up and get her bags. But now lugging her luggage was solely her responsibility. She thought about yelling downstairs for Preston's help, but he would chastise her for bringing too many clothes, and she didn't want to hear his ranting, so she just struggled by herself.

She managed to get the bags down the stairs, one at a time, and when she reached the bottom of the landing for the second time, she was exhausted and felt as though she'd put in an hour's workout at the gym. Ariel put her elbow on the banister and rested a few seconds before taking another step.

"Can you help me take my luggage outside?" Ariel asked, as Michele walked out of the office area.

"*Excuse me?*" Michele raised her voice and crossed her arms at the same time. She exhaled hard and said, "In case you haven't noticed, I'm not wearing a doorman's uniform, and hauling suitcases does not fall under my job description."

"Michele, I know you're not a doorman. I was just asking you for a little help," Ariel said.

"Like the help you were trying to give me when you told your friend Meri that you can't wait to have me fired?" she said venomously.

Ariel looked shocked. She had no idea that Michele had overheard her conversation. One look at the twisted expression on Michele's face, and Ariel could tell that she was pissed. She didn't know what to say to smooth things over, so she didn't say a word.

"You were so big and bad on the phone with your friend . . . so what do you have to say now . . . *Nothing!*" Michele hissed.

Ariel was caught with foot in mouth, and couldn't deny her words. "Uh, Michele, I seriously think that you misconstrued what I said."

Michele rolled her eyes, and snapped her neck simultaneously. "You want to talk *seriously?*" she said, quoting Ariel's word. "How about I seriously think about telling Preston about you and Trey? How's that for being taken seriously?"

Ariel's jaw dropped. Ever since she, Trey, and Michele had made their pact to keep quiet, Michele hadn't uttered a single word about their betrayal. Ariel had misgivings about trusting Michele, but Trey assured her that Michele would keep their affair a secret. Now the cow was finally confirming her suspicions. "How does telling Preston the truth have anything to do with my conversation? One thing has nothing to do with the other," Ariel said, in the calm, professional voice that she reserved for clients.

Michele flipped her hair to one side. "Don't you think I know that they have nothing to do with each other?" She rolled her eyes again.

"Then why would you mention the, the . . ." Ariel was having a hard time saying the word ". . . affair?" she whispered.

"I just want you to see what it feels like to be blindsided. Like when I overheard your double-crossing conversation."

"You wouldn't!" Ariel said, in a quietly raised voice. She wanted to shout, but she didn't want to alarm Preston.

"Oh, yes I would! Just try me!"

"Why would you want to hurt Preston like that?"

"Isn't that the pot calling the kettle black? You're the one who hurt him by fucking his son. And now, you're trying to make me out as the bad guy; isn't that a bitch?! I've got a mind to go into his office right now and tell him everything!" Michele turned toward Preston's office.

Ariel grabbed her by the arm. "Wait a minute. Don't be too hasty. At this point, it'll be your word against mine and Trey's. I'm sure that Trey isn't on board with you helping to jog his dad's memory. So you can go in there and say whatever you want; I'll just deny everything and you'll look like a zip-dang fool," Ariel said calmly, hoping that she'd given Michele food for thought.

Michele was quiet for a few seconds, as if weighing Ariel's words. She hadn't thought her plan through. Ariel had a major point, and that was until Preston began to recall what happened on his own, it would be her word against the two of them. Michele knew that she had to tread lightly, until she had an ironclad plan; otherwise she'd be out on her pretty ass, with no job and no man. Since Preston didn't have a recollection of the forty-eight hours preceding his stroke, he'd probably think that she was making up the entire story just to cause trouble in his marriage. It was no big secret that Michele and Ariel were adversaries. "Whatever!" was her only comeback. She was caught between a rock and a hard place, but was trying not to let Ariel know that she had won this round. She turned on her heel and strutted away, while she still felt empowered.

Ariel felt weak in the knees, and slumped back on the banister for support. She hadn't expected a confrontation with Michele and was totally taken off guard. She hadn't spoken with Trey and had no idea whether or not he would back her up, but she had to play that card; otherwise, Michele probably would have told Preston the truth and nothing but the truth. Since her husband was showing no signs of regaining his memory and their love life was back on track, Ariel felt safe in going to New York, especially now that she had put Michele back in her place. Besides, she'd only be gone for a few weeks—back in time for her next ovulation—and was confident that nothing significant would happen in that time.

10

"SO, HOW does it feel to be free from the old ball and chain?" Laird asked Preston. He had stopped by the town house instead of calling, hoping to get a glimpse of Michele, but she was out of the office running errands.

"I wouldn't exactly call Ariel a ball and chain, but it does feel good not to have to worry about another person. Well, I shouldn't say worry. What I meant to say is that, it feels good not to have to consult her about dinner every night," Preston said, clarifying his statement.

"I know exactly what you mean. Most nights Leona is preoccupied with her own agenda, but on those days when she's at home, she's asking me about dinner before I've even had lunch. What is it with women and food? It seems they're always trying to feed you something." Laird chuckled.

"I'm sure it has to do with their maternal instincts."

"I already have a mother who happily resides miles away in sunny Boca Raton. If anything, I need another lover, not another mother," Laird said seriously. "Speaking of food, that's why I stopped by. I'm taking you to dinner, and I'm not taking no for an answer. Since your wife is out of town and mine has other plans this evening, we're going to have a boys' night out."

"Sounds good to me." Preston smiled. He was beginning to miss his wife, and was happy for the distraction. "Let me send this e-mail, and I'm ready to go."

Laird's midnight blue Mercedes sedan was parked in the driveway, and the two men happily hopped into the car like two college buddies on their way to the local pub. "Where're we going?" Preston asked, once they were en route.

"A really unique restaurant called À Votre Service."

"I take it it's French?" Preston asked.

Laird smiled. "Yes, it's very French. Hope you're into international cuisine; thought we'd try something different." The last time they went to dinner a few months ago, they had gone to a traditional steak and seafood restaurant.

"I love French food. It'll be a nice change from the usual steak house."

"Yes, À Votre Service is definitely a nice change. I'm sure you'll enjoy it."

The restaurant was tucked away on a quiet Georgetown block, in a century-old town house. A uniformed valet was waiting to park the car the moment they drove up. And as soon as they stepped out of the car, a well-dressed maître d' appeared at the doorway, and ushered them inside.

The interior was quaint but elegant. There were only about ten tables in the entire restaurant. Preston looked at the tables and noticed that they were not the normal height. They were tall, almost the height of a bar, and were draped in long, ecru linen cloths. Atop each table was a vase of blood orange calla lilies. The deep color of the flowers complemented the burgundy walls and velvet drapes perfectly. Soft lighting emanated from ornate wall sconces, and seductive French music played softly in the background.

Preston looked around. "I think you picked the wrong restaurant," he whispered to Laird, as they waited to be seated.

"Why do you say that?"

"Because this place is a little too romantic for two straight men going out to get a bite to eat; maybe we should leave and come back with our wives," Preston suggested. He felt a little uncomfortable. Georgetown was known for having gay establishments, and he didn't want to be seen having a cozy dinner with another man. The last thing he needed was to get a reputation of being gay.

"Trust me. This isn't a place we'd want to bring our wives."

Before Preston could ask why not, the host approached them. "Good evening, Congressman Forester. Should I seat you at your regular table?"

"Yes, please, Jean-Luc."

Preston and Laird followed Jean-Luc to a choice corner table in the rear of the restaurant. Once they were seated, the host told them that the sommelier would be right over with the wine selections of the evening.

"Look, Laird," Preston said, leaning in once they were seated, "I'm not in the mood for any wine. Let's get out of here, before anyone sees us, and head over to Smith and Wollensky and get a nice juicy steak," he said nervously.

"I thought you said that you were not in the mood for steak tonight. Look, Preston, just relax, and stop being paranoid. Trust me; you're going to have a great time this evening," he said, with confidence.

Preston began to fidget in his seat. He was finding it hard to relax. He didn't want to wind up on somebody's blog as another down-low politician. He looked around the room, and didn't see too many women customers. Most of the tables were occupied by men. Though they didn't appear to be gay, it was suspicious nonetheless.

"*Bonjour*, Laird," a beautiful French woman said, and handed him a leather-bound wine list.

Laird looked at her and licked his lips. She was gorgeous, with flawless porcelain skin, long auburn hair, emerald-green eyes, and a body built like Barbie's. Her waist was small, her hips round, and her rack was well endowed. Laird put his arm around her tiny middle. "*Bonjour*, Sasha; *ça va?*" he asked, in a perfect French accent.

"I've been good, and you?" she replied, leaning into his embrace.

Preston watched the exchange between them, and it was obvious that Laird was a regular. This woman seemed to know him well enough to refer to him by his first name and let him touch her in an intimate way. Preston knew that Laird was a hound dog and couldn't help but wonder if he was having an affair with the stunning sommelier.

"Sasha, this is my good friend Preston," he said, purposely omitting Preston's lofty title, immediately putting them on a first-name basis.

She walked over to Preston, and smooched him on each cheek, French style. With her mouth close to his ear, she said softly, "*Bonjour*, Preston."

Her French accent made the hairs on the back of his neck stand at attention. "Uh, hi," he said nervously. She was standing so close that he could smell her hypnotic perfume, which was no doubt French. He instinctively took a deep whiff, and inhaled the sexy scent. *I see why Laird wanted to stay.* This woman was intoxicating, which was ironic, since she was a wine expert.

Sasha walked back over to Laird. "Shall I choose a bottle for you two?"

"*Oui. Merci*, Sasha."

"You are more than welcome. I'll send over your waitress," she said, brushing Laird's cheek with another kiss before she sashayed away.

"Man." Preston did a slow whistle. "She's exquisite. Now I see why you wanted to stay." Preston wasn't a committed hound like his friend, but he appreciated a good-looking woman, nonetheless.

"Yes, Sasha is indeed beautiful, but she's not the reason we're staying." He smirked.

Preston naturally thought that Laird was referring to the food. He knew that a good French chef could make magic in the kitchen with gastronomical creations such as bouillabaisse, beef bourguignonne, and chicken *cordon bleu*. "Is the food that good?"

"It's mouth-watering, *especially* the appetizers."

"*Bonjour*, gentlemen," said not one, but two beautiful waitresses.

They looked like identical twins. They were as tall and thin as models with faces fit to grace the cover of *Vogue*. They wore short, tight ivory skirts, and burgundy bustiers, the exact same color as the decor. "Would you gentlemen like an appetizer?" they asked in unison.

"Yes, we would," Laird answered for the both of them.

Instead of spouting off a list of specials, the women kneeled down, lifted up the linen cloth, and disappeared underneath the table. Preston looked at Laird, and was getting ready to ask what they were doing, but before he could open his mouth, the zipper on his pants was being zipped down.

Laird noticed the shocked expression on Preston's face. "*Now* you'll understand why I wanted to stay," he said.

Preston was speechless. It suddenly hit him why the tables were so tall—to allow the waitress easy access, and to conceal your business from the rest of the guests. He didn't know what to say. He sat speechless as the waitress took his dick out of his boxers and began to lick the shaft. He wanted to tell her to stop, but the sensation felt too good. Now that his schedule had eased up, his libido had returned with a vengeance, and he couldn't get enough sex. His limp dick came to life. She began kissing the swollen head, and then slipped the length of him into her mouth. She sucked long and hard, until he was on the verge of coming. He tried to pull out, but she held on to the base of his dick, and wouldn't release it. She kept sucking, as if she were forcing him to come in her mouth. After trying to resist the urge to cum, Preston couldn't hold back any longer, and exploded down her throat. Once she had finished her business, she cleaned his cock with a napkin, tucked the dick back in his pants, and came out from underneath the table.

"How was your appetizer?" she asked, smiling coyly.

"Uh, uh," he stammered. Preston didn't know what to say. He had never cheated on Ariel, and felt a twinge of guilt creep up his spine. "It was uh, nice. Thank you." *Nice*, Preston said to himself; he couldn't believe that he had just described one of the best blow jobs he'd ever had as *nice*.

"You're more than welcome, monsieur."

Once her twin resurfaced, the women walked away like they had just served a basketful of mussels, instead of serving up BJ's.

"*That's* why I wanted to stay." Laird smiled big, nearly showing all thirty-two teeth. "Like the name of the restaurant implies, everyone here is definitely at your service."

"I wish you would have warned me," Preston said, ready to chastise his friend.

"If I had told you what was going to happen, you wouldn't have come."

"You're right about that! I'm a married man, and have never cheated on my wife, unlike some people," he said, pinning Laird with a knowing look.

"Preston, you're too uptight; you need to loosen up. Ninety-nine point nine percent of married couples cheat, men and *women*. And if it makes you feel any better, a blow job isn't exactly cheating; it's not like you fucked her," he said, justifying their lewd act.

Laird was right, but Preston felt guilty anyway. He shook his head. "Man, you're something else."

"What can I say? I love sex, and not necessarily with my wife."

"Well, my wife and I have a very healthy love life. And, just so you know, this will be my last time coming here. I don't intend to get into a *situation* that I can't get out of. Ariel and I are both committed to our marriage, and I plan to keep it that way. So as far as I'm concerned this incident tonight never happened, if you know what I mean." He gave Laird a serious look.

"Don't worry, tonight never happened."

"Good. Now let's order," Preston said, eager to put the naughty blow job out of his mind.

11

ARIEL WAS so glad to be back in New York that she happily
walked the twenty blocks from the firm's corporate condo on Central
Park West to Meri's penthouse on Park Avenue. The sidewalk was
bustling with hordes of people rushing to and fro, and she increased her
step to keep up with their hectic pace. New York was such a pedestrian
city, and walking was the preferred mode of transportation, especially
during rush hour, when midtown traffic was backed up for blocks.

As she made her way up Fifth Avenue, she said hello to some of her
old friends—Cartier, Takashimaya, Van Cleef & Arpels, and Bergdorf
Goodman. Seeing the luxury purveyors lined up on the avenue made
her feel like she was finally home, since most of the stores were New
York staples. Ariel had had a Bergdorf's charge since she graduated
from law school. She was in a good mood and decided to stop in the
store and buy herself and Meri a gift du jour.

Ariel knew the layout of Bergdorf's like her very own house, and
went directly to the counter that carried luxurious scarves. A scarf
was a safe gift, since size wasn't an issue and you could wear the silk
ones year-round. She stood over the counter, peered down into the
case, and spotted a multicolored beauty.

"Good afternoon, Ms., can I show you something?" asked the sales associate.

"Yes, I'd like to see that one," she said, pointing to the scarf she wanted.

The sales associate took out the oblong silk scarf and spread it across the counter. "This is a Loro Piana and it just came in yesterday."

Ariel fingered the smooth material, and loved the feel of the soft silk. The black, purple, and aqua combination with black fringes on the ends was perfect for Meri. It was sassy, yet classy, just like her friend. For herself, she chose a Renato Balestra turquoise and coral double chiffon scarf. "I'll take these two," she told the woman.

"Will that be cash or charge?"

Ariel handed over the plastic. "Can you gift wrap them?"

"Sure. Is the house wrapping okay?"

"That'll be fine."

Once the gifts were paid for, wrapped and packaged, Ariel bounced out of the store with the shopping bag in hand, and made her way to Meri's penthouse. Nearly twenty minutes later, she was finally at her destination.

"Hi, Frank, how have you been?" she asked the doorman.

"I'm good, Ms. Vaughn. I haven't seen you in a long time; where have you been hiding?" he asked, smiling.

"Actually, it's Mrs. Vaughn Hendricks now. I've gotten married and moved to Washington. I've been back a few times, but you must have been on vacation, because someone else was at the desk." Unlike some of the snooty east side doormen, Frank was pleasant, and he and Ariel had built a friendly rapport over the years.

"Congratulations, that's great news!" he said, giving her a hug. "You can go on up. Ms. Renick is expecting you."

"Thanks, Frank. I'll see you later."

When Ariel arrived at Meri's floor, she walked down the plush hallway, which resembled an upscale boutique hotel, with its ivory and silver foil designer wallpaper, and plush gray carpeting. She couldn't believe how much she had missed coming over to her friend's house for their chats over lunch and cocktails. It was late in the day, so instead of lunch, Meri's chef, Jacques, was whipping up a gourmet meal for a long, relaxing dinner. The door was ajar, which wasn't unusual when Meri was expecting company. Ariel walked right in. "Hey there. I'm here. Where are you?" she called out.

"Hello, daarling. I'll be right out. Fix yourself a drink," Meri said, her voice coming from the bedroom area.

Ariel set the shopping bag on the sofa, and went over to the beveled-mirrored bar on the far wall of the living room. Meri's bar was fully stocked with top shelf vodka, scotch, rum, tequila, and various other liquors. There was even a mini—subzero refrigerator filled with Veuve Clicquot rosé, Dom Pérignon, Cristal, and various other champagnes. She felt like celebrating. She was back in her hometown, getting ready to have dinner with her dear friend, and best of all, she had an ironclad plan to keep her marriage from falling apart, once Preston regained his memory. Ariel took two chilled flutes from the fridge, brought them along with a bottle of Gosset Grande Réserve over to the sofa, and set them on the cocktail table. She poured a flute full, took a sip of the exquisite champagne, and relaxed back onto the sofa cushions.

"What are we celebrating this evening?" Meri asked, entering the room.

"Being back in my hometown," Ariel said, taking another sip. She looked up and asked, "Where are your clothes?"

Meri was wearing a long, floor-length chocolate brown robe with ivory mink around the collar and cuffs, and matching fur-puff high-heeled slippers. "In the closet," she said casually as she took a seat next to Ariel on the sofa.

"And why are they in the closet? You knew I was coming over," Ariel said, slightly annoyed.

"I knew you were coming over, but Paul surprised me with an afternoon visit, and after we ate lunch, he ate me out, and then I took him into the bedroom and fucked his brains out. I swear that man has a perpetual hard-on. He can keep his dick erect for hours, and you know one thing I can't turn down is a stiff one! We were fucking like Energizer Bunnies and time got away from us. He's asleep now, getting ready for our all-nighter," Meri said matter-of-factly.

Ariel had known Meri for years, but it still surprised her how free Meri was with the details of her sex life. She had no sexual inhibitions like some women. She was extremely liberated and wasn't shy when it came to discussing her many lovers. "Meri, you're one of a kind." Ariel laughed. "Do you want me to leave so that you can get back to your *business*?" she asked, raising her eyebrow.

"No, no; he's in there snoring. I worked him over good, so good in fact that he's sleeping like a drunken truck driver. Besides, I need a few hours to do my Kegel exercises to tighten up again," she said, pouring herself a glass of champagne.

"T.M.I," Ariel said, putting her hand in the air. "Meri, that's just too much information. I don't need to know that you'll be flexing your vaginal muscles while we're having dinner."

"Oops, sorry," she said, putting her hand to her mouth after the fact. Meri looked at the shopping bag on the sofa. "Somebody's been to Bergy Goody."

"I stopped in Bergdorf's on the way here, and bought us a little treat." Ariel reached into the bag, took out the gift-wrapped scarf, and gave it to Meri.

A wide grin spread across Meri's face, like a kid opening a present Christmas morning, as she unwrapped the box. "Daarling, this is beautiful," she said, wrapping the scarf around her neck. She leaned over and hugged Ariel. "Thank you so much!"

"You're very welcome. I'm glad you like it."

"I do, I do." She smiled. "So, daarling, what's been going on in our nation's capital? Any good gossip?"

"I don't have any gossip, but I do have some news."

"Really?" She took a sip of champagne. "Do tell."

"I had a run-in with Michele the day I left town."

"Oh?" She raised her eyebrow. "What happened?"

"It all started when I asked her to help me with my luggage, and the next thing you know, she's talking about telling Preston about me and Trey." Ariel then explained what transpired between them.

Meri looked concerned. "So basically, she threatened you. Do you think it was wise to leave Washington while she's on the warpath? Maybe you should've stayed to keep an eye on her, and keep the young hussy in her place."

"I'm not worried. I set the wench straight. She knows better than to tell Preston anything. As long as he has no memory of what happened, it'll be my word against hers," she said confidently.

"For your sake, I hope you're right. To be on the safe side, I think you should have a conversation with Trey while you're in town to make sure he's on the same page as you. And the sooner the better. You should always be two steps ahead of Ms. Michele. She's a clever one, so you'll have to be three times as smart," Meri said, dispensing a dose of wisdom. She was older than Ariel, and had experienced her fair share of relationship crises in her lifetime, so she was well versed in dealing with drama.

"That's a good idea." Ariel nodded her head in agreement. The joyous feeling she had earlier was slowly dissipating, as she thought about Michele alone with Preston. "I would go back to Washington in the morning, but I've already started working on a project with one of the New York partners, and can't leave now," she explained.

"In that case, I suggest you go to the Black Door tonight, and talk with Trey to circumvent a potential catastrophe," she said, with concern in her voice.

Just hearing the name of the club made goose bumps spring up on Ariel's arms. She hadn't been back to the Black Door since she ran out on Trey after they had made love and his mask fell off. She'd seen Trey the few times when he came to D.C. to visit Michele, and they were cordial with each other. And of course she'd seen him last year at the grand opening of Hirschfield Multimedia. Ariel was at the opening as a guest of one of the partners, and was surprised to see Trey. Their being at the same party was coincidental, but timely. She was in New York for business, and had planned on stopping by the Black Door to talk to him. Preston had been treating her indifferently, and she immediately thought that he had regained his memory. She needed to consult Trey as to how they should proceed. When she spoke to him at the party, and told him of her suspicions, he didn't appear to be alarmed. Initially he said that he didn't know what they were going to do. After a second thought, he said for Ariel to keep a close eye on Preston for any behavioral changes. And unless Preston straight-out asked her about the affair, she should under no circumstances confess to cheating on him. Ariel agreed, and when she returned to Washington a few days later, Preston was back to his normal self.

"You're right. As much as I want to stay for dinner, I need to take care of my business, and unfortunately that business is at the Black Door." Ariel poured another flute of champagne, and guzzled it down in one smooth gulp. She needed the alcohol to drown the butterflies that had started to flutter in the pit of her stomach. The thought of seeing Trey alone was making her nervous, but with Michele on the rampage, Ariel realized that she couldn't put off talking to Trey any longer.

"Daarling, I totally understand. Let me know what happens," Meri said, standing up. She walked Ariel to the door, and gave her a tight hug for support. "Good luck, daarling."

Downstairs, Ariel asked Frank to turn on the taxi light outside of the building, and within a few minutes a cab was pulling up to the curb.

"One-fifty-sixth and Riverside Drive," she said to the driver, then leaned into the backseat, closed her eyes, and prayed for strength. Even though their affair was long over, deep down inside, she still had a weakness for Trey. He brought out the sex goddess in her that she never knew existed. Though she and Preston had a healthy sex life, Trey made her want to do X-rated things she had never before dreamed of. Even the thought of their last tryst was making her wet. Ariel opened her eyes and tried to shake off the feeling of lust building up inside of her. *What's wrong with you? He's your stepson now! Get a grip!* she scolded herself.

"That'll be twelve fifty," the driver said, interrupting her reverie.

Ariel was so preoccupied that she didn't realize the taxi was parked outside the club. She looked out the window at the massive shiny black door of the building, and chills ran up her spine. She wanted to get out, but her body was frozen. The thought of entering the Black Door was paralyzing. She knew the decadence that lay beyond the threshold, and wasn't ready to enter that world again. "Driver, I've changed my mind. Can you take me to Sixty-first and Central Park West?"

Instead of venturing inside the Black Door and tempting fate, Ariel opted to return to the safety of the corporate apartment. As much as she needed to have a conversation with Trey, she wasn't ready for a face-to-face, at least not yet. *I'll call information, and get the number to the main office of the club,* she thought. A telephone conversation she could deal with, but seeing his handsome face up close and personal was a little too much to bear.

12

PRESTON WOKE up in the middle of the night in a cold sweat. The sheets were tangled around his feet, and his pajamas were soaking wet. The nightmare that jolted him awake was frightening. He wasn't being chased by headless monsters, trapped on a runaway train, or about to plunge to his death from a skyscraper, but the dream was frightening nonetheless. The realism of the dream made it more terrifying than fending off evil demons. He dreamed that Ariel was having an affair! In the dream she was in their bed making love to another man. Preston couldn't see the face of her lover, because he was underneath the covers pleasuring her orally. Preston knew the dream was a direct result of guilt working on his psyche from the random blow job he received the other night at the restaurant.

He shook off the absurd vision, and got up to change his pajamas. He then straightened the covers on Ariel's side of the bed and climbed in. His side was moist from perspiration, and he didn't feel like changing the sheets. Preston lay his head on the pillow, and within no time had drifted back to sleep, but instead of a peaceful rest, he began dreaming again. This sequence was almost identical to the one before, except this time Ariel was screaming out, "Yeah, baby, that's it, that's it!" Preston watched her body contort into a series of positions as she squirmed with pleasure. And when she reached climax, her body jerked back and forth uncontrollably as if she were possessed by a sex demon.

Once her lover had satisfied her, she slipped beneath the covers and returned the favor. Preston could hear the man moaning as Ariel sucked him off. When she finished, they both emerged from underneath the covers, and Preston was finally able to see the man's face. The mystery man was a mystery no longer. His wife's lover was none other than *his friend*! But the dream didn't stop there.

Laird spread Ariel's legs apart into a wide *V*, and lay his body between her thighs. He sucked her neck repeatedly until a crimson hickey appeared. He then grabbed his dick and entered her slowly. Preston watched Laird's butt cheeks flex in and out as he pumped deeper into her. Ariel reached around and began rubbing his ass, and when she was near orgasm, she dug her fingernails into his butt and didn't stop digging until a stream of thick red blood came oozing down his chalky white ass. They both screamed out simultaneously. Preston didn't know if Laird was screaming because of the pain she was inflicting, or if he was actually cumming. With one look at his wife's face, he knew that she was cumming, since he had seen a variation of that face many times before. Once their lovemaking session was over, they lay comfortably in each other's arms.

The vision of them together was enough to jolt Preston into consciousness, and he bolted straight up in bed. He opened his eyes wide and stared into the darkness; though he was wide awake, he could still see the disturbing visions of Ariel and his friend making love. *That's crazy. Why would I dream something like that?*

Dreams were usually a part of the subconscious, but there was nothing in the recesses of Preston's mind that linked Laird and his wife together as lovers. Preston kept blinking, trying to blink away the unlikely liaison, but it kept replaying in his mind like a loop of a bad movie.

It didn't make sense to him, since Laird and Ariel barely knew each other. Preston could count on one hand the number of times when the two of them were together in the same room. Dreams could be bizarre, and this one was the most bizarre dream he had ever had. Preston shook it off and reached for the bottle of Evian sitting on the nightstand. His throat was parched, and he drank the entire bottle of water in two gulps. He put the empty bottle back on the nightstand, and burrowed back underneath the covers. Preston closed his eyes, but sleep eluded him.

By the time he finally drifted off, the alarm clock was buzzing. It was five-thirty, and in total he must have only gotten about three hours of sleep. Preston wanted to stay in bed another hour, but he had a six o'clock appointment scheduled with his trainer at the gym. He had recently begun a workout routine, and didn't want to get off track, especially now that he was seeing the results of exercising. His love handles had trimmed down considerably, and his middle-aged belly was also disappearing. Preston's body was toning up nicely, taking nearly ten years off of his appearance. He wearily got out of bed, went into the bathroom, washed his face, and brushed his teeth. He always took his shower after he came back from the gym. He threw on his workout clothes and headed downstairs and out the door.

The gym was only a few blocks away, and within five minutes Preston was pulling into the parking lot. Though it was early, the club was crowded with members running on treadmills, pumping weights, and riding stationary bicycles in spinning class. Preston was early, so he went over to an empty floor mat, and began his warm-up stretches.

"I see somebody's trying to push back the hands of time," Laird said, walking over to the mat.

Preston looked up and frowned. He still had visions of the lewd dream in his head. He instantly got an attitude with Laird, as if the man were actually having an affair with his wife. "I thought it was time to hire a personal trainer to get this body back in shape," he said drily.

"I know what you mean; that's why I jog every morning. I might be old, but I still have a firm midsection and tight pecs," Laird said, flexing his muscles. "What are you doing tonight?" he asked, changing the subject.

"There's an upcoming case I need to review, so I'm staying in and ordering Chinese take-out."

"That sounds boring. Why don't you put the review off for one night, and let's go back to À Votre Service. I could surely use some more servicing. That last visit was awesome." He grinned.

Preston still felt guilty about accepting a blow job from a stranger, and there was no way he was ever going back to that restaurant. "No thanks; I'm going to take a pass."

"Why?" Laird hunched his shoulders. "Isn't Ariel still out of town?"

The moment Laird said her name, the hairs on the back of Preston's neck perked up. He knew he was being foolish, but he couldn't get the vision of them out of his mind. "Yes," he said curtly. Preston started to tell Laird about his dream, but decided against it. He didn't want to put any notions in Laird's perverted head.

"Since your wife is away, why don't you take the opportunity to play? If you don't want to go back to that restaurant, I know another little joint. It's not as sophisticated as À Votre Service, but the chicks there are just as beautiful, though freakier, if you can believe that. There's even a room in the back where, for a hefty fee, you can do more than just get your jimmy waxed, if you know what I mean." He winked.

Preston knew exactly what he meant, and the thought of making love to another woman was beyond repulsive. He was a one-woman man, and had no intention of ever sleeping around outside of his marriage. As it were, a random blow job was almost as bad as committing adultery, and he was paying for the deception with nonstop feelings of guilt. "No thanks. I'll pass."

Before Laird had a chance to try and convince him, Preston's trainer walked up. "Good morning, gentlemen."

"Good morning, Eric. I'm all stretched out and ready to get started," Preston said hurriedly, grateful for the interruption. Laird could be relentless, and he didn't want to hear any more of his persuasive reasoning.

"Okay, I'll leave you guys to your workout, but, Preston, think about what I said, and if you're on board, give me a call," he said, before heading over to the free weights.

An hour later, Preston's muscles were burning, and he felt five years younger. His trainer was a former boxer and knew just what it took to give the maximum workout in the minimum amount of time. Preston felt reenergized, and rushed home to shower and change. He had a breakfast meeting with the other justices, court, a lunch meeting with a former colleague, and then back to his home office to review a few cases. His day was full and since his wife was out of town he relished every minute of his schedule to keep himself busy.

By the time Preston got back to his office that afternoon, his battery was no longer energized, and he was completely exhausted. It was a combination of the steak and potatoes that he ate at lunch and a lack of sleep. He went into his office, closed the door, and decided to lie down on the sofa for a quick catnap before reading over the case histories. No sooner had Preston closed his eyes than he fell into a deep sleep, devoid of dreams. He was worn out since he hadn't gotten much sleep the night before, and he began to snore. The buzzing sound became so loud that he woke himself up. Preston opened his eyes and looked at his watch. He'd been asleep for over an hour, which was unusual for him since he rarely took naps during the workweek. He got up and went into his private bathroom to freshen up. When he came out, someone was knocking on the office door.

"Come in," he said.

"Oh, so you are here," Michele said. "I knocked earlier, but you didn't answer."

"I was taking a siesta."

"Really?" She looked at him strangely. "It's not like you to sleep during the day." Michele had been working with Preston for over a year, and during that time she'd never known him to take a nap.

"I take them on Sundays from time to time, but today was a rare occasion. I didn't get much sleep last night," he explained.

"Why? Did you have a late night out with the boys?" she joked.

Preston flashed back to the reason why he had had a restless night. The dream instantly played back in his mind like a bad porno movie. He thought about whether or not to tell Michele. On the one hand, he wanted to discuss the dream to get another person's opinion of what it meant, but then again, he knew it was just his guilt working overtime. "No, nothing like that. Just a bad dream, that's all."

"About what?" Michele asked, still standing in the doorway.

"Well . . ." he hesitated, knowing that what he was about to say would sound ridiculous, but maybe if he talked about it, he wouldn't have any more recurring nightmares. Before he could tell her the reason for his sleeplessness, the telephone rang.

Michele quickly walked to the edge of his desk, and picked up the receiver. "Good afternoon. Justice Hendricks's office, Michele speaking. How may I assist you?"

"Hello Michele, what a pleasure hearing your voice."

"Good afternoon, Congressman Forester," she said, ignoring his seductive tone.

She covered the phone with her hand, and mouthed to Preston "Do you want to take this call?"

His first thought was to have Michele say that he was in a meeting, but he knew there was no reason why he shouldn't talk to Laird; it wasn't like the man had actually slept with his wife. "Yes, I'll take it."

"Hold on, please. He'll be right with you." She pressed the hold button, picked up the contents of Preston's out-box, and left. Her hands were full of mail, so she couldn't close the door behind her.

"Laird, what can I do for you?"

"You seemed a little annoyed this morning, and I was calling to make sure everything is okay."

Preston was indeed annoyed with Laird, but for no good reason. He wanted to get over his unfounded feelings, so he told Laird about the dream—sans the nasty details.

As he was confessing his subconscious, Michele was at the door listening. She had gotten up to close his door, but when she heard Preston say that he dreamed Ariel was having an affair, she stopped dead in her tracks. Her first thought was that his memory had returned. She stood on the side of the door, out of his eyesight, and continued listening.

Laird let out a loud roar. "Now that's preposterous. You know how dreams are—one minute you're seeing snowflakes fall in the middle of July, and the next thing you're an undercover agent for the secret service looking for terrorist cells."

"That's true. I think it's just a result of my experience at the restaurant."

"Yeah, you're probably right. Well, let me put your mind at ease. I may be a dog, but I draw the line at sleeping with someone else's wife, let alone yours. All my lovers are free and single."

"That's good to know."

They chatted for a few more minutes and then ended their conversation.

Michele was disappointed. She wanted to hear more about Preston's dream, but he ended his conversation before elaborating further. She sat back at her desk and couldn't help but think that Preston's short-term memory was returning. She picked up the phone to call Trey, but got his voice mail. Michele hung up. She realized that there was really nothing to tell. She would just keep an eye on Preston for any sudden changes in his personality. Besides, she thought that it would be in her best interest if Preston's memory returned with Ariel out of the house. At least that way she would be able to paint the truth in her own colors.

13

TREY WAS spending the afternoon with Mason Anthony, the manager of the Black Door Two, the sister club located in the meatpacking district. BD2 catered to a younger, hipper crowd, and membership was thriving thanks to Mason's ingenuity. He had created new theme rooms that didn't exist in the main club, and the members loved the Mani/Pedi Spa suite where they could get toe-sucking pedicures and finger-licking manicures. They also loved reciting poetry in the Naked Poet Sanctuary. The Disco was a throwback to Studio 54, where members partied hard until daylight, and was a huge hit.

They were meeting at the driving range in Chelsea Piers, a sports and entertainment complex located along the West Side Highway, near Chelsea. Trey arrived first and went to the upper level that overlooked the Hudson River toward New Jersey. The view was scenic, with boats cruising up and down the river and houses dotting the shoreline along the Jersey side. He went inside the netted cage, took out his Big Bertha, and began practicing his swing. Trey had recently taken up golf, and was a natural. His form was perfect. He gripped the club, placing his right hand over his left, dropped his head, and with his eyes focused on the little white ball, he angled his body and swung. The dimpled ball sailed over the netting, and hung high in the air, before sinking into the murky waters of the Hudson.

"Tiger, better watch out," Mason said, clapping his hands as he entered the cage next to Trey's.

"Yeah, you better tell him that I got game." Trey laughed.

"The way you're swinging, you'll be ready for the PGA tour in a few years."

"Years?" Trey wrinkled his nose. "I'll be ready to sport that green jacket by next summer," he said with a straight face, even though he knew he was nowhere near pro material.

After their jousting, the two men concentrated on perfecting their swing, and after an hour of practicing, they packed up their clubs and headed downstairs. Instead of having lunch at the Lighthouse, the restaurant located on the pier, which served mostly seafood, they headed over to the east side. They were in the mood for a juicy burger at Jackson Hole, so they tossed their golf bags in Trey's Range Rover and drove over to Third Avenue. A half an hour later, they were seated in the restaurant, ready to chow down.

"Man, these burgers are so big, feels like I'm eating a small calf," Mason commented as he wrapped his hands around the mammoth hamburger.

"Yeah, Jackson Hole is known for the size of their burgers," Trey agreed, biting into his own petite cow.

"So, man, I hear that you've been rocking Lexi's world," Mason said, picking up a napkin and wiping mayo from the corners of his mouth.

Trey looked at him strangely. "And how did you know that?" He hadn't breathed a word of their affair, and had planned on keeping it under wraps, since technically he still had a girlfriend.

"Didn't you know that Lexington and Terra are best friends? Women are like sieves; they can't hold water. They talk about *everything*," he said with emphasis.

Trey knew that Mason was dating Terra Benson, the tobacco heiress, but he didn't know that Lexi and Terra were friends. Truth be told, he didn't know much about Lexi. They had only fucked once, and not much talking had taken place during that time. All Lexi seemed to want was sex, and he was totally on board with that program. He wasn't looking for a commitment, just somebody to screw every now and then when Michele wasn't around. "No, man, I didn't know they were friends."

"Well, from what she's been telling Terra, I'd say you got the girl's nose wide open," he said, ribbing his friend.

Trey blushed. He didn't like his business in the street, but he trusted Mason to keep his mouth shut. "Just so you know, I didn't plan on fucking a client. As a matter of fact, when she came on to me at Hirschfield Multimedia's grand opening, I turned her down flat. But she called me at the club recently and invited me to come down to the Leopard Lounge. She looked so good that I just couldn't resist, but, hey . . . a man's gotta do what a man's gotta do."

Mason was also at the grand opening, but he was preoccupied with Terra. They had broken up, but that night reconciled their differences. They kissed, made up, and made love in one of the private offices to commemorate the moment. "I totally understand," Mason said, thinking back to that night over a year ago. "And don't worry, your secret's safe with me."

"Thanks, man, I appreciate it." As they were eating, Trey's cell phone rang. He took the phone out of his pocket, and looked at the caller ID. It was Michele. He didn't feel like talking to her. He was still a little pissed that she had blown him off to go to a party. He pressed the reject button to send her call to voice mail. No sooner had he put the phone back into his pocket than it rang again. He took it back out, and looked at the screen; it was Michele calling back, and once more he forwarded her call to voice mail. He didn't feel like listening to another one of her lame apologies, so he turned the phone off before she had a chance to call a third time.

"Man, somebody's blowing up your phone," Mason commented.

"That somebody would be Michele."

"Man, when are you finally going to give that girl her walking papers?" Mason knew that Trey was no longer into Michele—if he were, he would have never slept with Lexi—and didn't understand why he kept her hanging on.

He exhaled and said, "Soon, man, soon." Though Mason was a good friend, Trey had never told him the real reason why he was still involved with Michele. He was embarrassed to say that he had gotten caught feasting on his future stepmother's breasts, and that he was stringing Michele along so that she wouldn't tell his father the truth.

"Well, in my experience, I've found it's better to drop the deadweight before it drowns you."

Trey nodded his head in agreement, because that's exactly how he was feeling, like he was drowning, and Michele was the weight that was taking him under.

MICHELE KEPT HITTING redial, but Trey's phone went right into voice mail, a clear indication that he had turned off his cell. She was so frustrated that she slammed her phone on the desk. She needed to talk to him, but for some reason he was ignoring her, and it pissed her off. Michele wanted to tell Trey about his dad's dream. Somewhere in the recesses of Preston's mind, he was probably beginning to recall what had happened, and she decided to give Trey a heads-up.

She called the club, since he wasn't answering his cell phone, but the answering machine picked up. "Trey, call me as soon as possible; it's important," she said after the beep.

Michele started to dial Ariel's cell phone, but stopped. *Why should I tell her anything? Especially since she's planning on having me fired.* Michele knew that Ariel despised her, and she felt the same way.

She thought for a few minutes, and realized that it wasn't her decision to keep the truth from Preston in the first place. Trey and Ariel had basically forced her into secrecy. She only went along with the program because she was in love with Trey, and she thought that he was in love with her. A year ago, he was the doting boyfriend, catering to her every need. But now they were growing apart at a rapid pace. In the beginning of their relationship, she had hopes of one day marrying Trey—not anymore. She had been attracted to his physical being before getting to know him as a person, and now that the sheets had cooled off, she realized that she wanted more than just great sex.

Michele suddenly started to feel trapped. She had been forced to keep Preston in the dark; now she didn't see the sense in keeping her end of the deal any longer. She and Trey were drifting apart, and Ariel was going to have her kicked to the curb—that is, unless she helped Preston remember and then gave him her version of the truth. This, of course, would make her out to be as much of a victim as him. Michele would tell Preston that they made her lie. The more she thought about this idea, the more she liked it. As she sat there and plotted, another lightbulb went off in her head.

With a little prodding, I bet I can jog his memory. Michele smiled at that thought. With Ariel in New York, she'd have more than enough time to weave her magic. Michele had been looking for the perfect person to usher her into the elite circle, and who better than a Supreme Court justice to give her validation? Once she exposed Ariel for the liar she was, Preston would no doubt divorce her without a second thought, and she would be there to help lick his wounds. Michele had never looked at her boss romantically, and wasn't attracted to older men, but she was attracted to what they offered. Preston was powerful, rich, and sophisticated, and that combination was an enticing aphrodisiac. Michele was no fool, and realized that her relationship with Trey was dead in the water. It was time to move on, and she didn't have a problem moving from son to father. After all, if Trey could have an affair with his father's fiancée, then why couldn't she flip the script and fuck Preston?

ARIEL WAS on her way to meet a client and was running late. Traffic in midtown was at a standstill. There was an accident in one of the lanes, causing a major backup with buses, taxis, and cars lined bumper-to-bumper like a giant parking lot. She was tempted to get out and walk, but after the cab inched past the crash scene, traffic began to move again. She sat back and breathed a sigh of relief, but the flow only lasted for five blocks before the cars jammed up again. This time, instead of a fender bender, a bicycle messenger had fallen and spilled a backpack full of packages in the street. Some pedestrians stopped to help him retrieve the items, thus slowing traffic even more. Ariel looked at her watch; it was a quarter to three. Her appointment was in fifteen minutes, and they still had ten blocks to go. *I can run faster than this taxi is moving*, she thought.

"You can let me out at the next corner," she told the driver.

The second he pulled over, she tossed a ten-dollar bill through the Plexiglas partition, gathered her briefcase and purse, and jumped out without waiting for her change or a receipt. Luckily, she had worn flats with her pantsuit instead of pumps, and she began to trot down the street. She was moving so fast that she covered two blocks in less than two minutes. Ariel was so preoccupied with making it to her destination on time that she bumped the shoulders of several people as she whisked by, barely saying "excuse me" as she passed. She had tunnel vision, and barely noticed the other pedestrians walking alongside her, as she whisked past.

"Somebody's in an awfully big hurry."

Ariel stopped in her tracks at the sound of the voice, focused on the face in front of her, and stared. She was at a loss for words.

"So . . . how have you been?"

"Fine," she said, finally finding her voice.

"Ariel, this is Mason. Mason, this is my stepmother, Ariel," Trey said, making introductions.

She automatically extended her hand. "Nice to meet you." She looked at Trey's friend and couldn't help but notice how strikingly handsome he was. He was about six-four, with a bald head. A goatee framed his smooth, cocoa-brown complexion. He and Trey resembled each other, as if they were related. He looked familiar, and she tried to place his face. Then it occurred to her where she knew him from. *He's the escort I hired to take me to the Lancaster benefit last year.* Mason had been the perfect gentleman, and no one at the party knew that the man on Ariel's arm was a date for hire. At the end of the evening, he gave her a business card for the Black Door, and told her to call the number on the back in the event she needed more than an escort.

"Nice to meet you too," he said, giving no hint that they had met previously.

The way Trey introduced her as his "stepmother" Ariel assumed that he hadn't told Mason about their affair. Standing in the presence of Trey and Mason was making her nervous and she began to alternate her briefcase from one hand to the other. Ariel tried not to look at Trey, but she couldn't keep her eyes from darting up to his gorgeous face; she then quickly diverted them back to the ground before he caught her staring. Though he was her stepson, there was no denying that he was one handsome man. His hair was cut to perfection; it was extremely low and resembled a five o'clock shadow. He stood there smiling for no apparent reason, and his matching dimples pierced his smooth chocolate skin. Trey looked as if he were sculpted from a giant Hershey bar, and she wanted to sink her teeth in and take a savory bite. Ariel hated that she still harbored feelings for Trey, but as much as she tried to erase their love affair from her memory bank, the images of them fucking at the Black Door were permanently etched in her brain. Ariel wondered if Trey reminisced about their liaison as well. The way he was smiling at her, made her think that he was having a private flashback of his own.

"So what brings you to New York?" Trey asked, still smiling like he was happy to see her.

"I'm here on business," she replied and looked away, trying to avoid eye contact. She was afraid that her eyes would reveal her repressed feelings, and the last thing she wanted was to get involved with Trey again.

"How long are you going to be in town?"

"For a week or so. I'm here working on a case."

"Oh, I see. Well, maybe we can get together for a drink or dinner while you're here." Even though their tryst was over, Trey still admired Ariel. She was a smart, classy woman, and he wanted to keep her as a friend, if that were at all possible. The few times he'd seen her in Washington, she was pleasant, and though they hadn't really discussed how their affair ended, he assumed that she was okay with his decision to stay with Michele.

"That would be fine. As a matter of fact, how's tonight?" She needed to tell him about her run-in with Michele. "Can you meet me at Olives at the W, on Park Avenue South?" Ariel figured meeting at a public place like Olives, a popular restaurant and bar that stayed crowded, was much safer than meeting him at the Black Door.

"Sure. What time?"

"Five-thirty."

Trey thought for a second. He had to run back uptown to the club and wouldn't be back by then. "I can't do five-thirty. Is six o'clock okay?"

"Sure. Six is fine. I'll see you then," she said, and quickly walked away. She wanted to turn around to see if they were still standing there, but decided against it, just in case Trey was watching her.

Ariel was only five minutes late to her meeting and would have been on time if she hadn't run into Trey and Mason. She blamed her tardiness on the traffic, which was an acceptable excuse for New Yorkers, since everyone in the city had gotten caught up in the mayhem at one time or the other.

She was meeting with a client to discuss new developments in their case. The senior partner also working on the case was out of town so she was spearheading today's meeting. The client was a *Fortune* 500 corporation involved in a class-action lawsuit. Former employees were suing, claiming that the company was guilty of unfair labor practices. Initially, there were fifty litigants, but after Ariel hired the best investigator in the city to do background checks, twenty people dropped their claims. The PI discovered that nearly half of the plaintiffs had filed discrimination lawsuits in the past, and she had a sneaking suspicion that the entire suit was bogus.

The investigator was also in the conference room, going over his findings in explicit detail. Ariel was grateful that he was basically running the meeting, since she was distracted with images of Trey.

She thought back on the evening when Michele had caught him feasting on her boobs. Michele was in shock at catching her man with another woman, and quickly fled the scene, with Trey following close behind. At that time, Ariel wanted him to choose her, and not run after Michele, but he didn't. Ariel knew that their affair was wrong, but when it started, she had no idea that her lover was Preston's son. Once she learned of his identity months after their first encounter, it was too late. By then she had already fallen in lust with him. Ariel knew that Trey had made the right decision in choosing Michele, but it didn't make dealing with the rejection any better. She had been rejected by her mother at birth and put in the foster care system, so any type of denial stung like a stingray's barb. Had she met Trey in another time and place, there was no doubt that they would be together, but that wasn't the case. She was committed to Preston.

An hour later, the meeting was adjourned, and she made a beeline straight out of the building. She hailed a taxi; unlike earlier, traffic was sailing smoothly and she arrived at the W fifteen minutes early. She took a seat on an oblong velvet cushion near the window and waited.

As she was waiting for the server so that she could order a drink, Todd English, the owner and chef of Olives, spotted her sitting by the window. Ariel had met Todd a few years ago, when her firm did some work for one of his restaurants. Todd was tall and strikingly handsome, with thick dark hair and a killer smile.

"Hello, beautiful," Todd said, sitting next to her on the window seat and giving her a smooch on the cheek.

"Hey there," she said, giving him a friendly kiss in return. "Looks like business is booming." She looked around the crowded lounge.

"Yes, things here at the W have been good. I can't complain," he said, smiling modestly. "Are you hungry? Why don't you come in the dining room and let me treat you to dinner," he offered.

"Thanks, Todd, but I'm waiting for someone, and I'm really not hungry. I had a late lunch," she lied. Ariel hadn't eaten since breakfast, but her stomach was tied up in knots at the thought of meeting with Trey, and she couldn't eat a thing.

"Oh." He looked disappointed. "Well, at least let me have the waitress bring over a plate of hummus, flat bread, and an assortment of olives."

"Hmm, that sounds delicious."

"And, speaking of delicious, the bartender is shaking up a new drink called the Velvet Cane."

"The Velvet Cane, that sounds interesting. What's in it?" Ariel hadn't been out for cocktails in a while and wasn't hip to some of the latest martinis.

"It's Moët and Chandon White Star, poured over a raw sugar cube, and drizzled with Ten Cane rum. It's refreshing. I think you'll enjoy it."

Ariel wanted to tell him to bring over an entire tray. She needed to calm her nerves before Trey arrived. "Thanks Todd, that would be great."

"No problem, Ariel. I hate to run off, but I've got to get back to the kitchen and make sure the osso buco is braised according to my brilliant recipe." He chuckled, and kissed her on the cheek again before rising to leave.

A few minutes after Todd left, the waitress came rushing over with the appetizers and a Velvet Cane. Ariel took a sip and loved the martini instantly. She sat and enjoyed her cocktail while waiting for Trey.

The hotel was located across the street from Union Square. She sat at the huge picture window and watched people rush in and out of the small park. Some of them were going to the cafés and restaurants that dotted the perimeter of the park, and some were headed toward the subway station. In the distance, Ariel spotted a tall man, wearing a black leather coat, jeans, and a black turtleneck. The coat swung open in the breeze, and the way he strutted confidently with his head held high, reminded her of Samuel L. Jackson in *Shaft*. When the man came into focus, she realized that it was Trey, and her heart began to race from nervous energy. She took a big gulp of the martini, and turned so her back was against the window, so he wouldn't see her ogling him. Ariel put the drink on the table, then quickly retrieved her cell phone from her purse, flipped it open, and dialed her voice mail.

Trey breezed into the lobby looking like a movie star, and scanned the room for Ariel. He spotted her and walked over. He stood there for a second as if waiting for an invitation to sit down; when she didn't acknowledge his presence, he sat across from her on the cushion anyway.

Ariel pretended to be on an important call, when in actuality she was just listening to her old messages. She finally looked in his direction and mouthed, "Just a minute." Ariel nodded her head up and down, as if she were listening intently. She wanted to buy a little more time to compose herself. Outwardly she appeared calm and collected, but inside, she was an emotional wreck. She hadn't been this close to Trey since that episode in her apartment. After the last message played, she flipped the phone shut, cleared her throat, and said, "Hello."

"Hi, Ariel, how are you?" he asked, with sincerity in his voice.

Ariel looked into his small, seductive eyes, and felt a tug at her heart. He was so damn sexy that she wanted to lean over and kiss his full lips. There was no denying that a part of her—a big part—still wanted Trey. *What are you thinking? He's your stepson, for crying out loud! What happened at the Black Door is ancient history. GET A GRIP!!* "I'm good, thanks. Listen, Trey, the reason I wanted to meet with you is to tell you about a conversation I had with Michele," she said, getting right to the point. Ariel then went on to tell him about the confrontation that transpired between her and Michele the morning she left for New York.

"That's probably why she called me this afternoon."

"Really?" Ariel looked surprised, but should have known that Michele would have gone blabbing to Trey. "What did she say?"

"I don't know. I didn't talk to her."

"What do you mean? I thought you just said that she called you today."

"She did, but I sent her calls to voice mail," he said matter-of-factly.

"Calls?" Ariel asked, alarmed. "How many times did she call?"

"Twice before I turned off my phone, and—"

She cut him off. "Oh no!" she nearly shrieked. "Trey, you have to call her back right away. What if she told Preston about us?" Ariel asked, panicking.

"Clam down. Michele isn't stupid, and she wouldn't tell my dad anything without talking to me first. You made a good point by telling her that it would be her word against ours," he said, putting his hand on top of hers.

Ariel should have snatched her hand away, but she didn't. Even though she knew it was a comforting gesture, their skin-to-skin contact felt good, and she wanted to relish the moment, even if it were fleeting. "What are we going to do? Should we tell Preston the truth before Michele does?" she finally asked, breaking the spell.

Trey removed his hand, rubbed his chin with his thumb and index finger, and thought for a moment. "Well, the truth would be better coming from us. At least we could soften the blow by explaining that we didn't know each other's identity at the time, and that our affair was innocent."

"Isn't that an oxymoron? Who ever heard of an innocent affair? Anyway, that would explain away the Black Door, but what about the incident at my apartment? We could talk until we used every word in the dictionary, but there's no way of explaining why you were at my place, sucking on my—" she stopped mid-sentence, and shook her head as if she were disgusted with herself.

He knew exactly what she was about to say, and jumped right in. "You have a point."

"All I can say is that we got caught up in the moment, but Preston will probably want to know why I went to the Black Door in the first place. Had I never stepped foot inside the club, none of this would be happening," she said, nearly on the verge of tears, wishing that she could turn back the hands of time.

Trey wanted to know the same thing. He had never asked Ariel that question, because their affair took him off guard, but now that it was over and he had a clear head, he finally asked, "Why did you come to the club, since you were in a relationship?"

Ariel looked down in embarrassment. Her sins had caught up with her, and she felt like a scorned woman with a bright red *A* tattooed boldly across her chest. "Basically, I went there just to look around and relieve my sexual frustration, nothing more. Preston was preoccupied with securing the nomination for the Supreme Court, and I was lonely. It all started off innocently enough, until I met the man in the black mask. Had I known that that man was you, I would have never allowed myself a moment of weakness," she said, with the tears that had welled up in her eyes earlier falling slowly down her cheeks.

Trey took a white handkerchief out of his back pocket, and handed it to her. "Look, Ariel, it's not the end of the world. We're only human with mortal flaws. When are you going back to D.C.?"

She dabbed her face with the cotton cloth, and composed herself. "I'm working on a case with one of the senior partners, and won't be able to leave for another week or so."

"Let me know when you make your plans to leave, and I'll go back to Washington with you. We'll tell my dad together. I think a united front will be much better than you going it alone."

"What about Michele?" Ariel asked, still concerned about her nemesis.

"Don't worry about Michele. I'll deal with her." Trey had been blowing his girlfriend off lately, but now he'd have to reverse his role, and become the caring boyfriend once again, so that she wouldn't reveal their secret before they had a chance to tell Preston face-to-face. "Maybe I'll invite her up for the weekend."

"That's an excellent idea. At least she'll be away from Preston for a few days." Ariel exhaled a sigh of relief. She knew that once she and Trey put their heads together, they would come up with a reasonable solution. Ariel had neutralized Michele as a threat, and felt slightly better, but her nerves were still frayed, so she picked up her drink and polished it off. She offered to buy Trey a Velvet Cane, but he declined, saying that he had to go back to work. Once he was gone, Ariel ordered another cocktail. Even though they had committed the ultimate act of betrayal, Trey was one of the good guys. He wanted to make things right with Preston, and so did she. Ariel knew marrying Preston once he lost his memory was a gamble. She had been playing a high-stakes game, now it was time to cut her losses and tell him the truth. She had hoped to be at least pregnant when that day came, but with Michele on the warpath, she didn't have much of a choice. Her only comfort was in knowing that she and Trey were in this together. They couldn't be lovers anymore, but at least they were allies. Ariel raised her glass and silently drank to their newfound friendship.

SHE WAS in New York on business, but her business had nothing to do with corporate boardrooms, conference calls, or spreadsheets. It had to do with bedsheets, and not the five-hundred thread count variety. She was a frequent visitor to the Black Door, but had yet to visit the sister club, BD2, in the meatpacking district. She told her husband that she was spending a few days in Manhattan shopping, lunching, and visiting with friends. For obvious reasons, she omitted that she was also going to do some fucking as well. She loved her husband, but sex with him was like painting by numbers—you knew exactly where the next color was supposed to go before you finished the picture. In other words, their sex life was beyond predictable. She craved the exhilaration the Black Door offered. With its exotic theme rooms and sexy servers, it was anything but predictable.

"Welcome to BD Two," said the beefy greeter the moment she stepped off the freight elevator. "Can I take your coat?"

She unfastened the rhinestone buttons on the fuchsia evening coat and slipped her arms out. Underneath, she wore a silver mesh halter chemise, which matched her silver mask. The dress was so short that it barely covered her bottom. She knew the outfit was designed for a younger woman, but inside the confines of the Black Door, any article of clothing was appropriate, or none at all. Some members wore nothing more than their masks, a thong, and stilettos.

The greeter walked up close behind her, and asked, "Do you need tweaking?"

She smiled broadly, and nodded her head yes. She purposely left her panties in the hotel in anticipation of getting tweaked. He was nearly six and a half feet tall, and towered over her. He wrapped his muscular arms around her, engulfing her in his embrace. His large masculine frame made her feel like a sexy feline, and she backed her ass up into his crotch. He then reached underneath her micro-minidress, and his hand immediately landed on her smooth triangle. She had gotten a Brazilian wax earlier that day, and her pussy was now as clean as a cue ball. He stroked the smooth skin back and forth with his thumb, until he felt the tip of her clit poke out like a turtle emerging from its shell. He took his thumb and index finger and began kneading the soft, sensitive tissue until she started moaning.

"Oohh, daddy, you found my spot. Don't stop!"

Once her clitoris was totally engorged, he slipped his middle finger inside of her vagina and found that she was dripping wet. A moist box was a sign that he had done his job to perfection, so he stopped and said, "Now you're tweaked."

"Why'd you stop?" she whined.

"Because you're wet and ready to enter BD Two," he said, backing away.

"But I want you to fuck me right now," she demanded.

"My job is to tweak, not to fuck. You'll have to find a server for that. We have a new chamber called Between the Sheets, and I'm sure you can find a willing participant there." He opened the door to the club, and pointed her in the direction of the new theme room.

Music was emanating from the disco, and she bopped her head to the beat as she made her way down the corridor. The sound of Gloria Gaynor reminded her of Studio 54 back in the seventies and early eighties. She continued down the hallway, and stopped at a door that was wrapped in a black satin sheet, turned the doorknob—the only part of the door that was exposed—and walked inside.

"Would you care to change into a sheet?" asked a young Hispanic server, standing inside of the doorway with a black satin sheet draped over his arm.

He was clothed in only a thin sheet wrapped around his waist; she admired his bare chest, which was toned and sculpted into a series of undulating muscles. He looked good enough to eat, and she thought about propositioning him, but obviously he was working the door, and she didn't want to get turned down twice in the same night. She quickly scoped out the room for a victim, and noticed that everyone was either dressed toga style, draped in sheets, or on beds between black satin sheets, more than likely nude. "I'd love to change."

He held up the sheet and used it as a shield as she slipped out of her dress. He then wrapped the sinuous fabric around her body so that she resembled a Greek goddess. Once he secured the toga, he picked up her dress from the floor and hung it in a nearby closet.

There were various sized beds—round, oval, square, king, queen, and twin—strategically placed throughout the large room, and she gracefully maneuvered her body around each one. A sexy French song by the hot new artist BabyKat was playing in the background, everyone seemed lost in the hypnotic music, and nobody noticed her as she scanned the room looking for a partner. All the servers were engaged, pleasuring the oversexed members. They were humping, pumping, sucking, and fucking. She slowed her pace and nearly stopped at the bedside of a couple that was going at it sideways. The server had the woman turned on her left side, and his body was angled horizontally to hers, right near her ass. He was easing his dick into her pussy from behind. The way they were positioned reminded her of a moving T Square. She could see the rim of his penis as he pulled out, and his huge balls as he eased back inside. He was plunging in and out and in and out of the member's vagina like an expert plumber. The sound of his bloated scrotum slapping against the woman's ass was making her hornier. She wanted a good plunging of her own, and licked her lips at the sight of them.

"You don't have to stand there and drool. If you like what you see, you can have some of the same action," a server said, approaching her.

She looked at the person in front of her, and wondered whether that person worked at the club or not. She couldn't decide, so she asked, "*You* work here?"

"Yes, I do."

"Oh. Since when did they start hiring women?" Ever since she'd been coming to the Black Door, she had never seen a female server.

"My name is Christy," said the auburn-haired beauty. "I'm the first woman to ever work at the club, but I assure you that I can do everything the male servers can do." She smiled a crooked smile below her purple half-mask, and added, "Probably even better."

"And how is that?"

"Because I've got a twelve inch strap-on with the girth of an overgrown plantain, if not thicker," Christy said, and whipped back her toga, revealing a lethal looking prosthetic penis.

She had never seen a dick that long and thick before—real or fake—and she couldn't help but to reach out and touch it. She ran her hand along the length of the shaft, and it felt authentic, even down to the bulging veins. It was totally erect, and she wondered how a cock that large would feel inside of her pussy. She looked into Christy's face, and though she could only see her mouth—which was decorated in bright red lipstick, with a heavy coat of gloss—she thought that Christy was attractive enough to fuck, and continued stroking the fake dick. She hadn't been with a woman since college, and didn't consider herself gay or bisexual, but she was bi-curious. Curiosity was making her mouth water, so she bent down and licked the tip of the strap-on. One thing she couldn't resist was a big cock, and even though she knew it wasn't the real deal, she wanted to experience it anyway. After she finished deep throating the long schlong, she said, "I want you to fuck me."

Christy didn't say a word. She grabbed her prey by the hand, led her to an empty bed, laid her on her back, and mounted her like a man. Christy rubbed the oversized dick with a handful of K-Y Jelly, and then eased the tip inside of her partner's pussy. Once she was all the way in, she began pumping like a man, until the woman underneath her started moaning with pleasure. She was humping so hard that sweat began pouring down her chest onto her exposed nipples. "You like this hard cock?" she asked in between breaths.

"I love it. It's sooo good!" Her husband's penis wasn't nearly this big, and barely filled her up, but this dick was so large that it hit her G-spot over and over and over. She was in climax heaven, and with her eyes closed, she couldn't tell that a woman was doing the fucking.

"I told you, I can do anything a man can do."

"Can you suck a clit?"

"Like a pro." Christy slid the dildo out, spread her partner's legs further apart, and began feasting on her clitoris.

Five minutes later, she started screaming, "Oh shit, I'm cumming! I'm cumming!! After she recovered from her sixth climax, she leaned up on one elbow and said, "Christy, I think you're going to be my new best friend."

"The pleasure was all mine," Christy said.

She watched as Christy wiped the dildo clean, and then she readjusted the belt around her waist to tighten the cock back in place. Once she had secured the strap-on, she disappeared toward the front of the room, no doubt looking for another victim.

TREY HAD been blowing up Michele's phone all night, and most of the following day. She purposely sent his calls to voice mail, just like he had done to her. Every time she hit the reject button on her phone, she felt empowered. He'd even called her work number. Fortunately there was caller ID on the phone, and she let the automated recording answer instead of picking up. Michele was on a new mission, which didn't include Trey. She'd made up her mind to seduce Preston, and didn't want to deal with any distractions from Trey. She thought about coming right out and telling him that it was over, but she didn't want to tip him off. Trey would probably want to know why she was dumping him without notice, and he of all people couldn't be privy to her plan.

For some reason, he had finally decided to return her calls, but she was no longer interested in telling him about Preston's dream. He had left numerous messages, but she deleted every single one before listening to them. If her scheme had any chance of succeeding she needed to cut Trey loose, cold turkey—no patch, no placebos.

Her phone rang again, and again she looked at the caller ID. It was Fiona, so she picked up.

"Hey girl, what's up?"

"That's my question to you," Fiona said, sounding a little put off. "I haven't heard from you since the CBC affair. I hope you're not still upset that Thompson gave away the extra ticket."

Michele had been humiliated beyond belief, and had yet to tell her friend what happened at the door. Now that some time had passed, and she'd gotten over the embarrassment, she told Fiona everything.

"Girl, I am so sorry," Fiona said, as if it were her fault.

"Don't worry about it. I'm working on a plan to ensure that that will never happen to me again in my life!" she said with conviction.

"What are you talking about? What plan?"

"A plan that will soon have my name on every VIP list in town."

"And how's that going to work?" Fiona asked, still clueless.

"It's going to work, because I've found the perfect sponsor," Michele said, nearly bubbling over with excitement.

"Sponsor?"

"Yes, someone to usher me beyond the velvet ropes."

"And who might that be, pray tell."

Michele hesitated for a second. She and Fiona shared mostly everything, but she didn't know if this was something that was shareable. Michele realized her scheme was far-fetched, and thought twice about verbalizing it, but if there was one person who wouldn't judge her motives, it was Fiona. She covered the mouthpiece with her hand, and whispered, "Preston."

"Preston!" Fiona shrieked through the receiver.

So much for judgments. Michele could tell by Fiona's tone that she was surprised. "Yes, Preston. Why do you sound so shocked?"

"First of all, he's your boyfriend's father, *and* your boss. Have you lost your mind?"

"On the contrary, I've finally woken up. Trey is never going to be the man I want him to be, and truth be told, I don't think he'll ever pop the proverbial question, not that I would accept anyway. I know what I'm saying is a stretch, but hey, what do I have to lose?" She waited a few seconds to hear what Fiona was going to say, but there was silence on the other end, so she continued. "Come on, think about the situation. Ariel cheated on Preston with Trey. Trey lied to his father about his business dealings. Preston had a stroke and forgot those two *major* details. So what do you think is going to happen once his memory returns?" she asked rhetorically, not expecting an answer. "Well, I'll tell you. Preston is going to divorce Ariel with a quickness, and who do you think will be there to help him grieve the loss? *Moi!* That's who," Michele said, full of herself.

Fiona couldn't believe her ears. She was aware of Michele's desperation to be embraced into the fold, but she didn't think Michele would go this far. "Girl, you know that I love you, and I only want the best for you, but . . ."

"But what?" she asked, full of indignation.

"I think you're taking this a little too far. What happened between Ariel and Preston is their business, and—"

"And nothing," Michele huffed. "It would've been their business if my man wasn't involved, which I saw up close and personal with my own eyes. Trey and Ariel roped me into this lie for their own benefit. Now it's time that I get some satisfaction out of the deal. I'm tired of being their puppet on a string. Now I'm ready to pull some strings of my own."

Listening to Michele rant, Fiona knew that talking her out of this outrageous plan was futile, so she asked the million-dollar question. "So how are you going to sway Preston over to your side?"

"I really don't want to talk anymore about this over the phone," she said, looking over her shoulder, making sure Preston was still in his office with the door closed. "Just know that I've thought long and hard over the past few days, and I've devised the perfect scheme. But with Ariel out of town for probably one more week, I have to move fast. And speaking of moving fast, I've got to go, time is a-wasting." She chuckled. "Fiona, don't worry. I've got everything under control. I'll talk to you soon," she said, hung up, and focused her attention back on her computer.

Michele had been doing research on the Internet all morning, but the material she was looking for had nothing to do with work. It had taken her nearly an hour, but she finally found the perfect article. She hit the print icon on her computer, and waited for the information that she had Googled to download. Once the article printed, she folded it, wrote a note on a yellow sticky with her left hand so that her handwriting would not be recognizable, and stuck the note on top of the article. Michele switched screens on her computer so that Preston couldn't see what she was working on in case he came out of his office. She addressed the envelope with the same script, put a stamp on it, walked outside, and put it in the mailbox that was less than a half a block away. Once she heard the envelope drop into the blue box, she smiled a sly grin, and walked back to the town house.

Michele sat at her desk, and pulled up the screen she had been working on earlier, and printed out a different article. Instead of mailing this one, she slid the pages in with Preston's mail. *Showtime,* she said to herself, and knocked on his office door.

"Come in," she heard him say through the closed door.

"Good morning, Preston," she said, in a professional voice.

He looked up from the newspaper he was reading, and stared at her in disbelief, almost doing a double take at her outfit. Michele wore a gray gabardine pantsuit with a white mock turtleneck. The three-button jacket was buttoned up, with a pearl brooch on the left lapel. Her hair was swept back in a neat bun, exposing a pair of tiny pearl earrings that matched the pendant. Her overall appearance was extremely conservative, even down to her gray flannel round-toe Ferragamos with the demure patent-leather bow. The suit wasn't too tight like most of her clothes; it fit perfectly. He was used to seeing the imprint of her nipples through her snug silk blouses, but today her breasts were shielded behind the wool blazer and turtleneck, with no cleavage in sight. She even wore a pair of square, black-framed glasses. If he didn't know better, Preston would have thought that a stranger had entered his office. Usually, she looked like a party girl ready for a hot date, but today Michele resembled a prim Republican.

Obviously, she took my suggestions regarding her wardrobe to heart, Preston thought. He was glad that Michele had toned down her style of dress, but she had gone from one extreme to the other. The outfit made her look ten years older, and wiser.

"Nice pantsuit." He smiled.

"Thank you. I thought about what you said, and you were right. I'm in Washington now, and need to dress like a political aide, and not a barmaid," she replied, without cracking a smile.

"Well, I wouldn't say that you dressed like a barmaid, but I must admit that I like this style better. When did you start wearing glasses? They make you look like a librarian."

"I've been wearing glasses since grade school. Normally, I wear contacts, but my eyes were irritated this morning so I decided to wear my glasses instead," she said, adjusting the arm of the frames.

"Oh, I see."

"Here's your mail." She handed him a stack of correspondence. "If you need anything else, I'll be at my desk," she said, sounding like an efficient robot without any emotion.

He couldn't help but stare at her transformation; even her demeanor was subdued. Her usual bubbly personality was replaced by a more reserved one. She wasn't full of idle small talk, just handed him the mail and left.

Once she was gone, Preston shook his head, still marveling at her drastic change. Though he approved of her new look, a part of him would miss her daily peep show (after all, he was a man and wasn't immune to the female anatomy). Preston sorted through the various letters, business periodicals, and law reviews. He thumbed through a copy of *Newsweek*, and then put it aside. There was nothing exciting in the morning mail, so he picked up the stack of papers to put them in the "file" bin, but a piece of paper slipped out and fell on the floor. He picked up the document; it was an article from the Internet. He looked it over, and began reading. Preston finished the first page, but the article wasn't over. The story was intriguing, so he fished through the stack of papers for the second page. He breezed through the rest of the article and couldn't help but wonder what it was doing in his mail, since the story had nothing to do with politics. The piece was entitled "Off the Radar," and it focused on underground sex clubs. One establishment in particular, the Black Door, seemed familiar, but he didn't know why, since the story mentioned that men were excluded from membership. Preston knew there was no way that he had ever been inside, but the name rang a bell nonetheless. *What's this doing in my mail?* he wondered. Preston pressed the intercom. "Michele, can you come in please?"

"Did you need me, Preston?" she asked, once she entered his office.

He held up the computer printout. "Did you see this?"

She squinted her eyes, "What is it?"

"An article on underground adult entertainment clubs; is this yours?"

"Uh, yes." She put her hand to her mouth as if embarrassed. "A friend of mine is doing her dissertation on sex in America, and I agreed to help with the research. I must have accidentally put the printout in your mail." She walked over to his desk. "I'm sorry; I'll take that," she said, and reached out for the pages.

"No problem." He handed her the article. "Michele, can I ask you something?"

"Sure, Preston, what is it?"

"For some reason, this place called the Black Door sounds slightly familiar and I don't know why. Have you ever heard of this club before?"

Michele hunched her shoulders. "Can't say that I have." She folded the pages in half, and stuck them in the folder that she carried. "Did you need anything else?"

"No, that's all."

Once Michele was seated back at her desk, she took the article out of the folder, and smiled slyly. The first phase of her plan had worked brilliantly. She purposely changed her style of dress to please Preston. She hated the drab gray color and detested covering up her "assets," but the outfit was an essential part of the plan. Preston was a sophisticated man with upscale tastes, and she wanted to appear refined to draw him closer. The way he stared at her when she walked into his office was a clear indication that her dull wardrobe had a positive effect on him. Besides, she had to appear like someone he'd be proud to be seen with in public.

The second phase was to plant a seed in his mind, and that's exactly what the article did. Michele knew that she couldn't come right out and talk about the Black Door without raising suspicions, so she found a story on the Internet about underground sex clubs. She didn't admit to knowing about the Black Door, because she wanted Preston to discover Trey's deception on his own. If she said too much, she would seem like a blabbermouth. And who liked a tattletale? Instead, she planned to drop hints and chip away at his memory until the picture of Trey and Ariel's betrayal was as clear as a piece of Steuben crystal. She had done research on short-term memory loss, and read that subtle reminders of the past could help restore a person's recollection. Michele had planted a few more land mines to help with his recovery. She only hoped that his memory returned before Ariel did, and if it didn't, she would have no other choice but to seduce him. He was a man after all, and what man could resist her brand of loving?

17

ARIEL HAD had one hell of a trying day. She'd spent the morning deposing witnesses, which was something she hadn't done in ages. Most partners rarely took depositions, except in special cases, and this case was major, so she had made an exception. She and the other partner on the case spent the entire afternoon behind closed doors, huddled over documents and discussing strategy. They were going to trial in a few days, and their case had to be airtight. After strategizing for hours on end, they were confident that they had an open-and-shut case. They then dashed off to meet with the client over dinner. By the time Ariel stepped foot into the corporate apartment, all she wanted to do was take a shower, put on her nightgown, and crawl into bed. And she did just that.

Ariel was underneath the covers, ready to turn out the light and get some rest when it occurred to her that she hadn't spoken to her husband all day. She'd been so busy that she hadn't even missed hearing from him until now. She reached for the phone on the nightstand and dialed her home number. After a few rings, he picked up.

"Why haven't you called me?" she asked right away, skipping the pleasantries.

"Well, hello to you too. I did call but I kept getting your voice mail, so I decided to wait until you called me," he explained.

Ariel had completely forgotten that her cell was turned off. She didn't want any distractions while working on the case. "Oh, I'm sorry. I didn't want to be interrupted, so I didn't turn on my phone this morning. I should have put it on vibrate in case you called. Do you forgive me?" she asked in a pleading tone.

"I figured as much. Of course I forgive you."

Hearing his words of forgiveness made Ariel think back on her meeting with Trey, and she silently prayed that Preston would utter those same words once they told him the truth. Ariel knew that it was a lot to ask for, but she asked anyway. *Please, God, let Preston understand, and have mercy on us. Please let him forgive our betrayal.*

"Hello? Ariel, are you there?"

Ariel was deep in thought and didn't realize that her praying had created dead air between them. "Oh, yes, honey. I'm here. So, Judge Hendricks, or should I say Justice Hendricks," she said, addressing him by his formal title, which was also her pet name for him, "what have you been up to since I've been gone?"

Preston's mind instantly flashed back to À Votre Service, and the delicious blow job he had had. A flourish of guilt washed over him; he felt so bad that he started to confess his dirty little secret. He quickly weighed the pros and cons of telling Ariel the truth. On the one hand, if he told her, she would no doubt be devastated, but on the other hand, he would relieve his constant guilt. "I have something to tell you—"

"Hold on, honey. Someone's calling," she said, cutting him off, and answering the other line.

"That was Meri," she said, returning to the line a few minutes later. "I told her I was on the phone with you, but she kept blabbing. You know how Meri is. Now what did you want to tell me?" she asked, getting back to their conversation.

"That I miss you terribly." While Ariel had him on hold, Preston changed his mind. A confession, though it would ease his troubled mind, would destroy his wife, and he loved her too much to devastate her.

"Aw, honey, I miss you too."

"Really? What do you miss?" he asked, dropping his voice in a deeper register. Thinking about À Votre Service had gotten him heated up. He wanted to get laid, but since going back to the restaurant wasn't an option, he thought the next best thing was phone sex with his wife.

Ariel smiled. She knew that tone in Preston's voice meant he was feeling naughty. "Well . . . let's see . . . I miss your strong arms around me when we're lying in bed."

"And . . ."

"And I miss how your dick feels against my butt when you start to get hard."

"And . . ."

"And I miss how it feels when you put it inside of me."

"Hmm," he moaned. "You're always so wet, when I'm inside of you. Are you wet now?"

Ariel had also gotten heated up, and talking dirty to her husband had made her moist. "Yes."

"Good. I want you to play with your clit, until you come. Can you do that for me?"

"Yes." She put her hands underneath the covers, closed her eyes, and began kneading her pleasure point. "Ohh, I wish you were here. It feels s-o-o-o good."

Preston was stroking his pole, and the sound of his wife's voice was making him harder. He increased the pace. "Yeah, my dick feels good too. Let's come together. Are you almost there?"

"Yes-s-s," she sang, with her head now laid back on the pillows.

"Come on, honey, stroke that clit. Don't stop. Don't stop. Cum for me. Ohh, I'm almost there," he said, pulling his dick harder and harder.

"Oh, yeah, I'm there. I'm there."

"Me too. Ugggghhh," he moaned as he came.

There was only heavy breathing on the line, as they each recovered from their respective orgasms.

"That was great," Preston said. He had relieved his sexual tension, and was ready to go to sleep—like the average man. "Honey, I'm going to turn in now. I'll call you first thing in the morning."

Ariel was exhausted too, and didn't protest. "Okay, good night."

The next morning she felt refreshed and energized. As she was drinking her second cup of coffee, and reading the business section of the *Times,* the phone rang.

"Good morning," she said, knowing it was probably Preston.

"Good morning yourself, how did you sleep?"

"Like a woman who had had some great phone sex," she said, smiling.

"Yeah, it was great, wasn't it?" Preston's career had overshadowed his sex life for so long that it felt good to finally be able to please himself and his wife. "Listen, the reason why I'm calling this morning is to see if you can come home for a day or two."

"I don't know. This case is pretty intense. What's going on?"

"The president elect is having a cocktail party, and I'd love to walk in with my beautiful wife on my arm," he said, looking at the invitation.

"When is it? Maybe I could catch the train, come down for the evening, and return the next day."

"Oh, that would be great! The party is tomorrow evening."

That was the day before the trial, and she had a debriefing meeting with the client. "Honey, I'm so sorry, but I can't make it tomorrow since it's the day before the trial."

"I understand," he said, sounding like a boy who was told that Christmas had been canceled.

"I knew you would; that's what I like about being in the same business as you. We both know how grueling this profession can be." The minute those words left her lips, she realized how hypocritical she sounded. She was anything but understanding when Preston was seeking the nomination for the Supreme Court. On those days when he blew her off to rush to Washington for an impromptu meeting with Senator Oglesby, she was livid. And when he had to take the senator's calls, and would be on the phone for hours, she wanted to put a hit out on the senator. He was only trying to help Preston secure the nomination, but she viewed his constant presence as an un-welcome intrusion. It was Preston's preoccupation with his career that drove her to the Black Door and her eventual affair with Trey. Now that the tables had turned, and she was busy with work, she couldn't help but wonder if Preston was seeking love elsewhere, like she had done. Out of the clear blue she asked, "So, have you been going out?" Even though Ariel knew that if Preston was cheating he'd never confess. What man would? But she had to ask anyway; think-ing that she'd be able to detect a change in his voice, if he were lying.

Preston thought the question odd, but answered anyway. "No, honey. Where would I go without you anyway?" he said, with no hes-itation.

"Good," she said, with a grin in her voice. After their phone sex session last night, she knew that he was telling the truth. "Well, you have my permission to go to the party and have fun, but not too much fun."

"Thanks for allowing me the privilege of going to the president elect's party." He chuckled. "Okay, gotta run. Love you."

"I love you too." Ariel hung up and went back to reading the morning paper.

UNBEKNOWNST TO PRESTON, Michele had been lurking outside of his door. Luckily, she had come to work early and overheard his entire conversation. She knew about the party weeks ago and was dying to go. The presidential election had been such a heated competition, with a narrow win for the candidate, that everyone was dying for a chance to meet the new president up close and personal. The cocktail party had been written up in all the society columns as the place to be, and Michele was going to use Ariel's absence to her advantage.

She tapped lightly on his door, and heard him say, "Come in."

"Good morning, Preston. I'm going to make a pot of coffee, just wanted to know if you'd like a cup?" she asked, walking into the office.

He looked up at her. Michele was dressed in a navy pinstripe skirt suit, with a white oxford shirt. Her hair was pulled back in a chignon, and she was wearing her glasses again. Preston thought that after his talk regarding her wardrobe had worn off, she would go back to wearing her skintight clothes, but she didn't. As a matter of fact, her outfits seemed to get more conservative. It was almost like he was working with an entirely different person; even her demeanor had changed. It was as if she had matured from a college coed into a professional woman. Not that she wasn't professional before, but now she seemed more seasoned, and he liked the transformation. "I'd love a cup. Thanks. Also, can you file these papers?"

She walked to his desk to take the stack from him, and saw the invitation to the party. "I certainly hope you're not going to toss that invitation in the trash."

"Of course not; I plan on going. As a matter of fact, I'd planned on going with Ariel, but she can't make it."

"Oh, that's too bad. I'm sure you don't want to go alone, since most people will be with their spouses, assistants, or significant others," she said, throwing in the word *assistant* and hoping that it would make a subliminal impact.

"No, I really didn't want to go alone, but at the same time, this is one cocktail party that shouldn't be missed," he said.

Damn, didn't he hear me say "assistant"? Michele wanted to lay another land mine, but she had to tread lightly and not appear desperate. "I talked to Senator Oglesby's assistant and she's going with him, since his wife is out of town."

Preston put his thumb and forefinger on his chin. "Really? Is that right?" he asked.

She watched his face closely, and could tell that he was considering the idea. She held her breath, and was on pins and needles, hoping that he took the bait. "Yes, that's right." She nodded her head.

"Well . . ." he looked at her. "If the senator is taking his assistant, I might as well take mine. That is, if you're free tomorrow night." Months ago, Preston would have never dreamed of taking Michele anywhere for fear that she would embarrass him with one of her overtly sexy dresses. But now that she had toned down her image, he didn't have to worry about her wearing something inappropriate.

"Yes, I'm free," she said calmly, even though inside she was scream- ing with joy. "I've done research on the president elect's camp, and will be able to assist you with the names of people who were not in the limelight during the campaign," she offered as to why he should take her, just in case he suddenly had a change of heart.

"Oh, that would be great! I'm familiar with most of the people, but sometimes my memory takes a holiday." He grinned.

"Don't worry, I got your back." She smiled. "I'll bring my clothes for the evening so that we can leave directly from here."

"Excellent idea. Thanks, Michele. I really appreciate you going with me. I didn't want to go alone; now I won't have to. With you fill- ing out the blanks in my memory, if need be, it'll be like we're work- ing," he said, justifying her presence. Now that they had defined her role, he had a viable answer as to why his assistant was there, and felt completely comfortable with the decision.

"Not a problem. Let me go in the kitchen and start the coffee."

"Okay."

In the confines of the kitchen Michele mouthed, *"I got my first date with Preston! Move over, Ariel, I'm taking your man like you took mine!"*

IT HAD been a few days, and Trey couldn't believe that Michele was still ignoring his calls. Whenever he called—day or night—her cell phone would ring several times, and then go into voice mail. She obviously saw his number pop up on the screen and chose not to answer. He was getting extremely frustrated, and a little paranoid. It wasn't like Michele to dismiss him like that. *What if she's told my dad everything?* he thought. Normally she relished every second speaking with him. He had her dick-whipped from day one, and she was firmly under his spell, or so he thought. Something had changed, and he couldn't help wonder if someone else had her hypnotized. Under normal circumstances, he would have loved it if Michele had moved on and was someone else's burden, but since they were partners in a cover-up scheme, he needed her commitment now more than ever. He dialed her number for the tenth time that day.

"Hello, Trey," Michele answered in a deadpan tone.

Trey was elated, and paid no attention to her attitude. He couldn't believe that she had finally picked up. "Hey, baby! Where have you been? I've been trying to call you and I keep getting your voice mail. Is everything all right?"

"Yes. Why do you ask?" she said, sounding drier than before.

"Because every time I call, I get your voice mail, which is so unlike you. Have you been sick or something?" he asked, still wanting to know why she was ignoring his calls.

"No, I haven't been sick. I've been busy. I'm sure you know about being *busy*," she said, putting emphasis on the word. "You've sent my calls to voice mail so many times that I've lost count." Even though Trey couldn't see Michele, she was rolling her neck and pursing her lips, as if she were telling him off to his face.

Trey's mouth dropped. Michele had never spoken so harshly to him before, and he didn't know what to say. "Well, I'm not busy this weekend. Why don't you come to New York, and we can spend some much-needed quality time together," he said, almost pleadingly.

Any other time Michele would have jumped at the chance to see Trey. Last year he was the love of her life, but life had taken a different turn, and now she had another agenda that didn't include him.

"Can't. Busy," she said, cut-and-dried and without supplying further explanation.

"Well, why don't I come down there instead?" Trey was desperate to talk to Michele to persuade her to keep her mouth shut. He didn't want her telling his dad anything. He had to tell Preston, man-to-man, what happened. Look him in the eyes and ask for his forgiveness.

"Can't. Busy," she said again. "Look, Trey, I'm going to an important event this evening and need to get ready. Good-bye."

Before he could say anything else, she had slammed the phone in his ear. She dismissed him so fast that he didn't have time to recover. Trey slumped back in his chair, and tried to think of another strategy, but kept coming up blank. *I need to talk to Ariel. Maybe she can help me find another way to see Michele.* The phone was still in his hand, so he just pressed the receiver button, and dialed Ariel's cell, but it went straight to voice mail. *"Damn it!"* he shouted, and slammed the phone back in its cradle.

"What's got your knickers in a knot?"

He looked up and realized that his office door was open. "What are you doing up here? This area is private," he said, putting down the receiver.

"Yeah, I know. I came to play, but it doesn't sound like you're in much of a playing mood," Lexi said, walking across the threshold, and closing the door behind her.

"You're right. I'm not," he said curtly. Though Trey enjoyed their last encounter, he wasn't in the mood for fucking. He had more important things on his mind.

"Oh, come on, Trey; it can't be that bad." Lexi took an uninvited seat in one of the chairs sitting in front of his desk, and crossed her long legs.

Trey didn't say a word, as he watched her settle in. She wore a micro-miniskirt, which rose so high when she sat down that he could clearly see her silver thong. Her legs were shaved smoothly, and it appeared that she had on a coat of bronzing lotion, because her calves were glistening in the light. "Lexi, thanks for stopping by. I don't mean to be rude, but I need to make an important call," he said, picking up the phone.

"I don't want to interrupt you, but isn't customer satisfaction a part of your job?" she asked, swinging her top leg back and forth.

"Yes it is, but there are servers downstairs who can supply your every need."

She took off her mask, and placed it on the edge of his desk. "I'm not in the mood to be with a masked, no-name hunk tonight. I want someone who's familiar with what I like," she said, looking him dead in the eyes. Lexi wanted Trey and refused to take no for an answer. She knew just what it took to sway him.

Trey watched as she uncrossed her legs, and threw her right leg over the arm of the chair. She then put her hand between her legs, lifted her butt, and took off her thong. She sniffed the thin piece of fabric before tossing it to him. He dropped the phone, caught her thong midair, and instinctively held it up to his nose. She had a tangy, sweet scent, like lilacs laced with ahi tuna. His mood began to change. The memory of the conversation with Michele was quickly fading with each whiff.

"You like the way my punany smells?" she asked in a soft whisper.

"Um-hmm." He nodded his head.

His response was exactly the answer she was looking for; the way he was enjoying her thong told her that his mood had shifted, and he was now ready to play. She stood up, unfastened her skirt, and let it drop to the floor. Standing naked from the waist down, she walked over to the side of his desk, and put one stiletto-clad foot on the edge of his desk, and began playing with her clit. Lexi knew that most men loved to watch women masturbate, so she began to put on a show that he couldn't possibly resist.

Trey could clearly see her clit emerge, since she had a fresh, Brazilian wax, and there was no pubic hair impeding his view. He swallowed hard, as he watched her knead the small piece of pink flesh with her thumb and forefinger. After a few minutes, she began to moan with the pleasure of her own touch. Unable to take the teasing any longer, he reached out and pulled her over to him. She was still masturbating, but he slapped her hand away, replacing it with his. He slipped his middle finger inside of her, while still massaging her clit. She was dripping wet, and he wanted a taste. Trey leaned down, and began sucking her moist triangle like he was drinking from the fountain of youth. Not only did she smell good, but she tasted heavenly as well.

"Ohhh, that feels so good," she moaned. "You know just what I like, baby."

He stopped, but only long enough to unbuckled his belt, unzip his jeans, and whip out his dick, which was only semi-hard. "Sit on my cock."

Lexi did as instructed, and began rotating her hips around and around, until her pussy lips were kissing the head of his rising erection. Once he was totally firm, she reached down, gripped his pipe, and inserted the tip into her wet pussy.

Trey put his hands on her hips and began pushing her farther down on his erection. Once he was all the way inside, he held on to her ass, and stood up while holding her firmly in place.

Lexi wrapped her legs around his waist and held on for the ride of her life.

His jeans dropped to the floor, as he turned them around and pressed her back against the wall. He then began banging the fuck out of her.

"Oh *shit!*" she screamed, as his dick touched her G-spot. "Fuck me harder; fuck me harder."

"Don't worry, baby, I'm-a give you all of this dick." He then swung her around and laid her on the desk. He grabbed her ankles, and spread her legs into a deep *V*. He stood between that *V*, pumping, and pulling her closer with each thrust. The pussy was so good that he could feel his army of men on the verge of charging. He wasn't ready to cum just yet, so he stopped mid-thrust.

"Oh . . . shit . . . why'd . . . you stop? I was . . . just . . . getting ready to cum," she said, between pants.

"Because neither one of us is cumming yet," he said, like a man in charge. He licked his index finger and eased it into her rectum, to shut her up. The way he wiggled that finger around and around stopped her words cold. She shut her eyes, laid back, and enjoyed every second of the digital stimulation. "You like that, baby?" he asked, as he watched her squirm from side to side.

"Um-hmm."

Once Trey felt that he had gotten his men under control, he slowly began pumping again. He kept his finger in her ass, while plunging her pussy. Her anus was so tight, and her pussy so wet, that the sensation felt good times two, and he was finding it hard to control his erection much longer.

"Damn, Trey, you know just what I like," she said, again on the verge of cumming.

"And you know I can't resist this pussy." He picked up the pace, and fucked her harder and harder until they came simultaneously.

He slumped down on her, and held her tightly. "Damn, you got some good stuff," he whispered in her ear.

"And the dick ain't bad either," she joked.

"Ain't bad? Baby, you know this is the best dick you ever had," he said with confidence.

Lexi smiled, because he was right. Out of all the lovers she had

had in the past, Trey was by far the best. She had become addicted to his dick and wanted it on a regular basis. But she wasn't going to come right out and say that, for fear a true confession would scare him away. At this point she was more than satisfied fucking him at the club. It was better than nothing. A man like Trey would run for the woods if he thought she was trying to trap him.

Just as he was gearing up for round two, his cell phone rang. He thought about answering it, but was in a better mood now and didn't want to break the spell. He knew he should have answered the phone, just in case it was Michele calling to reconsider his invitation to come to New York. But then again, she could have been calling to give him another earful of her ranting. He was now in a better place than he was fifteen minutes ago, and didn't feel like listening to any more of Michele's harsh words, so he let the call go to voice mail. Besides, Lexi had gotten him hot and horny, and he wanted some more pussy. "Since you think the dick is just all right, why don't we go for two out of three," he said in her ear. With the way Michele had treated him earlier, Trey didn't feel any remorse for fucking another woman. In fact, he was beginning to feel a slight connection with Lexi. She was witty, and seemed to come to his rescue just when he needed to relieve some tension, and he was grateful for the distraction.

"Hmm, sounds good to me," she said, wrapping her legs around his back, starting the beginning of round two.

19

THE WORKDAY couldn't go by fast enough for Michele. She had been in a dreamlike state ever since Preston invited her to the cocktail party in honor of the president elect. She could hardly sleep the night before, and floated through the morning and afternoon on autopilot. She couldn't concentrate on mundane office tasks, since all she could think about was changing her clothes and accompanying Preston to the cocktail party of the year. Unlike the debacle that unfolded while trying to get into the VIP reception at the Congressional Black Caucus event, Michele didn't have to worry about getting past security using someone else's name. Tonight, she would be on the arm of a Supreme Court justice, and no one would dare deny her entry. She felt like Queen for a Day, and if her plan worked, she would not only be Queen for a Day, she'd be the new Mrs. Hendricks for a lifetime. With that thought permeating throughout her brain, she hummed a no-name tune until it was time to change clothes.

Michele shut down her computer, walked into the foyer, and retrieved her garment bag out of the hall closet. She went upstairs without permission, which was something she would have never done if the Mrs. was in town. Since Preston was in his office on a conference call, she took her time and roamed slowly down the long hallway. She stopped outside of the master suite, opened the door, and eased inside. The room was larger than most New York studio apartments. The walls were painted a soothing robin's-egg blue, with white trim. The drapes and duvet were in a matching combination of blue, chocolate, and white. The dark-brown furniture was sleek and modern. The room was neither overly feminine nor masculine; it was the perfection combination of both.

The vaulted ceilings and ivory marble fireplace gave the bedroom a romantic feeling. Michele walked over by the French windows. The setting sun was casting a radiant glow throughout the room, and she couldn't help but fantasize about making love to Preston in the king-sized bed. She wanted to lie across the bed and pretend that they were in the throes of passion, but was afraid of making an imprint in the fluffy comforter. Instead, she strolled over to Ariel's dresser, and ran her hands across her personal belongings. Michele picked up a bottle of perfume and spritzed her neck, wrists, and between her boobs with the expensive scent. *Pretty soon, all of my things will replace hers,* she thought.

With time ticking by, Michele left the master suite, and went down the hall to the guest room, which was much smaller, but also well-appointed. She took the gown out of the garment bag and laid it across the bed. She had showered earlier that morning, so she took a bird bath instead. She put on a strapless bra—something she hadn't worn in years—before slipping into her evening gown. She sat on the edge of the bed and put on panty hose and a pair of black silk pumps. Michele walked over to the mirror.

"Ugh." She grimaced at her reflection. "This dress ain't me," she hissed. Her mother had bought that gown when she graduated college. And she hadn't worn it since.

Michele wore a black gown with a moderate neckline. The front was cut so high that she could hardly see any cleavage. There were no thigh-high slits or dazzling bugle beads to make her stand out from the crowd. The dress had no redeeming features to accentuate her assets, but she knew that Preston would approve.

She combed her hair up into a pompadour with loose tendrils framing her face. Michele dusted her face with translucent powder to get rid of the sheen on her nose and forehead. She then clipped on a pair of small rhinestone earrings. Satisfied with the look she wanted to portray, she gathered her belongings and headed downstairs. Unlike Ariel, she was ahead of schedule, instead of behind.

Preston's office door was still closed, so she tapped lightly.

"Come in."

Michele opened the door and entered with a little hesitancy. She was nervous. She wanted this night to be special, but didn't want to tip her hand. Her cards had to be played with the skill of a Monte Carlo pro, not an Atlantic City amateur. Her future was at stake and she couldn't afford to make any clumsy mistakes. "It's almost time to go; are you finishing up?" she asked, in a professional manner.

Preston looked up from the document in his hand, and did a double take. "Wow!" he heard himself say. Michele looked stunning. The classy way in which she was dressed reminded him of his wife. Her outfit was something that Ariel would have definitely worn; it was conservative yet sophisticated. For a split second, she brought to mind Audrey Hepburn in the opening scene of *Breakfast at Tiffany's*. He cleared his throat. "Michele, you look stunning."

"Thank you, Preston." She looked at her watch. "The party starts in forty-five minutes, and we don't want to be late," she said calmly, pretending to brush his comment aside, but was dancing a Scottish jig in her mind.

"You're right. Let me go upstairs and quickly freshen up. I'll be right down," he said, heading out of his office.

Once he was gone, Michele jumped up and down and clapped her hands like a kid whose parents had given her a surprise birthday party. "My plan is working; my plan is working," she sang in a soft whisper.

Michele was standing in the foyer when Preston came walking down the stairs fifteen minutes later. A knot formed in her throat as she watched him strut toward her. He wore a black tailored suit, a crisp white shirt, and a steel gray silk tie. Michele knew that Preston had started working out again, but hadn't really noticed the effect until now. Most of his work shirts were a little loose, but he must have had this shirt tailored to fit his new, improved physique, because it hugged his pecs ever so slightly. And the pudgy midsection she was accustomed to seeing was gone, replaced by a taut middle. If she didn't know any better, Michele would have thought that Preston had gotten one of those extreme makeovers, taking years off of his appearance. He looked more like Trey's older brother, instead of his father. *He looks so good, I could fuck him right now on those stairs,* she thought.

"Are you ready?" he asked, buttoning his jacket.

"Yes. I already called the driver, and he's waiting outside," she said, as if she were still on the clock.

"Well, let's get out of here." He smiled, glad to be leaving on time for once. If Ariel were going with him, she'd still be upstairs doing God knows what. Michele, on the other hand, was prompt and ready to go.

In the limo on the way to the Four Seasons, Preston tried not to inhale Michele's perfume, but it was too intoxicating for him to ignore. The scent seemed oddly familiar, and then it occurred to him that she wore the same perfume as his wife. Preston thought it ironic that two women, who were polar opposites, would enjoy the same fragrance. He started to comment on it, but decided not to. Preston had already given her one compliment, and didn't want to continue with the flattery. Even though they were going out for the evening, she still worked for him, and he didn't want to give her the impression that he was interested in anything other than work.

While she had the chance, Michele wanted to ask when Ariel would be home, so that she could gauge how much longer she had to work her plan. However, she needed a reason for asking; otherwise her question would seem odd. She thought for a second, and then said, "*Washington Confidential* called today and they want to schedule an interview with you and Mrs. Hendricks, but I didn't put anything on your calendar since she's out of town." Michele decided an indirect approach was best, so she told a little fib.

"I'm glad you didn't schedule anything. Ariel is going to trial tomorrow, so it's hard to say how long she'll be in New York. Could be another few days, or a few weeks. Call them when you get back to the office, and postpone the interview until next month, just to be on the safe side."

Excellent, Michele thought. Preston told her exactly what she needed to know. "No problem. I'll call the editor first thing in the morning."

The cocktail party was being held in the Presidential Suite at the Four Seasons Hotel, and every important name on the Hill was invited. The limo eased up to the curb; Preston got out, and then reached inside for Michele's hand. The moment she stepped out of the car, she felt like a fairy princess easing out of her golden carriage. He held her by the elbow like a true gentleman, and guided her toward the entrance. Two secret service men were guarding the door. Michele felt her heartbeat increase. She couldn't help but think about her embarrassment at the CBC affair. *What if they don't let me in?*

"Your names please?" asked the stone-faced man to the right.

Michele didn't say a word. She just hung back and let Preston do the talking. She knew from past experience that if a person's actual name was not on the list, entry would be denied. She had forgotten to remind Preston to include her name, and was now racked with nerves. Once again, Michele was on the fringes of penetrating the social elite. She held her breath and said a little prayer.

"Justice Preston Hendricks, and my assistant, Michele Richards," he said, in a booming authoritative voice.

The guard flipped a few pages on his list until he found their names. "Go right on in, Justice Hendricks, and have a wonderful evening."

"When did you add my name to the guest list?" Michele asked, once they had passed security.

"I called the secretary of the planning committee early this morning and told her that you would be replacing my wife this evening."

What a Freudian slip! Michele smiled at the thought. *Yes, I'm replacing her, but it won't be just for tonight!* "Thanks, Preston. I completely forgot to remind you."

"Michele, you don't have to remind me of everything. I do have a mind of my own," he said, teasingly.

They took a private elevator to the top floor. The doors opened right into the foyer, and Michele's eyes nearly popped out of her head when she stepped off the elevator. The suite was *huge*. It seemed to span the length of the building. Floor-to-ceiling windows framed the massive living room. Various sized crystal chandeliers hung through-out the suite. The decor was traditional, yet modern. The furniture looked as if it came directly from the showroom of Roche-Bobois. And the artwork appeared to be original pieces by Picasso, Monet, and Degas.

They were greeted immediately by a uniformed server with white gloves, who offered them each a flute of Dom Pérignon. Michele fol-lowed Preston's lead as he made his way through the intimate group of politicians and their spouses. She spotted a few familiar faces. Laird and Leona Forester and Senator Oglesby, who was drinking and chatting with his assistant. She also recognized some people who were at Angelica Oglesby's birthday party. Preston stopped to chat with the senator, and Michele stood close—but not too close—by his side.

"Fancy seeing you here," Fiona whispered in her ear. "And you look great," she said, noticing Michele's conservative gown.

Michele smiled. "Thank you. I took your advice to heart, and I must say that it worked. I've finally arrived."

"And with Preston, no doubt."

"I told you I had an ironclad plan. Now do you believe me?" she whispered back.

Fiona slowly nodded her head. "Girl, I've got to give it to you. You got nerve. Just be careful. You're playing a dangerous game."

Michele noticed that Preston was ending his conversation. "Duly noted. Now I've got to go," she said, and turned to follow Preston as he mingled through the crowd.

Michele stayed on his heels, and watched as he greeted his fellow colleagues. He didn't introduce her once, but she didn't care; all she cared about was being in the presence of greatness.

As Preston was being introduced to the president elect, a couple of photographers snapped their picture. Michele didn't know if she had gotten in the frame or not, since their lenses were focused on the two heavy hitters, but she had shown her pearly whites just in case she made the cut.

An hour and a half later, she was ready to go. Preston was behind closed doors speaking with the president elect, and she was left alone. The party was boring. Fiona and her husband were gone, and nobody was talking to her. Now that she was on the other side of the fence, the view wasn't necessarily better, just different.

"Hello, Michele," Laird said, easing up behind her.

She turned around to face him. "Hello, Congressman." She smiled. Michele didn't particularly care for Laird, because he was always leering at her like she was an entrée on an all-you-can-eat smorgasbord. However, tonight, she was happy to see him, and not because he was talking to her. No . . . unbeknownst to Laird, he was a part of Michele's well-thought-out plan. "How have you been?" she asked, taking a half a step closer.

He licked his bottom lip, while eyeing her up and down. "I'm good. Real good," he said, with a sexual lilt to his voice.

She looked around the room, making sure his wife wasn't within view, and then lightly rubbed his forearm. "I just bet you are." Michele cleared her throat. "I was wondering if you could help me?" she whined like a damsel in distress.

His cheeks flushed a crimson color. He grinned a wicked grin, and whispered, "I would help you with anything, anywhere, anytime."

"Well, a friend of mine is doing her dissertation on sex in America, and I've agreed to help her with some research."

Laird's entire face turned red. He couldn't believe Michele wanted to talk to him about sex. He looked at her chest, but her lethal arsenal was battened down, so he couldn't get any cheap thrills. It didn't matter to Laird, since he knew what she had to offer underneath that dress. He had seen the impression of her nipples pressed against her clothes on more than one occasion, and could envision himself tickling her tits with his tongue. If his wife hadn't been there, he would have taken Michele into one of the many bedrooms and fucked her brains out. "I would love to help you with sex—oops, I mean with the re-search. Why don't we meet later tonight, after I take Leona home? Where do you live? Maybe I could come by, bring a bottle of Patrón, and we could do a couple of shots while we do some 'research.' " He grinned.

"Well, actually, I just wanted to ask you a few questions. Have you ever heard of any underground sex clubs?" she asked, getting right to the point. Michele had no interest in doing tequila shots with Laird.

"Yes, I know a few. Do you want to go with me sometime?" He looked around the room to make sure his wife wasn't within earshot. He didn't see her, and assumed that she was in another room. He quickly rubbed his drink across Michele's right boob. "I know we could have a blast. You're one sexy woman," he said, practically drooling.

Michele wanted to slap his hand away, but she had to play into his unwelcome advances. "Hmm," she leaned into his ear. "Congressman, you're so naughty." She then returned to the question on the table. "Well, the type of clubs that my friend is researching are for women only. Do you know any?"

"Women only?" He looked at her oddly. "Is your friend gay?"

"No, she's not. There just seems to be a trend toward women's clubs and she wants to find out more. I know you've been on the East Coast all of your life, and was wondering if you've ever heard of any-thing like that before."

Laird thought for a moment. "As a matter of fact, I got this article in the mail the other day that focused on females' clubs. I started to throw it away, but the attached note said that I might find it interest-ing, and once I started reading, I couldn't put it down. The article talked about these various theme rooms, where women get fucked," he said, lowering his voice, "and I love to read about anything that has to do with sex. But more than reading about it, I love doing it!"

Michele had opened Pandora's box, and didn't know how to get Laird back on track. She needed for him to talk about the details of the article, not his personal preferences. "Well, if you can remember the name of the club, maybe I could go, and then tell you all about my experience." She looked him dead in his deep blue eyes, and whispered, "If I knew exactly where this club is I could personally show you what I learned there. I'm sure a man like you could appreciate learning new tricks." She dropped her hand and let it brush against his crotch.

He swallowed hard at her touch, and then blurted out, "It's called the Back Door, but it's in New York. No, that's not the name; it's the Black Door," he corrected himself.

"The Black Door, now that's an interesting name. What else did the article say?" Michele knew exactly what the article said, since she was the one who had mailed it in the first place.

"Let's see . . . well, the article said that the club is for 'the women who like to lunch' crowd," he said, giving up as much detail as he could remember. Laird wanted to get laid, and if telling Michele about that article was his ticket to pleasure, then so be it.

"I'll have to tell my friend about this place. Did the article mention exactly where it's located, and who the owner is? I'm sure she would like to talk to the person in charge," Michele said, trying to extract as much information as she could.

"It's located in upper Manhattan, and the owner is Trey somebody. I don't remember his last name."

"Trey, are you guys talking about Trey?" Preston asked, joining them.

"Yes, I was just telling Michele about a club in New York called the Black Door, owned by somebody named Trey," Laird said, filling Preston in.

"What did you say?" Preston asked.

Perfect timing, Michele thought. She couldn't have planned this any better. Preston reemerged from his meeting just in the nick of time to hear Laird's story. Even if Preston hadn't joined them precisely at that moment, she had planned to keep Laird talking until Preston's meeting was over.

"I was reading an article about a club for women called the Black Door, and it's owned by a guy named Trey, but I can't remember his last name," Laird repeated.

Suddenly, all the color drained from Preston's face. He took hold of Michele's arm, and said, "Come on; we have to go."

"Why are you guys leaving so soon? We were just starting to have a little fun." Laird grinned.

Preston didn't say another word, just led Michele through the room and into the waiting elevator. He was beyond speechless, and didn't utter a word until they reached the town house.

20

"so how was it seeing your lover again?" Meri asked facetiously.

"He's *not* my lover, and I wish you wouldn't say that," Ariel said sternly. Even though she still harbored feelings for Trey, she felt guilty about their affair and wasn't in the teasing mood.

"Okay, ex-lover. So how did he look?" Meri asked again, refusing to let the question drop. Not only did she enjoy talking about her sexual exploits, she also took pleasure in living vicariously through others.

Ariel exhaled hard out of frustration. She couldn't tell Meri not to refer to Trey as her ex-lover, since that's exactly what he was. "He looked all right."

"All right? Now come on, Ariel, as fine as Trey is, I'm sure he looked more than just all right." Meri remembered Trey from the engagement party she threw for Ariel and Preston. That night, she nearly came in her panties when she saw his fit body and handsome face. He was just her type—young, handsome, and virile.

Ariel didn't want to admit that she still had feelings of lust for Trey. Sexually, he had taken her places that she'd never been before, and secretly, she wanted to revisit them, but he was the wrong person to serve as a tour guide. He was her stepson now and completely off limits. She knew that Meri would misconstrue the statement, and probably encourage her to explore her feelings for Trey. Meri wasn't a fan of Preston. She liked him as a person, but thought that he was too old for her friend. Occasionally, she would tell Ariel that she needed a younger man to toss her around the bedroom.

"Why are you asking me how Trey looks? You know as well as I do that he's an attractive man. Anyway, I didn't call to discuss his appearance. I called to tell you that we came up with a solution to the Michele problem," she said, changing the subject.

Obviously, Ariel didn't want to talk about her stepson in a sexual manner, so Meri didn't press the issue. "That's good to hear. What have you guys concocted?"

"Once the trial I'm working on is over, Trey and I are going to Washington together and we're going to tell Preston the truth. As ugly as it might sound, we realized that hearing the entire story from us would be better than him hearing a twisted version from Michele."

"Hmm," she thought about what Ariel said, and then added, "That sounds fine and well, but don't you think that you should have a sit-down with Preston and tell him the truth by yourself? After all, he is your husband."

"You're right, that's why I wanted to wait until I was pregnant. I'd planned on telling him the good news and bad news at the same time, hoping that the good would balance out the bad. But with Michele on the warpath, I can't wait until I'm with child. And to be honest, I can't face Preston alone either."

"I see," Meri said, still not convinced that Ariel's plan of action was the right way to go. "Ariel, there's something that I've been meaning to ask you for a while. Now don't get mad, but why did you marry Preston when you knew that one day his memory would return, and that you'd be in this predicament? Why put yourself through all this grief?"

Ariel had asked herself the same question again and again over the course of the past few months. "I'm not mad. That's a fair question.

Well . . ." She exhaled hard into the phone. "Whether or not I married Preston, his memory was eventually going to return, and one day I'd have to answer for what I did."

"Yes, I realize that, but at least you wouldn't be living under the same roof with him, with the possibility of being kicked out," Meri said bluntly.

"True. I married Preston because I love him. I know that's hard to believe especially since I slept with his son, but Preston has always been there for me. I've never mentioned this before, but when I was a wet-behind-the-ears law clerk, he took me under his wing and guided me in the right direction. And when I was challenged with the tough cases as an attorney, it was Preston who I consulted. I know it sounds like I'm just grateful to him professionally, but I'm not. Before his nomination, he was caring and nurturing and always put me first. Preston has unconditional love for me, and I trust him wholeheartedly. I knew in marrying him, I'd be rolling the dice, but it was a chance I had to take. Anyway, if I would've backed out of the wedding, he would have questioned my reasoning, and since he didn't know about my affair at the time, I couldn't give him a good enough excuse as to why we shouldn't get married. So I went ahead with the wedding, because ever since I was a little girl, all I've ever wanted was a family of my own. Something I never had," Ariel said, with a faraway tone, as if she were remembering her parentless childhood.

"Daarling, I know you had it rough growing up, knowing that your real mother gave you away, but do you really think that Preston can get over your betrayal and forgive and forget?"

"I pray that he can. I don't want to lose him. He's my rock, and I need that in my life. My affair with Trey was just a fling, even though part of me wanted it to be more. I now realize that a man like Trey will probably never settle down with just one woman. And even if Trey wasn't related to Preston, chances of us becoming a serious couple were really never in the cards. Our attraction was purely based on sex and nothing else. Preston is the man for me, and I plan on keeping my husband."

"I understand. My second husband was the love of my life, and I did everything to keep him happy. Unfortunately, he died before we could grow old together."

"Growing old with Preston is exactly what I want to do. And hopefully have a few babies in the process."

"I wish you the best, Ariel," Meri said sincerely. "Since time is indeed of the essence, maybe you should drop whatever you're working on in New York, and take the train back to D.C. before Michele puts a bug in Preston's ear."

"That's not necessary. Trey plans to call Michele and invite her up to New York to spend a few days with him. As lovesick as the girl is over him, I'm sure she's packing as we speak," she said confidently. Trey was handling Michele, so Ariel was no longer worried.

"I hope you're right, daarling," Meri said skeptically.

"Why are you sounding so doubtful?"

"Daarling, like I've told you before, I've been around the block more than a couple of times, and I know how delicate matters of the heart can be. I'm sure you've heard the phrase, 'It's a thin line between love and hate.' Well, I'm here to tell you that no truer statement has ever been spoken. One minute you're in love, and the next you despise the very person you couldn't live without the day before," Meri said, speaking from experience.

"Stop being so paranoid, Meri; everything is going to—" she heard the call-waiting beep, and stopped mid-sentence. "Hold on; I have another call."

When Ariel clicked back over to Meri a few seconds later, her tone had changed from spirited to serious. "I'm going to have to call you back. It's Trey."

"Sure, daarling," Meri said, and hung up.

"Hi, Trey, what's going on? Did you talk to Michele?"

"Yeah, I talked to her."

"Well, what did she say? Is she coming to New York for a few days?" Ariel asked frantically. She was dying to hear about their conversation, but Trey was giving her the abbreviated version.

"No, she's not coming up," he said drily.

"*What?*" She raised her voice. "Why not?" Ariel wanted to know.

"First of all, she didn't answer or return my calls, and when she finally did pick up the phone, she was as cold as Siberia. I invited her to come for a visit, but she declined, saying that she was going to an important function."

"What could be more important than seeing you? I remember a time, not so long ago, that Ms. Thang would have run over her own mother for a chance to spend time with you. What happened?" Ariel got up from the bed, and began to pace back and forth.

"I know. These days, she seems more interested in hobnobbing."

"You think she's dating someone else?" Ariel asked, trying to think of a plausible explanation. Knowing Michele, if she was holding Trey at arm's length, she probably had a bigger catch on the hook.

"Could be. Suddenly, she's treating me like an annoying ex-boyfriend, so I wouldn't be surprised if she did have someone else. And frankly I couldn't care less, as long as she keeps her mouth shut."

Meri's words replayed in Ariel's ears, "It's a thin line between love and hate." And from the sound of things, Michele's affections, for some reason or another, had shifted. "The trial I'm working on should be over by next week. Once I'm done, we can go to D.C. and tell Preston the truth."

"From the indifferent way that Michele is acting, I don't think we should wait until next week. There's no telling what could happen between now and then. Can you assign someone else to the case?"

"I'm afraid not. There's no way I can back out of the trial now. It's a major case, and the client would be livid, not to mention the other partner, if I pulled out at the eleventh hour."

"Well, things at the club are pretty calm. Why don't I go to D.C. and have a talk with my dad?"

Ariel stopped pacing and thought for a second. "The plan was to tell him together. Do you think you should go alone?"

"Under the circumstances, I think it's better that he learns the truth from one of us, before his memory returns. We've skated on thin ice for far too long; now it's time to come clean. I'm sick and tired of appeasing Michele and having her hold this lie over our heads. I feel like her prisoner. So, I'd rather go it alone than chance her telling my dad her version of what happened."

"That makes sense, but I still think that we should tell him together. I'll come down for the weekend, since we're not in court, and we'll have our meeting then," Ariel said nervously. The thought of finally telling Preston the truth made her stomach curdle like spoiled milk.

"I'm going to go down ahead of you, to talk to Michele and make sure she hasn't mentioned anything to my dad."

"That's sounds like a good idea. Okay, I'll talk to you later."

Even though they shared an ugly secret, Ariel trusted Trey, and knew that he had her best interests at heart. He didn't want to hurt his dad any more than she did. Unfortunately, their untimely liaison would probably hurt Preston to the core, but that was a chance they both had to take.

21

PRESTON WAS quiet all the way back to the town house. He just stared out the window without uttering a sound. Michele didn't know what to believe. She prayed that her plan was effective, and that hearing Trey's name associated with the Black Door had triggered his memory. She knew that once Laird got on the subject of sex, she wouldn't be able to shut him up. Michele had heard of his reputation as a hound dog, and knew that he was the perfect pawn to use in her game. Besides, he had the hots for her. Even though he had never verbally approached her, she knew men, and the way he was always eyeing her boobs, she knew that he would do anything to sample her goodies. She had teased Laird more than she planned, but she had no choice. She knew that from now on he would be hot on her tail, but she'd deal with him when the time came. Her mission was accomplished, and Laird was part of the collateral damage.

When the driver pulled into the driveway and stopped, Preston opened the door and got out. He didn't reach back for her hand like before, just walked like a zombie to the front door. Michele told the driver good night, and said that his services were no longer needed for the evening. She wasn't about to go home, not when Preston was on the possible verge of regaining his memory. She then quickly caught up to Preston as he was unlocking the door, and went inside with him.

Preston turned on the lights, and went directly into the den. He opened the liquor cabinet, poured himself a triple shot of Johnnie Walker Blue, and plunked down on the sofa.

Michele poured herself a small shot of scotch and sat in the chair across from Preston. "What's the matter? Why did you want to leave so abruptly?" she asked. Her tone was soft, almost a whisper.

He didn't answer her, just put the snifter up to his lips and took a healthy gulp. Michele watched him clench the glass as if it were his long-lost friend. She didn't want to pressure him into talking, so she just watched as he drank the brown liquor like it was tea. He polished off the first glass, then returned to the bottle and poured another triple shot. He sat back on the sofa, and his eyes began to glaze over, as if the liquor was taking effect.

"Did you know about Trey and my wife?" he asked, in a faraway voice.

"Know what?" Michele asked, playing the dumb role. Part of her plan was to act as if she knew nothing about the affair. If she wanted to win Preston over, she had to pretend like she was clueless. She wanted Preston to confide in her. If he thought that she was in cahoots with Ariel and Trey, he probably would clam up, and she couldn't take that chance.

"That they are having an affair," he said, looking past her.

"An affair!" She sound alarmed. "What makes you think that?"

"The minute I heard Laird mention Trey's name and the Black Door, I suddenly remembered everything."

"Remembered what?" she asked, prodding him to make sure his entire memory had indeed returned.

"Last year, I was in New York, sitting in my office, reading the newspaper, and you called saying that Trey was taking you away for the weekend. I remember thinking that he must have gotten caught with another woman, and was trying to appease you. But you were so happy that I didn't say anything. After we hung up, I got a fax from Senator Oglesby."

"What did it say?" she asked, cutting him off.

"It said that Trey was the owner of a club called the Black Door. The senator then told me that I could forget about my chances of securing the nomination, because the press would have a field day with this information. I was devastated. I went over to Ariel's apartment for some solace, but she was drunk. The minute I mentioned Trey and the Black Door, she blurted out that she was fucking him, and—"

Michele put her hand to her mouth as if she were shocked. "What? Are you sure?"

"Yes," he said, looking at her for the first time since they had walked into the house. "That must have been the moment that I had the stroke, because the next thing I remember is waking up in the hospital."

"Wow! What a story. What are you going to do now that you know?"

"I'm going to confront them and find out exactly what happened. My memory is still a little fuzzy, and I want to know the entire truth." He put the snifter on the table, and dropped his head into his hands.

Michele could hear him sniffling. She got up, sat next to him on the sofa, and put her arm around his shoulders. "It's going to be okay," she whispered, as she rubbed her hand across his back.

Preston's sniffles turned into loud wailing. He burrowed his head into Michele's chest, and began crying like a baby.

Michele rocked him back and forth, all the while smiling a sly smile of victory. She continued rubbing his back until his wailing turned into whimpers. She held on to him until he cried himself to sleep.

Once she heard him snoring lightly twenty minutes later, she unsnapped her bra with one hand, and took it off underneath her dress. His head had fallen into her lap, but she gently lifted it up, and positioned his mouth near her chest. His mouth was agape, so she held on to her titty and tried to slip it into his mouth. Preston didn't respond. "Damn," she whispered. Michele didn't want to be too forceful, but she wanted him to react like any warm-blooded male. She thought for a second, and then took a chance.

Michele began kneading the soft flesh between his legs. His dick felt like mush, but she kept working her fingers until she felt him come to life. Before he reached a full erection, she stopped and pretended to be asleep.

Though he was asleep, Preston felt a wonderful sensation between his legs. He thought he was dreaming, but it felt so real. He opened his eyes, and was surprised to see Michele's cloth-covered tit near his mouth. *What the hell is going on?* he thought. He looked up at her and she was asleep. Her arms were clenched around his shoulders, and he couldn't move without waking her. He felt awkward, so he laid there for a second trying to figure out what to do. He then moved his head away from her breast. He looked down into his crotch and saw that he had a full-blown erection. His dick was throbbing badly, and he needed to release the tension, so he slowly reached into his pants and began to stroke himself. Preston looked up at Michele to make sure that she was still asleep, and she was—or so he thought.

Michele began watching his every move, and getting turned on by the second. She knew that Preston was trying to be discreet, and she was trying to figure out how she could join him without him shying away from her. *Actions are better than words*, she thought. Michele released Preston from her embrace. She covered his hand with hers, and before he could protest, she quickly unzipped his pants and took out his cock. Michele nearly gasped; his dick was bigger than Trey's and twice as thick. She dropped between his legs and began feasting on his erection.

Preston wanted to protest, but he wasn't thinking clearly. The betrayal of his wife and son had his mind reeling. Thoughts of revenge kept entering his head, and what better way to get back at them than to fuck Michele. His reasoning was irrational, but he didn't care. He wanted to soothe his wounded heart, and if screwing another woman would ease his pain, then so be it.

He grabbed her by the hair and pushed her farther down on his cock. Michele had a deep throat, and didn't gag. She just sucked harder and harder.

She could feel that he was on the verge of cumming, so she stopped. She got up and slipped out of her gown and underwear. She wanted Preston to see her arsenal up close and personal. She knew that once he got a glimpse of her rack, he would want more than just a blow job.

Preston was rendered speechless. Her breasts looked better than he thought. They were big and round with just the right amount of sag. Her nipples were firm and thick, like they were made for sucking. He rubbed the shaft of his penis up and down as he watched Michele undress. Standing in front of him with nothing on but her shoes, she looked like a porn star. Her body was perfect and he wanted a taste.

Michele saw the lustful way in which Preston stared, and knew that she had him exactly where she wanted him. She smoothed one hand over her nipples, and slipped the other hand between her legs and into her vagina. She took her fingers out, and stuck them into his mouth so that he could taste her juices.

"Hmm," he moaned as he sucked her fingers.

Michele pulled his pants legs, indicating that she wanted him to take them off, and he did. She then straddled him, sitting directly on his humongous cock. She bent her knees, and put her feet on the sofa so that her pussy lips opened wide, covering his cock. She then began to bounce up and down.

Preston watched her breasts move freely, and all he could think about was fucking her. He stuck his fingers in her ass, and she didn't object. He worked her ass until it was loose. He then got up and flipped her facedown on the sofa. He pulled her ass close to him. He then took the head of his dick and slowly replaced his fingers. He worked his cock slowly into her ass.

"Ohhh, baby," she purred.

Preston expertly worked his cock until he was all the way in her back door, and then began moving his pelvis around and around in a circular motion, until she started bucking back against him.

Michele had only had anal sex a few times in her life, and had never really enjoyed it. But the way Preston was feeding his dick into her made her more aroused than she had ever been before. His dick was hitting so many nerve endings that she didn't know whether to cry out in pain, or scream in sheer pleasure. So she did both. "Ohhh . . . that hurts . . . sooo . . . *good*!" she shouted.

Preston's eyes were closed. He was in a zone. Ariel had never let him butt fuck her, and this was a treat. He grabbed Michele's hips, and pulled her closer and closer until he felt his balls slapping against her ass. He then reached around with both hands and grabbed her nipples.

"Oooohhh!" she screamed out, as he pulled her nipples so hard that she thought he was going to rip them off.

Preston heard her pain, and eased out of her ass. He turned her over, and began gently sucking her breasts, like he was trying to soothe them. "Is that better?" he moaned between sucks.

"Yes, but my pussy's getting jealous."

Preston didn't say another word, just eased down between her legs, and began feasting. He had his tongue and hand so deep into her canal that she began to squirt cum. "Yes, baby, that's it; cum for me."

Michele wiggled against his touch and came like a wild woman. No man had ever made her squirt before, and her body jerked back and forth from the sensation.

Preston then took his dick and entered her. She was so wet that his cock slipped right in. He fucked with such force that they both fell off the sofa, but he didn't stop. He humped and pumped until they were both bathed in sweat. Her pussy was clenching his dick, and he couldn't control himself. He came with such force that he thought his cum was going to shoot out through her nose. After they came, he turned her over to her side, spooned her right there on the imported rug, and drifted off into a lust-induced sleep.

22

SHE WAS still in New York. She should have been back in D.C. a few days ago, but couldn't pry herself away from BD2. The sister club to the Black Door was on fire. The energy of the club was palpable, and the sexual tension was contagious. The moment she entered the gated freight elevator, she could feel her body temperature increase a few degrees in anticipation of the possibilities that lay ahead. During her last visit, she had spent the entire evening in the Between the Sheets chamber with a beautiful young woman named Christy; now she was back for more.

She walked right past the greeter. She preferred not to be teased by the brawny doorman. She wanted to be teased *and* pleased, so she went directly into Between the Sheets, looking for her lady love. But her intended target wasn't there.

"Did you want to change into a sheet?" asked the young Hispanic server approaching her. The last time she was there, he greeted her at the door and offered her a satin toga. This time, she walked into the room so fast that she brushed right past him in an effort to find the woman in the purple mask.

"No, thank you." She looked around the room again, and then decided to ask him. "Have you seen Christy?"

He looked shocked that she knew the name of the new female server, since most servers didn't exchange names with clients. "Uh, she was here earlier and mentioned that she was going to the mani-pedi suite."

"And where is that?" She wasn't as familiar with BD2 as she was with the original club.

"Make a right when you leave this chamber; go down the hall, make a left, and it's the third door on the right. You can't miss the frosted aqua door."

She did as instructed and sauntered down the hallway until she found a beautifully frosted glass door. She pushed the door open and stepped inside. She expected to see people fucking and sucking like in some of the other chambers. Unlike the Between the Sheets chamber, which was dimly lit, with gyrating bodies everywhere, this chamber was serene and tranquil, like a spa. The walls were painted a soothing sea-foam blue. On the far wall, there was an oversized waterfall, and the sound of the flowing water brought to mind waves lapping softly on a sandy beach. A recording of a Japanese koto was playing gently in the background, adding another layer of ambiance to the atmosphere. She was taken aback. She didn't expect this chamber to feel so Zen-like. The last thing she wanted was to calm down. Her adrenaline was pumping and she wanted sex, not a relaxing rubdown.

I've got to get out of here before I fall asleep. Just as she reached for the doorknob, a woman appeared from behind a glass-brick wall.

"Leaving so soon?"

She turned around, and faced a woman who was dressed as a geisha, with white facial paint, bright red lips, dramatic black eyebrows, and an elaborate headdress. Her kimono was a vibrant combination of plum, tangerine, and cherry, with gold flecks. Her outfit was complete even down to her feet. She wore the traditional *tabi* white socks, and wooden *okobo* clogs. "Yes. I was looking for someone, but I don't see her."

"And how do you know that person is not here?" the geisha asked, in a soft tone. "Please come with me." She fanned her arm out, welcoming the new guest. "I promise you won't be disappointed."

She was intrigued, and followed the geisha. Behind the glass block wall was a short hallway with two doors on each side. The geisha opened one of the doors, led her inside, and then walked out, closing the door behind her.

The room was just as tranquil as the outer lobby, except the lighting was softer. The only piece of furniture was a white leather pedicure chair perched on a platform. She stood there for a few seconds, not knowing what to do. She leaned on the edge of the chair, and folded her arms. *If Ms. Geisha doesn't come back soon, I'm leaving.*

Just as she was ready to make her exit, the door opened. "Going somewhere?"

"Not anymore. I've been looking all over for you," she said, uncrossing her arms.

Christy walked into the room and closed the door. "So I've heard." She smiled.

"How did you know I was in here?"

"The reception area is equipped with cameras, and I saw you on the monitor. I told Ginger to bring you back."

"Who's Ginger?"

"She's the geisha, and a good friend of mine."

She looked at Christy's outfit. "And where's your geisha ensemble?" Christy wore a short white silk sheath with nothing on underneath, a pair of Lucite wedges, and her purple half-mask.

"I'm not a geisha. They just hired Ginger to add a new element to the mani-pedi suite. I don't usually work this area. I was in the back taking a break, then I saw you on the monitor, and . . ."

"And what?"

"And I wanted to see you again. I enjoyed the last time, and thought we could have a little more fun tonight," Christy said, walking a little closer.

"I thought so too, but . . ." She looked down at Christy's crotch. "Where's your strap-on?" She had enjoyed the fake dick and wanted more. She was disappointed when she didn't see the massive dildo.

"Trust me, I don't need it tonight, I've got other skills," she said with a devilish grin. "Get in the chair."

She looked at Christy oddly. "Why do you want me to sit down? I thought we'd go back to Between the Sheets since we enjoyed ourselves there last time."

"It's too crowded in there tonight. Let's try something new. Now get in the chair."

"Oh, okay," she said skeptically and climbed the three short steps. As she was ready to sit down, she noticed that there was a hole in the seat of the chair, and hesitated.

"Go ahead and sit down," Christy instructed.

She sat in the unique doughnut-looking chair, with her ass out. She didn't have on any underwear and could feel air hitting her vulva. She watched Christy squat underneath the chair, and seconds later, felt Christy's tongue tickling the hood of her clit. She now understood why the chair had a hole in the seat.

Christy took her fingers and parted the rose folds of her lover's pussy, and then stuck her tongue deep into the moist cuntal orifice. She then trailed her tongue from the tip of her lover's clit to her sphincter, and back again. She sucked and licked and sucked and licked until her lover was moaning in ecstasy. "You like the special chair?"

"Hmm, I love it."

Christy finger fucked herself, while getting her lover off, and when they both came within minutes of each other, she wiped her mouth, and reemerged from underneath the chair. "I bet you never had a spa service like that before," she said, sitting on the edge of the platform.

"No, I haven't." She was surprised at how comfortable she was with Christy. She had always had male servers at the Black Door, and enjoyed every second of them, but there was something about this girl that had her wishing for more. She knew that she needed to get home, but didn't want to leave her new lover. She and her husband had been on the outs lately, and there was nothing exciting waiting for her when she returned.

"It was great seeing you again," Christy said, getting up to leave.

"Wait a minute. I know this isn't customary, but I was wondering if you'd like to go back to D.C. with me for a few days? We could continue our play date in Washington. My husband will be busy with meetings, and I need something exciting to do."

"I don't know. We're not supposed to see clients outside of the club; it's against the rules."

"Who's going to know? I won't tell if you don't." She winked.

"I certainly won't tell, but didn't you say that you're married?" Christy asked, looking at her skeptically. She didn't want to be the cause of any marital issues.

"Yes, I'm married."

"So, what's your husband going to say when you bring some chick home? I don't want to get in the middle of your domestic bliss," she said sarcastically. "Does he know you're bisexual?"

"Trust me, the bliss is long gone. And he won't know a thing. I'll put you up at the Ritz. And just so you know, I'm not bisexual, just adventurous, that's all. I haven't been with a woman since college, and that was a hundred years ago." She chuckled. "Besides, with him working and hitting the bottle, I doubt he'll even notice my spending a few hours at the Ritz."

"Well, it would be fun to get away from this place for a few days. Why the hell not?" Christy said, warming up to the idea.

"Excellent! Okay, this is the plan. I'm leaving early in the morning, and will go home, give my husband some charity pussy—that is, if he's not too drunk to get it up." She laughed. "Then, I'll meet you at the hotel."

"Sounds like you got everything covered on the home front. I'll see you tomorrow night in D.C."

The women exchanged last names and cell phone numbers, and kissed good night. Christy went back to work, while her lover left the club, went back to her hotel, and began packing for her return trip home. Lately she had been spending more and more time away from home, since that was the last place she wanted to be. Her once happy marriage was now just a front, and she knew that it was partially her fault.

23

MICHELE WOKE up first, looking over at Preston, who was curled up on the rug still asleep. He was naked from the waist down, and she peeked over at his resting penis and smiled. Her plan had worked brilliantly. Not only had Preston's memory returned, but she was able to exempt herself from Trey and Ariel's cover-up scheme. As far as Preston was concerned, she knew nothing about the affair, and she planned on keeping it that way. Michele wanted Preston to confide in her, which would only draw them closer. Even though they had made crazy love last night, she knew that that wasn't enough to drive a permanent wedge between him and his wife. Michele had to play on Preston's emotions, and make him think that Trey and Ariel were still seeing each other behind his back. Betrayal was a much bigger and better wedge to pry them apart than a one-night stand, and once that happened, he would be all hers.

Michele quietly got up, slipped on her evening dress, and tiptoed into the kitchen. She was still buzzing from the night before, and was dying to tell Fiona what happened. She picked up the phone, and dialed her friend.

"Hey girl, you up?" she whispered.

"Yes, I'm getting ready to go to the gym. Why are you whispering?"

"I'm at Preston's."

"Okay. But that still doesn't explain why you're whispering. Last time I checked you worked there, and were free to talk in a normal tone."

"Well, what I did last night definitely does not qualify for work." She walked over to the swinging door and poked her head out. She didn't see Preston walking around, and assumed that he was still asleep on the floor. She closed the door, went to the far end of the room, and whispered, "Unless you count fucking as part of the job."

Fiona gasped. "Girl, are you telling me that you slept with Preston last night?"

"Well, we didn't do much sleeping."

"How the hell did you pull that off? Where is his wife?"

Michele told Fiona about sending the article regarding the Black Door to Laird, and how he played right into her game. "The minute Preston heard Trey's name and the Black Door in the same sentence, his memory came back in a flash. It couldn't have happened at a better time, since Ariel is still in New York."

"That was a big chance you took. Suppose Preston hadn't walked into the conversation at that very moment, then what would you have done?" Fiona wanted to know.

"I had already thought about that. Laird has such a reputation as a man-whore, that I knew the second I brought up sex clubs, he would talk until he was blue in the face. And eventually Preston would join the conversation, which he did, so basically it was just a matter of getting Laird to open his big mouth, which was easy."

"Wow, Michele, I've got to give it to you, you pulled off a major feat. Helping to jog Preston's memory like you did was brilliant."

Michele blushed with pride, as if she'd won a Nobel Prize. "Thanks." Michele thought that she heard Preston stirring about. "Look, girl, I've got to run. I'll talk to you later."

After hanging up, she made a pot of coffee, and toasted a few English muffins. She put everything on a silver tray, including cups, orange juice, and a bottle of Tylenol in case Preston had a hangover from drinking too much scotch.

When she walked back into the living room, Preston was fully dressed and sitting on the sofa, holding his head in his hands. Michele took a deep breath. She didn't know how he was going to react to having fucked her. Either he would be extremely remorseful and apologetic, or would be so turned on that he'd want more. Knowing Preston as she did, Michele doubted that the latter would be the case.

"Good morning," she said in a soft voice.

"What time is it?" he asked, still holding his head.

Michele shifted the tray to her right hand, and looked at her watch. "It's six-thirty-two." He didn't respond; just kept holding his head as if it hurt. She set the tray on the cocktail table. "I made some coffee, nice and strong as you like it," she said, pouring a cup.

Preston finally raised his head and took the steaming brew. He sipped the coffee in silence with his head lying back on the sofa and his eyes closed. He looked as if he had a massive hangover and was trying to keep his head from exploding.

"Here are two Tylenol," she said, handing him the white pills and a glass of juice.

"Thanks. My head feels like Johnnie walked all over it," he said in a groggy tone.

Michele chuckled at his lame joke. She wanted to talk about last night and his newfound memory, but she didn't want to push the envelope. She decided it would be best to let Preston broach the subject, so she sat down, drank her coffee, and waited. Neither of them touched the English muffins, just drank one cup of java after another, until the carafe was empty. "Should I make another pot?" she asked as Preston took his last sip.

"No, thank you." He cleared his throat, and looked at Michele for the first time since she entered the room. "About last night, I, uh . . . want to apologize . . . I didn't . . ."

"Preston, you have nothing to apologize for. If anybody should be sorry, it's Trey and Ariel," she blurted out. Michele tried to refrain from talking about them, but she couldn't hold her tongue any longer—so much for decorum!

He looked to the floor and then back at her. "Do you think they're still involved?"

Michele thought for a second, trying to choose the right words. This was her moment, and she intended to shine. "Preston . . ." She hesitated for effect.

"Come on, Michele, if you know something, anything, please tell me. I've been in the dark for far too long."

"Well, I've been putting two and two together since you told me about their affair last night, and it's definitely adding up to four," she said cryptically.

"And exactly what does that mean?"

"It means that Trey hasn't been spending much time with me. Whenever I invite myself to New York, he has a lame excuse why I shouldn't come up, which leads me to believe that he's seeing someone else," she lied. "And if I had to guess, I'd say that that someone else is Ariel. Think about it. Why would she be working on a case in New York if it wasn't to be close to Trey? If she really wanted to, she could have declined that case. After all, she is a partner, and partners get to pick and choose. Don't they?" she asked rhetorically. "Those are the facts, and the facts don't lie," she said, giving him an earful.

Preston exhaled hard. He was trying to wrap his mind around the fact that his son and his wife were having an affair. But it still didn't make sense to him. Why would Ariel marry him if she was in love with Trey? It wasn't like she needed his money. She was well established, with assets of her own, and she wasn't the status-conscious type.

He thought back on that morning over a year ago when Senator Oglesby sent him the fax regarding Trey's ownership of the Black Door. He remembered reading the fax, and then going over to Ariel's apartment. She was upset about something and had been drinking. The moment he mentioned the club, she blurted out that she had fucked Trey at the Black Door. Preston had read that everyone at the club wore masks, which led him to thinking that Ariel didn't know

Trey's identity, which would explain how they got involved. But it didn't explain why they were still involved. "Did you know that Trey owns a club called the Black Door?"

Michele didn't know if she should lie or tell the truth. Since Preston hadn't asked her the night before if she knew about Trey owning the club, she decided on the truth. His owning the club didn't have anything to do with her. "When I first met Trey, he told me he was into real estate. It wasn't until after your wedding that I learned he owned the Black Door. Why do you ask?"

"I'm trying to figure out how Ariel knew about the Black Door, and why she would go to a place like that," he said, looking forlorn.

"She's obviously not who you think she is. Only a nymphomaniac would go to a seedy sex club," she said, turning up her nose at the thought, as if she were disgusted. "I mean, why would she want to fool around, when she has a smart, handsome, sexy man like you?" Michele purposefully threw in the word *sexy* to remind Preston about their heated lovemaking. He seemed to be focused on Ariel and Trey, and not on her, which was pissing her off.

"Ariel never appeared to be addicted to sex. I just don't understand." He dropped his head in his hands again.

Who cares about Ariel? Michele thought. She scooted closer to him, and began rubbing his back like she had done the night before. "Preston, she's not worthy of you. You're such a wonderful man. A man who needs to be cherished and not cheated on," she said softly in his ear.

He held his head up. "I need to talk to Ariel and Trey. I can't believe that they would purposely betray me. I need some answers. My memory is still a little fuzzy," he said, reaching for the phone.

Michele couldn't believe that Preston was willing to talk to either of them. He should have been enraged, but his reaction was totally different from what she expected. It was like he hadn't heard a word she had said. Even with her talking up Trey and Ariel's affair, Preston was willing to give them the benefit of the doubt, as if the affair had never happened. Michele needed to stop him from calling Ariel or Trey. If he talked to them, he would know that she was lying about

her involvement. "Preston, wait," she said as she took the phone out
of his hand, "there's something else I need to tell you."

"Yes?"

"I wanted to spare you the pain, but there's something you don't
know. . . ."

"And what's that?" he asked, looking at her oddly as she replaced
the phone back in its cradle.

"Remember a few months ago, when you went to the country
with Senator Oglesby? Well, that weekend Trey came down, and I
was so happy that he had come for a visit. The next morning, he'd
gotten up early and left a note saying that he had gone running. I
didn't think too much about it. I had some work to finish up from the
day before, so I got dressed, left my apartment, and went to the town
house. I opened the front door, and there right on the staircase," she
pointed toward the front of the house, "Trey and Ariel were fucking
like two dogs in heat. I was devastated and ran out in shock!" She
forced a tear out of her eye. "I was going to tell you, but I was too
ashamed. Not only were you being cheated on, but I was too. And to
be honest, I still haven't gotten over the pain." She wiped the lone
tear from her cheek. Michele hadn't planned on ad-libbing, but she
needed a plausible story to link Ariel and Trey together in the present. And a tale of them fucking under Preston's roof would be enough
to send him over the edge—she hoped.

Preston jumped up. "*What!* Not in my own house!" he screamed.

Michele threw her hands up to her face as if she were crying,
when in actuality she was hiding a broad smile. Her off-the-cuff lie
was extremely effective, and Preston was finally steaming mad.

"How dare they have sex in my home? I can't believe it! And to
think I trusted both of them. Once I get through with them, they're
going to regret the day they betrayed me!" he ranted, flailing his
hands in the air.

Michele had gotten the desired response from him, but she still
didn't want Preston to breathe a word. If he confronted them at this
point, they would dispute her lies. She needed more time to pussy-
whip Preston. She wanted him totally smitten with her, so by the

time the truth came out, he wouldn't know exactly who to believe—her or his cheating wife and son.

"Do you think it's wise to confront them now?" she asked, looking at him pointedly.

"Why not?" Preston didn't see any reason why the cards shouldn't be laid out on the table. The game was over, and now it was time for the blinding truth.

"Look at their track record. They've done nothing but lie to you since day one, and what makes you think they won't lie once you confront them?" she asked, but didn't give Preston a chance to answer. "Your best bet is to catch them in the act. And in order to do that, you need to set up surveillance cameras. That way you'll have tangible evidence to support your allegations." Michele was speaking so fast that she nearly ran her words together.

"Hmm." He thought for a second. "I guess you have a good point. On the other hand, why do I need tangible evidence? You saw them firsthand, and Ariel has already confessed her affair to me."

Shit! Michele wasn't prepared for that question, but she wasn't going to be outdone at this point. "Don't forget that you're married to a partner in a law firm, and what if she uses her firm to rake you over the coals in a heated divorce suit? Just because she has money of her own, doesn't mean she won't go after yours. You know what they say, 'It's nothing worse than a woman scorned.' I realize that you're the scorned one, but you never know how she'll react if you ask for a divorce," she said, quickly throwing in the *D* word. "You've worked too hard to give up half of your fortune to an adulteress who's been sleeping with your *son*," she said, adding that little sting at the end.

Preston hadn't thought that far ahead, but Michele was right. If Ariel was determined to live her life with Trey, she wouldn't be living it with any of his hard-earned money. "I guess you have a point."

Michele silently breathed a sigh of relief. He was finally seeing her point of view and she was ecstatic. "Preston, we need to let them believe that everything is status quo. The best game plan is to let them think we know nothing, and once we've gathered enough evidence, they'll have no choice but to confess, and then the ball will be in our court," she said, subliminally incorporating herself into the equation.

Preston couldn't believe that his marriage had gone from happy to helpless in less than twenty-four hours. Not only had Ariel cheated before they got married, but she had also committed adultery with his son! He and Michele were busy talking about Trey and Ariel, and hadn't really touched on last night. He felt like a hypocrite. Here he was talking about his wife's affair, when he had fucked his assistant. He rationalized that his actions were justified, more like a knee-jerk reaction to his wife's betrayal. Besides, Preston had no intention of sleeping with Michele ever again. It was a onetime thing, and he planned on keeping it that way.

THE JUDGE had recessed the trial early for the weekend, and Ariel was elated. She had planned on meeting Trey in D.C. so that they could finally tell Preston the truth, but since she had a few extra hours to spare, she decided to go and visit Mrs. Grant, her foster mother. Mrs. Grant had no clue that Ariel was in town and would be pleasantly surprised. Ariel left the courthouse, jumped in a taxi, and headed over to Greenwich Village to Magnolia Bakery to pick up some of their famous cupcakes. Mrs. Grant still had a houseful of kids, and what child could resist the frosty sugary delight. Ariel enjoyed bringing treats for the kids. They were always so appreciative of every little thing that she brought over. It reminded her of being a child, and looking forward to visitors who came bearing gifts for the orphaned children. Most times it was just a pan of homemade oatmeal cookies, or a buttery pound cake, but to her it was monumental, since she didn't have parents to shower her with birthday or Christmas presents.

Loaded with an assortment of two dozen mini-cakes, Ariel hailed a taxi, and headed up the West Side Highway. Twenty minutes later, the cab was pulling up in front of Mrs. Grant's two-storied frame house. As a kid, Ariel thought that the house was humongous, but looking at it now, it seemed small and frail. The pale yellow exterior was in dire need of a paint job; the gutters were overgrown with vines, and a few of the windows needed to be replaced. She walked up the rickety front steps and pushed the bell, but it didn't ring. She balanced the pastries and her briefcase with one hand and knocked on the door.

"Baby girl!" Mrs. Grant exclaimed, opening the screen door. "What are you doing here?"

"I came to see you."

"Why aren't you in Washington with your husband?" Mrs. Grant asked, standing in the doorway.

"Are you going to let me in or are we going to stand out here on the porch for our visit?" Ariel asked, still balancing the cupcakes with one hand.

"I'm sorry, baby," she said as she held the door open wider, "come on in."

"Here, these are for the kids." Ariel handed over the pastry boxes. "Where are they anyway?"

"Chile, they in school, thank God." She chuckled.

Ariel gave Mrs. Grant a warm hug, and then walked into the tiny living room, which was littered with an assortment of toys. Ariel removed a doll and a set of LEGOs from the sofa cushion and sat down. "Mom, why haven't you gotten the house painted? I sent you money for repairs last year," Ariel asked, the moment she sat down.

"Now, don't go fussing at me," Mrs. Grant said, wiping her hands on her apron and sitting in one of the living room chairs. "I put the money you give me in the bank, to save for these kids' education. They all ain't gonna get scholarships like you did, and I wanna make sure that they get a good college education, so that they can take care of themselves, and not depend on the government for handouts the rest of their lives."

Ariel couldn't be mad at Mrs. Grant's intentions. She had a big heart and always put the welfare of her foster children before her own. "Mom, why didn't you tell me that? I would've taken the money and put it in a special account for the children, and paid for the paint job myself. This house is falling apart around you," she said, looking up at the water-stained ceiling. "I understand you want to help the kids, and I admire that, but you have to take care of yourself too. Before you say no, I'm going to have a contractor come over next week, and give me an estimate. I'll take care of the bill. You just make sure you show him everything that needs to be done. And I mean everything. Okay?"

Mrs. Grant looked slightly embarrassed at being chastised by her foster daughter. "Okay, baby girl. I will. Now I know you didn't come all the way out here to talk about this old house. How you been doing? How's your husband?" Mrs. Grant never missed an opportunity to talk about Preston. She was so proud to have a Supreme Court justice as a son-in-law, and often bragged about him to her neighbors and church members.

"I've been good, just busy that's all. And Preston is doing okay."

"Well, I'd say he's doing more than okay." Mrs. Grant got up, went over to the cocktail table, and rustled through the many papers and magazines that crowded the surface. She picked up a folded newspaper, and handed it to Ariel.

Ariel took the paper. "What's this?"

"Read it and see," Mrs. Grant said, and sat back down.

The paper was folded to the society page of the *Chronicle*, and it was an article about the cocktail party for the president elect. The article itself was basically a rundown of Washington's Who's Who, and was unimpressive to Ariel, but what caught her eye was the picture of Preston with the president elect. Her husband looked quite handsome in the black suit that she had bought for him a few months ago. "Actually, I was supposed to be at this party with Preston, but I couldn't go."

"And why not?" Mrs. Grant didn't understand why Ariel would let Preston go to such an impressive affair alone. Back in her day a woman's place was with her husband. "What's more important than standing by your husband when he's meeting the next president of the United States?" Now it was her turn to chastise.

"I would've loved to have been there, but I do have a career of my own," Ariel said, slightly annoyed. "Mom, things are not like they were when you were married."

Mrs. Grant cocked her head to one side. "And what's that supposed to mean?"

"It means that my world doesn't revolve around Preston. I wasn't put on this earth to supply his every need." As Ariel continued with her ranting, she looked at the solemn expression forming on Mrs. Grant's face and realized that she was offending the older woman. She then lowered her voice and changed her tune. "Mom, I'm sorry, I didn't mean to insult you. I realize that your generation has different views on marriage and family than my generation, but it doesn't make one opinion better than the other," she said, trying to smooth things over.

"Yeah, I guess you're right, baby. I just want you to be happy, and appreciate what a good man you have." She pointed to the article. "Just look how fine he is." She chuckled, putting her hand to her mouth.

Ariel looked at the picture again. She then did a double take. In the foreground were Preston and the president elect, but in the background, smiling like a contestant in a beauty pageant, was Michele. At first Ariel hadn't paid her any attention since her eyes went right to Preston, but there Michele was, smiling and profiling like she was hosting the party. "What the hell was she doing there?" Ariel said, underneath her breath.

"What did you say, baby?"

"Oh, nothing, Mom. Excuse me. I need to make an important call," Ariel said, getting up and going into the kitchen for some privacy.

Ariel called her home number, but the phone just rang. She then called Preston's cell phone, but her call went straight to voice mail. She started to call Michele, but decided against it, since Michele would probably gloat about schmoozing at the party with the important dignitaries. Ariel needed to talk to her husband and find out why he had brought Michele with him. She began to panic. *What if Michele told him the truth?* She dialed Preston's private office number.

"Hello?"

"Hey, honey, how are you?" Ariel asked once he picked up.

"Oh, hi. I'm fine, and you?" Preston decided to take Michele's advice and not tip his hand, so he pretended like everything was perfect.

He doesn't sound any different. I'm just being paranoid, she thought. "I saw your picture in the paper today."

"Really?" He'd been totally preoccupied dealing with his newfound memory, and hadn't read any newspapers.

"Yes, it was a picture with you and the president elect; also . . ." She hesitated, not knowing if she should bring up Michele, and then thought why the hell not. "Michele was in the picture too. What was she doing at the party?"

"She was there in a working capacity," he said point-blank.

Ariel still had the article clenched in her hand, and looked at the picture again. Michele did have on a conservative-looking dress, and wasn't showing any cleavage, like she normally did. "Oh." Ariel didn't have any other response. What could she say? After all, Michele did work for Preston. "Were there any other assistants at the party?" she wanted to know.

"As a matter of fact, Senator Oglesby brought his assistant, and so did a few of my other colleagues."

"Oh, okay." She felt relieved at hearing that Preston wasn't the only one with his assistant. "Well, I'm coming home today, since we're off for the weekend."

"You think that's necessary? Shouldn't you focus on the case? Don't get me wrong; I'd love to see you, honey, but you'll just be preoccupied with paperwork if you come home. Why don't you concentrate on winning your case and come home when it's over." Preston wasn't ready to see his wife just yet. He was still trying to wrap his mind around her disloyalty and until he sorted out his feelings, he preferred not to see her face.

"Well, I do have some files to go over, but I miss you so much—"

"I miss you too," he said, cutting her off. "Tell you what, once you finish your case, we'll go away for a mini-holiday. How does that sound?" Preston nearly bit his tongue as he said those words, but if he didn't want Ariel to become suspicious, then he had to pretend like their relationship was rock solid.

"That sounds heavenly." She smiled. "Okay, honey, I'll talk to you later. I love you."

"Me too," he said, and hung up.

After talking to Preston, Ariel felt much better. He had eased her paranoid thoughts about Michele, and she realized that she didn't have any reason to worry; everything was under control.

TREY WAS home packing for his dreaded trip to Washington. As much as he knew he needed to confront Michele, he wanted to delay the inevitable. She wasn't responsive over the phone, so he had no other choice but to see her face-to-face. Through her actions Michele had basically said that their relationship was history. Though she didn't utter those words, Trey could read between the lines. Obviously she preferred social climbing over him, and he was fine with her decision, especially now that he had some extra pussy on the side. Lexi was a pleasant distraction from his present problems and he welcomed the attention.

He tossed the last items of clothing and his iPod into a duffel bag and headed out. He heard his home phone ring as he locked the door. *If it's important, whoever it is will call my cell.*

While he waited curbside for a taxi, his mobile rang. He fished the tiny phone out of his jeans pocket. "Hello?"

"Hey, man. Where are you?" Mason asked, sounding like he was in a panic.

"I'm in front of my building, trying to hail a taxi, on the way to Penn Station. I'm going to D.C. this weekend."

"I'm glad I caught you."

"Why? What's up?" Trey asked casually.

"There was a water main break about a half a block away from the club and it's flooding the basement, and—"

"What? Which location?" he asked frantically, his casual tone now gone.

"The main club. Joe just called me. He said that he tried to reach you at home, but your phone rang a few times and went to voice mail."

"Did he say how bad it is?"

"No, I'm on my way there now," Mason said.

Trey stepped in the street, waved down a passing cab, and hopped in the backseat. "Okay, I'll meet you there." After hanging up from Mason, he dialed Ariel's cell.

"Hello?"

"Hey, Ariel, listen; I've got a crisis going on at the club, and don't know if I'll be able to get down to D.C. today," he said.

"I hope it's not anything serious." She sounded concerned.

"Me too, but I won't know for sure until I get there."

"Well, don't worry about going to D.C. I spoke with Preston earlier and everything seems to be under control," Ariel said calmly.

"Really?" Trey replied, sounding as if he didn't quite believe her. The last time they spoke, Ariel seemed convinced that Michele was on the verge of telling his dad the truth.

"Yes, from the tone of our conversation, I doubt if Michele has said anything to him. So, I don't think there's a need to rush down this weekend to confront her. My case should be over early next week and we can go down together as originally planned."

"If you think that's best, then it's cool with me. Give me a call when you're done with work, and we can coordinate the reservations."

"Okay, talk to you later," she said, hanging up.

As the taxi approached the club, Trey could see blue city utility trucks parked a few feet from his establishment. Orange cones were at each end of the block, preventing cars from entering. The cab stopped at the corner and let Trey out. He was so anxious to get to the club that he trotted down the block with his duffel bag swinging over his shoulder. Mason was standing on the front steps as he approached.

"Perfect timing; I just walked up," Mason greeted him.

Trey took out the front door keys and let them inside. They immediately went down to the basement to assess the damage. There were at least two and a half feet of standing water and sewage. They rolled up their jeans and waded through the water to get a handle on what had been destroyed. A few cases of liquor in the supply closet were semi-submerged, but the bottles were fine. Fortunately, Trey didn't store client masks in the basement; otherwise, the one-of-a-kind art pieces would have been ruined. He and Mason walked to the rear of the basement and up five steps to the Dungeon. Trey opened the door, and turned on the light. The sadomasochistic chamber where hard-core members, wearing latex, enjoyed being blindfolded and whipped with leather straps, while shackled on a wooden slab, was totally intact. Since the chamber was elevated on a platform, it wasn't affected by the water. After looking around, Trey turned off the lights, and they exited the room.

"Man, this cleanup is going to be one hell of a job," Trey said, surveying the sludge that had come in from the sewage system.

"Isn't the city supposed to pump out the water?" Mason asked.

"Yeah, they are, but once the water is gone we're still going to have all of this waste," he said, pointing to the debris on the floor. "And besides, I really don't want city workers nosing around in my basement. Even though the club is legit, some of the apparatus in the Dungeon could raise some interesting questions, and the last thing I need is for city inspectors to come knocking on my door."

"I guess you have a point. But if you don't get this cleaned up quickly, it's really going to start stinking. It smells like urine now. Imagine what the stench is going to be like in a few days," Mason said, wrinkling up his nose.

"Tell me about it," Trey said, shaking his head in frustration. "Let's go to my office; maybe I can find someone in the yellow pages who's discreet."

Once in his office, Trey found the phone book, sat behind his desk, and began calling company after company, but everyone he called was booked, and wouldn't be able to get to the club for a few days. The Black Door had a reputation of class and sophistication, and the horrific stench of sewage debris didn't mesh with the elite status of the club. Trey was in the middle of dialing another company when his cell phone rang.

"Hello?"

"Hey, handsome. What's happening?" Lexi was calling for another hedonistic round of sex. Their last encounter was off the chain, and she wanted more. Lexi had an aggressive nature, and when she wanted something or someone, she could be relentless.

"I can't talk right now," Trey said, ready to hang up the phone.

Sensing that he was busy, Lexi dropped her sexy tone. She remembered how upset he was the last time she entered his office and detected that same tone in his voice. He seemed in need of a friend, and she wanted to help if she could. "What's the matter? You sound stressed."

"Stressed is an understatement." Out of frustration, Trey went on to tell her his predicament. "And if I don't get somebody to come out soon, the odor will permeate throughout the entire building and I'll have to close the club until the cleanup is complete."

"You're not going to believe this," Lexi said, nearly shouting.

"What?" he asked, but wasn't really interested in hearing what she had to say. He had wasted enough time talking to her. "Listen, I've got to make some more calls. I'll talk to you later."

"Wait a minute, Trey. My cousin has an industrial-waste removal service. I'll give him a call right now and call you back," she said quickly, and hung up.

After about five minutes, Lexi called back. "Hey, Trey, I talked to my cousin and he'll be there within the hour."

"Thanks, but I need someone who's discreet. The Black Door isn't your ordinary club, and I don't want to have to answer a gazillion and two questions."

"Uh . . . hello! I know all about the club, and I told my cousin that this job is strictly on the DL, so don't worry, I got your back."

Trey didn't know what to say. Ten minutes ago he was in a panic and up to his ankles in waste; now his problem was solved thanks to a random booty call. "I don't know how I can thank you."

"I do. You can take me out to dinner. There's a new restaurant in the West Village that I've been dying to try," she said, with a ready answer.

Trey hadn't thought about seeing Lexi outside of the club, dinner with her would be like a date, and he wasn't sure if he was ready for all that. But on the other hand, how could he say no—after all, she had gotten him out of a serious bind. "Okay, just let me know when and where and I'm there."

"Okay," she said, smiling into the receiver. "Talk to you later."

He turned to Mason. "Man, you won't believe who just came to my rescue," he said, slightly shaking his head, as if he still couldn't believe the sudden change of events.

"Who?" Mason had been on his cell phone, and had no idea who was on the other end of the line.

"Lexi!" Trey grinned.

"Lexi? How did she rescue you?"

"That was her on the phone, and she called her cousin who has a waste-removal company, and he and his crew are on their way over right now."

"Wow, what a coincidence! I know you probably don't want to hear this, but Lexi is pretty cool. I've hung out with her and Terra a few times, and she's not half bad. If you want my opinion, she's a much better match for you than social-climbing Michele."

In Trey's mind, Lexi was nothing more than a convenient fuck. She seemed to like their arrangement, and he loved having sex without a relationship added to the equation. "Man, I don't know about all that."

"I know you're still a little gun-shy. Dealing with Michele, who wouldn't be? All I'm saying is, don't discount Lexi. I know you guys are having fun right now, but who knows? Once you dump Michele, maybe it could turn into something real," Mason said, sounding like he was trying to make a "love connection."

"Yeah, you never know. Maybe our lust will turn into true love, and we'll die old and happy in each other's arms," Trey said sarcastically.

"Well, never say never 'cause you never know." Mason winked.

Trey ignored his friend's comment, and turned his attention back to the yellow pages. He aimlessly flipped through page after page. He wasn't looking for anything in particular; he just didn't want to discuss Lexi anymore. Truth be told, after their last fuck-fest, he felt a little something for her. He didn't know if it was purely the pussy or if she was someone he could get to know and possibly have a relationship with. At the moment, he had too much on his plate to add another item. Whatever he felt—if anything—toward Lexi would just have to wait until he sorted out his present problems.

26

MICHELE COULDN'T have been happier had she won all six numbers in the Mega Millions lottery game. It took some finesse, but she had finally persuaded Preston to keep quiet about his restored memory. Now all she had to do was fuck him into submission before Ariel got back. She had slipped in a subliminal comment about him being a sexy man the morning after their heated night of lust, but he didn't react. Preston's sole focus was on Ariel and Trey. Michele had convinced him that they were still having an affair, and now he was determined to catch them in the act. Since his memory was still a little sketchy, Preston wanted hard-core proof, so that there would be no denying the truth. Looking back in hindsight, Michele regretted mentioning setting up surveillance cameras.

After she had gone home, showered, and returned for work, he insisted that Michele go out and buy the best equipment on the market, including recording devices for the telephone. He wanted to have everything set up before Ariel returned. Michele's plans for the afternoon included seducing Preston, not shopping for undercover gadgets. But since he was insisting, she had no choice.

Just as Michele was on her way out the door, Laird came walking in. He was the last person she wanted to see. Michele had used him as a pawn in her game; now it was his move.

"Hello, Michele," he sang her name, and sidled right up to her.

"Hello, Congressman." She faked a smile. He was standing so close to her that she could feel his warm breath on her cheek. She wanted to push him back a few feet, but couldn't. He could be useful in the future if her present game plan didn't pan out, so she decided to humor him. "Did you have a good time the other night?"

"I did, but it could've been better." He licked his lips.

"How so?" she asked suggestively, taking a step closer.

"If you would've let me come over to your place, we really could have capped off the night with a bang." He ran the back of his hand up and down her forearm.

"Oh, Congressman, you're such a naughty boy."

Laird looked around to make sure that Preston was nowhere in sight, then in a bold move, he grabbed Michele's breasts and squeezed them as if he were sampling down-filled pillows. "Hmm, I've been wanting to do this for s-o-o-o long," he said, closing his eyes while enjoying his cheap thrill.

She wanted to throw up all over his designer suit, but she just stood there while he fondled her boobs. "Congressman, I think we'd better table this until later," she said, stepping back and interrupting his lewd display of affection.

"Name the place and time, and I'll be there," he said, smooching her on the neck.

"I'm having my apartment redecorated, so you can't come over for a while," she lied. "But trust me, we'll have our moment. Congressman, I hate to rush off, but I have to run an important errand for Justice Hendricks." Before he could say another word, Michele quickly stepped away from him and dashed out of the door.

What the hell am I going to do about Laird? If I'm not careful, I might just have to fuck him to keep him on the line, Michele thought as she got into her car.

She had searched the Internet and found the top three surveillance shops in Washington, and had her list ready. She wasn't going to waste time trying to decide what to buy. Time was of the essence and she had another—more important—stop to make before heading back to the town house. She bought mini-cameras that were small enough to fit in the corner of a picture frame, and monitoring devices for each phone in the house, including the phone in their bedroom. Michele knew that she was wasting Preston's money, since there would be no footage of Ariel and Trey making love. Their relationship was long over, but she wanted to lead Preston on, so she bought enough recording equipment to bug the White House. Once that shopping assignment was over, she drove over to Coup de Foudre, one of D.C.'s exclusive lingerie shops.

"Hello Ms., can I help you?" asked the salesperson.

"Yes. I'm looking for something that's sexy yet sophisticated," she said, glancing around the shop.

"I know just what you mean. Follow me." The saleslady walked over to a rack of elegant-looking lingerie. She pulled out a black mesh chemise and held it up to Michele. "How's this?"

Michele took the delicate garment out of her hands, and walked over to the full-length mirror. The chemise was short and extremely sheer with an intricate lace design running down the front. She held it up to her body and turned from side to side, admiring herself in the mirror.

"Would you like to try it on?" the saleslady asked, pointing toward the dressing rooms.

"No, thank you; I'm in a hurry." She looked at the price tag and wanted to gag. The flimsy chemise cost almost as much as one of her business suits. She thought about going over to Victoria's Secret for a less expensive item, but she was playing with the big boys now, and had to step up her game. "I'll take it."

"Great choice! Jonquil is one of our favorite designers. I'm sure you'll enjoy wearing it. Please follow me to the counter."

As Michele was paying for the decadent little number, she saw a familiar face. "Hello, Mrs. Oglesby." She smiled.

Angelica looked at Michele, trying to place her face. "Uh, hi . . ."

"Michele Richards. I work with Justice Hendricks," she said, realizing that Angelica didn't remember her. "I was at your birthday party," she added, even though she wasn't on the invitation list.

"Oh, yes." Angelica smiled, unaware that Michele had crashed her party. "How are you?"

"I'm well, and you?"

"Life couldn't be better." She grinned.

As they were chatting, a statuesque woman with beautiful auburn hair strolled up to the counter. "What do you think of this?" she asked—before noticing Michele—holding up a tiny red see-through teddy.

Angelica glanced at Michele. "That's nice," she simply said, not wanting to elaborate.

Michele looked from one woman to the other. Angelica Oglesby was the epitome of sophistication with her blinding diamond necklace, Chanel suit, and Birkin bag, while the other woman wore jeans, a tank top sans bra, and a black leather jacket. From their outer appearances, it seemed unlikely that they ran in the same circle, but from their conversation, it was obvious that they were friends.

Angelica noticed Michele staring at them, and felt a little uneasy. "Well, Michele, it was nice seeing you again." She then turned her back and faced her friend, ending the conversation without making an introduction.

Michele paid for her chemise and left. *That was strange*, she thought about the encounter with Angelica as she drove away. She was on her way back to the town house when her cell phone rang. She had on her Bluetooth and couldn't see the caller ID. "Hello?"

"Michele, it's Preston. Did you pick up the surveillance equipment?" he asked, skipping the small talk.

"Yes. I have everything you asked for."

"Great. Well, just bring it with you in the morning. I'm exhausted and am going to turn in early. So take the rest of the day off, and I'll see you tomorrow."

"Uh . . . okay."

Preston hung up without saying good-bye. *"Damn!"* Michele hit the steering wheel with both hands. She had planned on going back over to the town house and modeling her new purchase for him, but he hung up so fast that she didn't get a chance to talk her way back over.

Once she returned to her apartment, Michele paced the living room floor, racking her brain until the sun set. She needed to think of an excuse to see him tonight. Preston had thrown her for a loop by telling her to take the rest of the day off. She had splurged on lingerie that she couldn't afford and wasn't about to let it go to waste. After a few hours of brainstorming, an idea came to her. Michele took the chemise out of the shopping bag and marched off to the bathroom.

Forty minutes later, she was showered, shaved, dressed, and ready to go. She sprayed her pulse points with a heavy dose of perfume. She tied a tan trench coat over the sheer negligee that she wore, and headed out the door.

In the car, on the drive over to the town house, Michele practiced her lines on the off chance Preston was still in his office instead of in the bed. If that was the case, she would just pick up a few random file folders, apologize for coming by so late, and leave.

The house was dark from the outside as she eased her car into the driveway. She got out and quietly closed the driver's door. With keys in hand, she tipped toward the entrance. Michele slipped her key—a key that was to be used only during business hours—into the lock and opened the door. The house was motionless, which was a good sign. She walked toward the office area. Preston's door was closed, but she tapped lightly anyway. There was no answer, so she gently pushed the door open. To her delight, he wasn't in there. Michele closed the door, and walked toward the staircase. Even though there were no lights on, she knew exactly which way to go. She knew the house like the back of her hand and navigated her way upstairs like a resident instead of a visitor.

Her breathing was heavy with anticipation as she reached the top of the landing. Michele turned to her right and ambled toward the master suite. "Showtime," she whispered in the dark, as she turned the doorknob and slipped inside.

Her eyes had long adjusted to the dark, and she could see the outline of Preston's body underneath the covers. Her plan had been to model her new purchase, but he was fast asleep. *I'll just have to show him the chemise in the morning*, she thought and eased out of the delicate gown, letting it fall to the floor. Standing there naked as the day she was born, Michele kicked off her shoes, and padded on the plush carpeting toward the king-sized bed. She lifted the edge of the comforter and slithered underneath the covers.

Michele inched her body near Preston's. She pressed her bare breasts into his back, but he wore pajamas so there wasn't any skin-to-skin contact like she had hoped for. Preston was snoring lightly, and didn't even feel her presence. Michele lay there for a second trying to decide what to do next. He was lying on his side, so she couldn't straddle him. She reached her hand around to his groin area, but didn't feel a bulge. *He must have his dick tucked between his legs—Shit!* Michele exhaled hard. She had gotten this far, but couldn't close the deal. Leaving wasn't an option, so she lay there a few minutes, until an answer came to mind.

She began to lightly suck his earlobe. Subtle moves like that were ideal for seduction. Michele was careful not to jolt him awake for fear he would toss her out. Gently arousing him was a much better tactic. Hopefully he would think that he was having an erotic dream, and get a hard-on. She continued sucking and sticking her tongue into his ear canal, until he began to stir. He turned over to his back with his eyes still closed and moaned lightly.

She eased the covers back, and sure enough there was a small tent in his pajama bottoms. Michele slowly unbuttoned his top. She leaned over and began sucking his nipples until they became hard.

Preston moved his head from side to side and mumbled something that she couldn't make out.

Michele stopped, rested on her elbow, and watched the tiny tepee in his pants become a major pergola. She wanted to mount his rigid erection, but it wasn't time yet. Michele wanted to get him so aroused that his libido wouldn't let him reject her. She stuck her index finger in her mouth and got it all wet, then reached into the slit of his pajama bottoms and rubbed the tip of his dick with her moist digit. She continued rubbing until she felt a little pre-cum surface.

Preston suddenly grabbed his erection and began jerking off in his sleep. Michele didn't want him to come without her, so she flipped his dick all the way out and mounted him.

With his dick inside of her, she held on to the headboard and began pumping like a man. His massive cock filled up her slippery canal, and she was on the brink of orgasm, but not yet.

Preston finally opened his eyes and saw Michele riding him like she was possessed. At first he thought that he was dreaming, but her naked breasts bouncing up and down were all too real. He wanted to say stop, but his dick was planted so far up her canal that it felt too good to stop. He grabbed her hips and pressed her down even farther.

Michele leaned over so that her nipples brushed his lips. When he didn't take the hint, she took her tit and forced it into his mouth.

Preston didn't want to suck her breasts—thinking that holding back would make their act of adultery any less wrong—but he couldn't stop himself. And then like a starving baby, he frantically went from one tit to the other, sucking and licking until her nipples were swollen from his touch.

"Oh yeah, baby," she moaned.

Preston could feel himself coming and tried to pull out, but she wouldn't let him. She clenched her knees together, and held on tightly to the headboard. He threw caution out of the window and exploded deep within her waiting ravine.

Michele wanted him inside of her for as long as possible. She closed her eyes and wrapped her arms around his shoulders. She could feel his dick trying to slip out, but she pressed her pelvis down and held it in place. Michele didn't say a word and neither did Preston. They both seemed lost in their own worlds. When his dick finally deflated, Michele climbed off and lay on her side. Preston didn't spoon her like before, instead he scooted to the other side of the bed and went to sleep.

Michele wanted to pretend as if they were a couple, so she turned and spooned him instead. She could feel Preston's body stiffen at her touch, but he didn't move away. She had succeeded in fucking him again, but still didn't have his heart. *A few more nights of my good loving and I'll have not only his heart, but his mind.* With that fantasy dancing around her head, Michele drifted off to sleep with a victory smile plastered across her face.

27

SENATOR OGLESBY was at À Votre Service sharing the evening with a vintage bottle of Zinfandel and a beautiful blonde. His wife had been spending a significant amount of time in New York, and unbeknownst to her, he knew exactly what she had been up to, thanks to the private investigator that he put on her trail. He should have felt guilty for being at the restaurant having his cock sucked, but he wasn't. Angelica had been cheating on him at the Black Door, so he found his own outlet to relieve his sexual tension.

Robert was reared back in the high-back chair with a glass of wine in his hand, and a smile painted across his face. He was not only enjoying the full-bodied red in his glass, but also the full-bodied blonde underneath the table giving him head. His wife hadn't serviced him in months, and it felt good having his balls licked. Robert knew he wasn't packing a heavy load, but the way she was sucking his dick—head first, then shaft, then back again—made him feel as if he had the biggest cock in town. Robert put his glass down, and clenched the sides of the table. He was on the verge of cumming, and braced himself, as he exploded down her throat.

"How did you like your appetizer?" she asked, emerging from

underneath the table, and wiping the corners of her mouth with a napkin.

"It was just what I needed." He picked up his wine and took a sip. "I hope it wasn't—" Robert stopped mid-sentence, thinking twice about his comment.

"No, your cock is perfect," she answered, sensing what he was about to say.

He smiled nervously, knowing that she was lying. Angelica had told him on more than one occasion that he had the smallest penis that she'd ever seen. "You're paid to lay on the compliments," he said, taking another sip of wine.

"I may be paid to service you, but my comments are free. Don't get me wrong, I'm not saying that your dick is huge, but size really doesn't matter."

"Yeah, that's not what my wife says."

"Well, if she wants girth and length, why don't you buy a strap-on," she said matter-of-factly.

"A strap-on? You mean a dildo? Aren't those for gays and lesbians?"

"They're for anybody who's into toys. Actually, the kind I'm talking about has an indentation inside where your dick goes, so it fits comfortably. Trust me, if your wife wants a big dick, this type of strap-on will fill her up, and she'll be begging you for more."

"Hmm," Robert said, rubbing his chin. The thought of wearing a fake dick had never occurred to him. "I just might have to do that. Thanks for the suggestion."

"No problem. Have a good evening," she said, and sauntered away.

Robert polished off the bottle of wine, and ordered another one to go along with his dinner. As he was finishing his meal, a man wearing a tan trench coat approached his table.

"Good evening, Senator," he said, pulling up a chair.

"What do you have for me, Sam?" Robert asked, getting right to the point.

Sam reached inside his briefcase, took out a thick file folder, and handed it to the senator. "Here you go."

Robert flipped open the folder, and thumbed through several detailed photographs. "When were these taken?"

"Over the past few days." He pointed to one picture in particular. "This was taken earlier this evening."

"Oh, I see," Robert said, studying the picture. "Thanks, Sam. Your check will be in the mail."

Their brief meeting was over in less than five minutes. Sam got up and left, disappearing into the night, no doubt headed to another surveillance assignment.

"SO, WHO WAS that chick at the lingerie shop?" Christy asked, lying butt-naked on top of the white, down-filled comforter.

Angelica was also in the buff, and strolled over to the bed with an ice-cold vodka martini in each hand. She handed Christy a drink. "She works with one of my husband's friends," she said, taking a sip.

Christy took an olive out of her glass and sucked it. "Is she cool?"

"What do you mean by that?" Angelica asked, sitting on the edge of the bed.

"Didn't you see the way she looked at us? I think she knew that we were together."

"Of course she knew we were together. I was talking to you, after all."

"I don't mean *together* as in at the store together. I mean *together* as in we're lovers," she explained.

Angelica touched the center stone in her diamond necklace. "I didn't get the impression that she was suspicious. I thought that my comments to you were benign. For all she knows, we were just two friends shopping for lingerie."

"For your sake I hope you're right. It would be unfortunate if nasty rumors about you being gay were spread around town. Your reputation would be ruined. This is D.C. after all, the land of images. And I'm sure you don't want yours tarnished."

Angelica took a swig of vodka. "And how do you know it's not already tarnished?"

"Oh, do tell. What nasty little secrets are you keeping?" Christy asked, leaning up on one elbow, eager to hear the details.

"Well, it's not a secret anymore," Angelica said, polishing off the last of her drink.

"Come on." Christy pinched Angelica's nipple. "Don't leave me in suspense. Give up the goods. Tell me everything, and don't leave out a single detail," she said, popping another olive in her mouth and chasing it with the ice-cold dry martini.

Angelica playfully slapped her hand away. "It all started at the Black Door. I had an arrangement with one of the servers. He would entertain me privately at my hotel room whenever I came to New York."

"Oh, so I'm not the first server you've propositioned?" Christy asked, faking a look as if she were hurt.

"Afraid not, doll, but you are my first female server, if that makes you feel any better." She leaned down and kissed Christy's silver belly ring.

"And what else? I know that's not where the story ends," Christy said, wanting to know more.

"I'd much rather tickle your belly button," Angelica said, running her tongue across Christy's stomach.

"You can do all the tickling you want, but first I want to know what happened."

"What? Are you writing a book? Why are you so intrigued?"

"I've heard so many stories from the servers' perspective, but I've yet to hear the clients' side. What can I say? I have a curious nature, that's all. Plus, hearing nasty stories really turns me on," she said, rubbing her furry triangle.

"Why didn't you say that in the first place? I love turning you on." Angelica trailed her tongue from Christy's stomach to her breast and kissed the soft skin in between her boobs. "Well . . . basically I started fucking this guy outside of the club. His dick was so big that I was addicted to his cock and craved him on a regular basis. Things were going good, until his friend got busted."

"Busted for what?"

"Remember that woman in the lingerie shop?"

"Yeah, what does she have to do with the story?" Christy looked confused.

"Well, she works for Justice Hendricks, who at the time was Judge Hendricks. Anyway, my husband was helping him secure the nomination for the Supreme Court. And when the investigators did a background check on the judge, they found out that his son owned the Black Door."

"And?" She hunched her shoulders. "What's the big deal? The club is legit."

"Yes, it's legal, but the judge had no idea that his son owned the club. And a club like the Black Door would be a media nightmare for a candidate running for the high court. So my husband told the judge that he could forget about his chances of running."

"I'm confused. If he didn't run, how is he a justice now?"

"That's where I come into the story." She got up and went over to the minibar to retrieve two more miniature bottles of vodka from the fridge to make more martinis, but there wasn't any left. "Hold on; let me call room service." After she placed the call for more liquor, she continued, "The judge's son blackmailed my husband. The server I was fucking was a friend of his, so not only did they tell my husband that I was a member of the Black Door, they gave him an earful about my other extracurricular activity. They said that if my husband didn't reinstate Preston's name back on the candidates list, then they would go to the press and divulge my membership."

"Oh shit!" Christy sat up in the bed. "What did your husband do?"

"What could he do? He certainly couldn't let my involvement in the Black Door become public knowledge, so he used all of his resources to keep the judge from being linked to the club, and lobbied hard for him to become a justice."

"No, I mean, what did he do once he found out you were a member of the Black Door?"

"He was hurt of course, and wanted to know why I needed outside stimulation."

"What did you tell him?"

"I told him the honest truth. And the truth was that his dick is just too small. When we got married, I was a virgin, and didn't know any better. The sex was adequate; but after I matured, and my sex drive really kicked in, he was no longer able to satisfy me. So I started experimenting with fake cocks, and the bigger they were, the harder I came. Don't get me wrong, I love my husband; he's a good provider. But I need more than a roof over my head and diamonds around my neck."

Christy put her hand to her mouth. "Oh my God! What did he say to that?"

"He didn't say anything, because he knows he's small. Since the truth was out, I started going to the Black Door more often, and he started drinking heavily; now's he's drunk nearly every night. I hate to think that I was the cause of his drinking, but deep down I know that I am." Angelica quickly looked away in embarrassment, and then back at Christy. "I've tried to get him to stop, but he ignores my comments."

"Wow, what a story! I thought it was going to be some kind of kinky sex tale, but that was so much better. Talk about never knowing what makes a person tick. You look like the perfect political housewife, when in actuality you are a world-class freak!"

"Yes, I'm a freak. A thirsting freak. Where is room service?" She reached for the phone and called down. "Oh, okay." She nodded her head and hung up. "They're on the way up."

There was an immediate knock on the door. Angelica grabbed the jacket to her suit, threw it on, and went to the door. Her mouth dropped the second she opened the door. "What the hell are you doing here?"

"The question is . . . is . . ." Robert Oglesby stammered, "what the hell are you doing here?" He staggered in, obviously drunk. "And who the hell is she?" he asked, pointing at Christy.

"A friend of mine," Angelica said, shutting the door.

"I knew you were screwing around again, that's why I hired a private investigator and had you followed. He told me you were here, and I came up to see for myself who's been keeping you away from home." He stared at Christy's naked body lying in the bed. "Are you fucking her too?!" he yelled.

Angelica took off the blazer, revealing her nude body, and strutted over to the bed. "What do you think?"

Christy looked at the two of them, and couldn't believe Angelica's gall. She had gotten busted and didn't care. "Uh, listen, guys. Why don't I let you have some privacy?" she said, feeling a little awkward. She had been in some sticky predicaments before, and knew from experience that it was best to let the couple talk things over between themselves.

"Don't leave. He wants to know what I'm doing here. Why don't we show him?" she said, climbing into bed.

Robert slumped down in a chair, as if he didn't hear a word his wife had just said. He took a flask out of his breast pocket, unscrewed the top, and turned it up to his mouth.

"Are you serious?" Christy whispered.

"Yep. He's so drunk, he'll probably think he's watching a porn video." Angelica turned toward Robert. "You wanna see how I like to be fucked?"

"How is she going to fuck you without a dick?" he slurred, and took another swig.

Angelica opened the nightstand drawer, and took out Christy's strap-on. She handed Christy the erect weapon. "Watch and see."

Christy was hesitant. Fucking Angelica at the club in front of other people was one thing but fucking her in front of her husband seemed disrespectful. Though she was in the sex-trade business, she still had a few morals left. "Uh . . . Angelica, I don't think this is a good idea," she said, looking over at Robert, who seemed lost in a drunken stupor.

"Don't worry about him. Can't you see that he's stoned out of his mind? Come on, let's put on a show. I feel like entertaining." She laughed, with no regard for her husband.

"Well, if you insist." Christy put on the fake dick. She had been in some freaky situations in her life, and wasn't too surprised by the sudden turn of events. Most men loved watching women fuck anyway. She dismissed her apprehensions, and pretended like they were back at the Black Door. Christy was a pro, after all. She tuned Robert out, while concentrating on Angelica. "Get over here and suck my cock," she said, pulling Angelica by the arm.

Angelica slid down Christy's body, and covered the plastic dick with her mouth. She sucked hard as if she were trying to extract cum. The more she sucked, the wetter she became. She started fingering Christy's clit at the same time, and didn't stop until her lover began moaning. Angelica peeked over at her husband. He had taken his tiny package out and was masturbating. "Come here, Robert."

He tried to get up from the chair but fell back. He tried a second time and was successful. He staggered over to the bed, with his pants dragging around his ankles. "Christy, take off the strap-on."

Christy did as she was told and handed the toy to Angelica, who strapped it around her husband's waist. She then laid back on the bed, and spread her legs. "Come over here and fuck me," she told him. It had never occurred to Angelica—until now—to have Robert wear a fake dick, but enjoying the strap-on with Christy made her want to experiment.

He couldn't help but think about his earlier conversation. It was as if the waitress was psychic. She had told him to try a fake cock, now here he was strapped up and ready to go. He obeyed like a willing pupil, and stuck the tip of the dildo into his wife's waiting pussy. He had never used a fake dick before, and didn't quite know what to do. "How's that?"

"Stick it all the way in," she said, grabbing his ass, and pulling him toward her. "Yeah, that's it," she moaned as he began pumping like a madman.

Not one to be left out, Christy sat on Angelica's face for a little oral stimulation. The three of them fucked for hours, and by the time they finished, Robert was no longer drunk with liquor, but drunk with lust. He had found a new toy, and used it on both Christy and his wife. He no longer felt like a "little dick loser." Now that some of his self-esteem was restored, he no longer felt emasculated. Though it would still take him time to get over his wife's involvement in the Black Door, at least now he'd be able to satisfy her sexually.

MICHELE OPENED her eyes and for a brief second, didn't know where she was. She looked around at the light blue walls, and at the brown, blue, and white comforter that partially covered her body, and realized that she was lying in Preston's bed. She immediately glanced to her left, but he was gone. She didn't hear the shower running, and assumed that he was dressed and downstairs working. She stretched her arms above her head and yawned. Though she had had a peaceful night's sleep, she was still tired. Michele's rest was interrupted when Preston tapped the bulbous head of his cock against her soft ass in the middle of the night. At first she didn't feel him, but he continued tapping until she began wiggling her rear in response. He then slipped his swollen cock into her buttery orifice, and slowly fucked her from behind. His movements were unhurried and deliberate, like he was trying to savor every second. They moved in sync, until succumbing to a heated climax. Though she was wide awake now, Michele could still feel him inside of her. He had exercised her vaginal muscles and they were still pulsating. She was craving more of Preston, and was getting horny just thinking about how well he had worked her over. She grabbed one of the down pillows and stuck it between her legs to stifle her rising passion. After another ten minutes of languishing in her lustful reverie, she glanced at the clock. It was minutes to eight. *I'd better get up now.* She still had to go home and change before being back at the office by nine.

Michele swung her feet over the side of the bed, bent down, and picked up her sheer negligee, trench coat, and shoes. She put on the delicate garment, tied the coat around her waist, and then slipped her feet into her fuchsia, ostrich-feathered mules. She crossed the room and opened the door, but before closing it, she turned around and took in the mess that they had made of the bed. The sheets and comforter were crumpled up, and partially draping the floor. She thought about making up the bed, but she wanted Preston to have a blatant reminder of their shameless night together the moment he walked into the room. She smirked and closed the door.

Maybe I'll model my outfit for Preston now since he didn't get a chance to see it last night, she thought, and walked toward his office. She knocked on the door, but there was no answer. She knocked a second time, and when he didn't answer, she slowly pushed the door open. "Preston, are you here?" she asked, on the off chance that he was in his private bathroom.

He must be at court. She went to the desk, and checked his calendar. Sure enough, he had a seven-thirty breakfast meeting, followed by a hearing, and then a lunch meeting. Michele was glad that he'd be out of the office until late afternoon. At least now she didn't have to rush home and try to get back within the hour. Besides, it would give her more time to get her script together. She and Preston had fucked like pros, but hadn't shared their thoughts. Obviously, he wasn't reserved with her anymore; at least last night he wasn't shy. The way his dick responded to her made her think that he was becoming whipped, and she smiled at the thought. Michele walked out of the office, and was headed for the foyer when the doorbell rang.

Michele thought it might be the FedEx man, running ahead of schedule. She tied the belt tight around her waist before opening the door. The smile that she had worn only seconds before, quickly vanished. "Hello, Congressman," she said drily. He was the last person—

well, maybe next to the last person, since Ariel was the first—she wanted to see.

"Good morning, Michele," he sang, as he stepped inside the foyer.

"Preston's at a breakfast meeting," she said quickly, trying to get rid of him.

He moved closer to her. "I didn't come here to see Preston."

Michele moved back a few inches to get some distance between them. "Well, I'm on my way out. I've got a few errands to run."

He looked down at her feet, and chuckled. "You won't be running far in those."

Michele had totally forgotten that she had on the sexy slippers. "I, uh . . ." she stalled, not knowing quite what to say.

"Is that the new dress code on the Hill?" Then in a bold move, he tugged on the belt of her trench coat. "Let's see what you have on to match those shoes."

Michele tried to snatch the belt from him but wasn't strong enough to pull it out of his grip. The belt wasn't knotted and loosened up with ease. She tried to hold the coat closed, to no avail.

"Hmm." His eyes took in her nakedness underneath the sheer chemise. "I love the way you dress for work," he said, taking the lapels of the coat and opening it wider so that he could get a better view.

Michele was totally embarrassed, and stood there speechless. Though she paraded around her goodies for all to see, wearing tight blouses and skirts, that was on her terms and she was in control. But standing before Laird, nearly nude, for once in her life, she felt ashamed. Besides, she had no explanation for wearing lingerie at work.

He stared at her bare breasts, and licked his lips. Her titties looked better than he had expected. Her areolas were dark, and her nipples were thick. He let go of her coat and began fondling her boobs. "Ohh, you feel so good." He then pulled her close. "Come on, baby, let me fuck you." Laird was so mesmerized by her, that he didn't even think to ask why she was dressed in the sexy chemise and slippers in the first place. At the moment, the only thing on his mind was getting his rocks off.

Michele could feel the stiffness between his legs pressing against her groin. She tried to squirm away, but he held her tight and continued grinding. She realized that there was no point trying to fight him; instead, she'd have to sweet-talk her way out of this situation. She eased her hand down to his crotch and began massaging him. She was surprised to feel how large he was. His package wasn't as big as Preston's, but it was substantial nonetheless. She closed her eyes, and thought about Preston. She could feel herself getting wet and horny all over again, and continued stroking him up and down.

"Hmm, that feels so good," he said, in her ear.

The moment Michele heard his voice, her eyes popped open. *What the hell are you doing? What if Preston walks in?* With that thought in mind, she suddenly stopped. "Laird, I'd love to fuck you right here, right now, but Preston is due back any minute and we don't want to get busted, do we?" she lied.

"I'm so hard right now, I wouldn't care if my wife walked in. All I care about is fucking your pussy," he said lustfully, still holding her tight.

Michele pushed against his chest. "The painters are finished with my apartment, so come by my place later this week, and we'll finish what we started. Okay?"

"Where's your apartment?"

She spouted off her address. Michele wasn't worried about him popping by unannounced. She lived in a doorman building, and there was no way he could get past security without her permission. "Okay?" she asked again.

"It's a date. And I promise you won't be sorry," he said, kissing her on the neck.

"All right, Laird, let me run," she said, finally breaking away from his clutches. Michele showed him the door, and once he was gone, she leaned against the back of the door, and breathed a sigh of relief. *Damn, that was close.* Michele was playing a dangerous game. She didn't realize how aggressive Laird could be. He was older and seemed harmless. Michele thought that she could flirt harmlessly with him, but now she knew without a doubt that he wanted more.

I'll just have to dodge him, until he cools off. She waited ten minutes to make sure the coast was clear before leaving.

At home, she thought about taking a quick nap, but decided against it. Laird had taken her by surprise. She was so busy fending him off, that she didn't have a chance to get her spiel for Preston together. Michele took an extra long hot shower. While the water ran down her body, she thought of two convincing arguments. One for if he rejected her and one for if he was willing to forgive his wife, and wanted to try and salvage his marriage. After showering and scheming, she stepped out of the stall, dried off, and went to her closet. Though she and Preston had made love twice—well, three times if you counted the early-morning fuck—she still wanted to continue dressing conservatively to really make him think that she had completly changed. The buttoned-up look was working to her advantage, and she didn't want to jinx her lucky streak. Michele chose a navy pantsuit with lavender pinstripes (which looked white from a distance), a pale lavender blouse, and a pair of navy, round-toe pumps. She grabbed her purse and briefcase and headed out of the door.

Michele noticed Preston's car sitting in the driveway as she drove down the block. Her nerves began to take over as she parked behind his sedan. She didn't know what type of mood he'd be in. After all, she had snuck into his bed in the middle of the night, and even though he had fucked her back, she still felt a twinge of guilt for seducing him. *Get a grip! Your plan is working brilliantly. Do you want to be the lady of the manor or not?* she asked herself. Michele sat in the car a few minutes longer to collect her thoughts. She had finally found her entry into the inner circle and wasn't about to back down now. She took a deep breath, and stepped out of the car. Michele stood tall with her shoulders back and her head held high as she marched up the walkway.

She stuck her key in the lock, opened the door, walked in, and immediately went to her office area. Preston's door was closed, but she wasn't sure if he was in there or upstairs. Once Michele sat down, she noticed that his private line was lit. Very few people called him on that line. Suddenly, she began to panic. What if he were on the phone with Ariel, confessing everything? *Calm down. He's not stupid. Men don't confess their affairs.* With that thought in mind, she began to breathe easy again. She logged on to her computer and was getting ready to check her e-mail when Preston buzzed.

"Michele, are you there?"

"Yes, Preston, I'm here."

"Can you come in please?" his voice boomed over the speaker.

"Sure. I'll be right in." She picked up a steno pad and pen, to look official even though she didn't plan on taking a single note. Michele opened his office door with trepidation. Though she was brazen the night before, at the moment she was nervous. She couldn't get a read on his voice over the intercom, so she didn't know what to expect.

When she walked in, Preston was holding the phone to his ear and nodding as if agreeing with the person on the other end of the line. He held up his index finger and mouthed, "Just a minute." Michele sat across from his desk, crossed her legs, and waited.

"Did you sleep well last night?" he asked casually, the moment he hung up the phone. His tone was that of a host asking a guest if the bed was comfortable.

Michele couldn't help but blush. "It was the best *sleep* I've had in a long time."

"Actually, I can say the same thing. *Sleep* like that doesn't come along every night," he responded, cracking a slight smile.

"You'd better believe it. *Sleep* like that is rare, and if I were you, I wouldn't take it for granted," she said, tossing the comment back in his court.

"Trust me, I appreciate good *sleep*." He dropped his head for a moment, and looked back at her. "In all seriousness, Michele," he said, putting an end to their verbal jousting, "last night was totally unexpected. I'd plan on making our first time the last time," he said, folding his hands on the desk in front of him.

"Look, I know you're probably feeling guilty, but like I told you before, you have nothing to feel guilty about. Trey and Ariel are in New York right now, doing Lord knows what, so why should you play the martyr and deny yourself? Life is too short to be miserable," she said, giving him food for thought.

Preston knew that she was right. He was being betrayed not only by his wife, but by his only son, and the thought made his blood boil. At this point, the only person he felt that he could trust was Michele; at least she wasn't lying and keeping secrets from him. "You're absolutely right. Life is too short, that's why as soon as Ariel gets home, I'm going to ask her for a divorce. Cheating can often be forgiven, but cheating with a friend or relative is the ultimate sin. I know I probably sound like a hypocrite, especially after last night, but at least I'm not going to lie and sneak around like she's doing."

Michele couldn't believe her ears. Preston said the *D* word, and she couldn't have been happier. "Yes, Preston, I think a clean break is best for everyone. Now Trey and Ariel can be together, and so can we."

Preston heard her words and nearly choked. There was no *we*; he had fucked her on the rebound, and beyond that, he had no future plans. "Listen, Michele, I truly appreciate you being honest with me, and allowing me to release my frustrations in a physical way. But, I'm still wrapping my mind around the fact that Ariel cheated with my son. So I'm nowhere near ready to jump into another relationship."

Shit! Why the hell did I say "we"? "Preston, I totally agree. I didn't mean *we* as in you and I as a couple. I just meant that now we can concentrate more on business and not be distracted by all of this personal stuff." Michele knew that she wasn't making any sense. She had already stuck her foot in her mouth, and it was too late for damage control, but she tried anyway. Preston was still sensitive, so she'd have to be more careful, and not tip her hand too soon. But at the same time, she needed to move quickly before Ariel came back home. "Preston, I can see that this conversation is making you upset. Why don't we knock off early today and go get some food," she said, trying to sound casual.

"I can't. I've got a four o'clock conference call," he said, sounding as if they had never fucked.

"Well, let's leave once you're done. I know this terrific little Italian place. The pasta is to die for, and it's small and quiet," she said, trying to lure him in.

"Michele, I don't know. I'd planned on having an early evening and . . ."

"Come on, Preston, it's only dinner. We'll drive separately, and once we finish eating, I'll go to my place and you go to yours. Okay?" she asked, trying to seal the deal.

He thought about it for a second. He loved Italian food, and since they would be driving in separate cars, he wouldn't have to take her home and be tempted to go upstairs for a "nightcap." Besides, he had told her exactly where he stood, and wasn't trying to lead her on. Their brief affair was over, now it was back to business as usual. "Okay, sounds good. We'll leave once my call is over."

"Great. I have some e-mails to return," she said, getting up to leave.

Once Michele was back at her desk, she wanted to scream. All the work she had done last night was in vain. Preston still wasn't hooked like she had hoped. However, Michele wasn't discouraged. She still had a few more tricks up her sleeve.

29

"CONGRATULATIONS, COUNSELOR," Meri sang through the phone.

"Thank you. The case was basically open and shut. We caught so many of the plaintiffs in lies, it wasn't funny. After we exposed them, they only had two creditable witnesses, and that wasn't nearly enough for a class action suit, so the judge dismissed the case. I'm so glad it's over; now I can get back to Washington and deal with more important issues," Ariel said.

"When are you going back?"

"This afternoon. Trey and I are catching the four o'clock train."

"Excuse me? Did you say you and Trey?" Meri asked, with a lilt in her voice as if she were surprised.

"He had planned on going down earlier and having a talk with Michele, but there was some kind of emergency at the club, and he had to stay in New York and handle his business. Now that the trial is over, we're going to D.C. together."

"Oh, I see. That's a long ride. Are you sure you can handle sitting next to your ex-lover for a few hours?" Meri asked, insinuating that Ariel still had feelings for Trey.

"Meri, what Trey and I had has long since been over." Ariel thought about whether or not to tell Meri about her recent fantasies. They were not fantasies per se, but recollections of the past. "Well . . ."

"Yes . . . come on; get it out. I can tell you want to say something," Meri prodded her.

"I must admit since coming back to New York, I've been reminiscing about me and Trey. I know it's wrong, but I couldn't help myself," she confessed.

"You know what they say?"

"No. What do they say?" Ariel asked, halfheartedly, not really wanting to know.

"That lust is stronger than love. I realize that you love Preston, but the sex with Trey was probably the best you've ever had. Am I right?" she asked knowingly.

Ariel shook her head *yes*, even though her friend couldn't see her reaction. "Meri, you have no idea how good it was. Ump," she grunted. "That man had me doing things I've only fantasized about. I swear if we had met in another time and place, *and* he wasn't related to Preston, we would probably still be together."

"So you do think that what you guys experienced was more than lust?" Meri had had her share of dynamite sex and knew that good lovemaking could make a woman think that she was in love, when in actuality she was just in love with the dick.

Ariel thought for a moment. "I don't know, Meri. Sometimes I think we had a deeper connection than just sex, and sometimes I think it was only sex. In either case, it really doesn't matter because I'll never know. I'm committed to my marriage, and pray that once Preston learns the truth, he'll forgive me," she said, with a twinge of sadness and regret in her voice.

"Don't worry, daarling, everyone's entitled to at least one mistake. And though yours was a doozy, you still deserve to be forgiven," Meri said, spoken like a true friend.

"Thanks. I pray you're right. I really want to start working on having a family. I truly believe that a baby will help us through this ordeal."

"Maybe so, but I know you realize that babies never hold a relationship together. I'm not trying to shoot down your hopes. There's a strong possibility that Preston will want a divorce, baby or no baby. Daarling, I don't want you to disillusion yourself," she added, trying to soften the blow.

Ariel was quiet for a moment, as if digesting Meri's words. "You're right, but I'm keeping my fingers crossed nonetheless. Well, let me run. I'm meeting Trey at the train station soon, and don't want to be late."

"Okay. Call me once the dust has settled, and let me know what happened."

"You know I will. Pray for me," Ariel said, before hanging up.

Penn Station was a flurry of activity. People were huddled underneath the big board waiting for gate assignments, and once the numbers ticked into place, they rushed off toward the designated gate. Vendors were hawking everything from jewelry to hot dogs to fake designer purses. There were local commuters going home to the suburbs, and long-distance travelers with luggage, on their way to destinations unknown.

Ariel had already gotten her ticket and was waiting for Trey near the big board, which was an unspoken meeting place. They had talked the day before regarding train schedules, but didn't exactly set up a specific area to meet. She'd assumed he would know where to meet. Ariel looked at her watch; it was seven minutes to four, and he was nowhere in sight. She took her cell out of her purse and dialed his number.

"Are you calling me?" Trey asked, walking up from behind.

Ariel closed the phone. "Yes. I was. I hope you have your ticket. It's almost time to board."

"Yeah, I do," he said, waving the pale blue ticket in the air. "We still have a few minutes; they haven't assigned the train number yet," he said, looking up at the big board. No sooner had he spoken than the numbers changed, their gate was assigned, and people started running. "Come on." He grabbed her hand. "We'd better hurry if we want good seats."

Ariel was speechless. She had gotten to the train station in plenty enough time to buy her ticket and walk to the gate like a civilized person, but now she was in a stampede with the masses. It was total pandemonium, and she felt like she was running with the bulls in Spain. They fought their way through the crowd and down the steps. When they reached the platform, people were nearly pushing their way onto the train.

"Come on; let's go to the last car," Trey said, running toward the end of the platform, with Ariel trotting closely behind.

The final bell sounded the second they stepped onto the train, and then the heavy metal doors closed. They had made their train with no time to spare. Trey led the way down the aisle, looking for two seats together, but there were only single seats scattered here and there. "Why don't you sit there?" he said, pointing to an empty aisle seat.

Ariel put her tote in the overhead bin and sat down. She watched as Trey made his way down the aisle, and finally found a seat. In a way she was grateful they were not sitting together. At least now, she wouldn't have to make small talk. She took a paperback novel out of her purse, turned to the bookmark, and began reading where she had left off. As the train made its way through the state of New Jersey, she continued reading and didn't notice as passengers moved on and off the car.

"Excuse me. Is this seat taken?"

Ariel was so deep into the story that she was unaware that the seat next to her was now empty. "Uh . . . I guess not."

Trey put his bag in the overhead bin. "I'm going to the club car; do you want a drink or something to eat?" he offered.

She wasn't hungry. "Would you mind bringing me a glass of cranberry juice?"

"Cranberry juice?" he asked, wrinkling his brow. In his line of business, cranberry juice was used as a mixer, not the main drink. "Don't you want a shot of vodka in it?"

"No thanks."

"Uh, okay."

Just as he was a quarter of the way down the aisle, Ariel called out to him. "Trey, on second thought, I will have some vodka with my juice." Now that they would be sitting together, Ariel decided a cocktail would make the ride go a bit smoother. She put the novel away and took out her compact. She quickly powdered her face, taking the shine off of her nose and forehead. She put the makeup away, and ran her hand over her hair, smoothing down any loose ends. After the run through the station, she was a little disheveled, and needed sprucing up.

"I bought some chips to munch on," Trey said, balancing the box of refreshments in his hand and easing past her to sit down.

"Thanks."

"Here's your drink. So, how did the trial turn out?"

Ariel filled him in on the details. "We would have won even if the judge hadn't dismissed the case. There was just too much damaging information against their witnesses. We had legal binders full of all kinds of incriminating evidence." Ariel was glad to talk about work, since it distracted her from thoughts of Trey. Meri was right; lust was stronger than love. As much as she tried to focus on work, and not think about that evening in her apartment with him, she couldn't help it. The scene kept replaying over and over in her mind. "Trey." She turned and looked him dead in the eyes. "Why did you run after Michele that day at my apartment instead of staying with me?" she asked, totally changing the subject.

Trey looked shocked. He wasn't expecting that zinger. He was comfortable talking about anything else but their affair. So much time had passed that he thought they would never revisit that dreadful day. But he should have known it wasn't dead in the water, and would resurface sooner or later. "Ump-hmm," he cleared his throat. "Ariel, you know as well as I do that we could've never continued with our affair. When Michele busted us, the only recourse was damage control. If I hadn't run after her, she would have gone straight to my father and told him everything."

"What did it matter? We're still in the same predicament," she said, sounding forlorn.

"Well, at least it bought us some time. If she had told him then, I'm more than sure that I wouldn't have a relationship with my dad, and I doubt very seriously if you'd be married."

"I guess you're right."

Trey put his hand on her knee. "Ariel, for what it's worth, that first night in the club when I didn't know who you were, I felt a strong magnetic connection. And if you didn't belong to my father, I think that we could have had something real, maybe a solid relationship."

Ariel finally heard the words that she was secretly dying to hear for months. She had always wondered how Trey felt; now she knew. His confession eased the conflict within her, and clarified her doubts. "Trey, thanks for being so honest. At least now I know I wasn't the only one feeling the attraction."

"No, you didn't imagine it; what we felt was real." He took his hand off her knee. "Ariel, I hope we can continue to be friends," he said with sincerity.

"Trey, I'd like that." She smiled. Though Ariel and Trey could never revisit "Lover's Lane," having him in her life on a platonic basis was better than nothing, and she was content in their newfound roles. "Now what's our game plan once we reach D.C.?" she asked, getting to the business at hand.

"When we get to the town house, we'll go straight into his office and simply tell the truth. We won't beat around the bush," Trey said, sounding like he was plotting out some kind of business meeting.

"I think I should start talking first, since he is my husband, and I married him under false pretenses, knowing that he had a memory lapse."

"You have a point, but I feel a sense of responsibility considering I own the club. And if it wasn't for the Black Door, none of this would've happened. I truly feel bad that you could possibly lose your marriage over our indiscretion. You and my father have been together for so long that I would hate to see your relationship end over a misunderstanding."

"*Misunderstanding* is an understatement." She chuckled.

"True, but it's not like we set out to deceive my father. The last thing I wanted to do was to hurt him," he said, sounding like a little lost boy.

Ariel heard the pain in his voice. "Trey, don't worry, blood is thicker than water. Preston has no choice but to forgive you. He might be pissed at first, but eventually he'll have to come around." This time it was Ariel's turn to console Trey.

"Let's hope you're right. In any event, I'll initiate the conversation."

"Okay, but what if Michele's there?"

"Then the three of us will tell him that we thought it was best to conceal the truth until after his confirmation. With Michele on our side, it'll make our case stronger."

"Let's hope you're right." Ariel still had doubts about the girl.

For the rest of the train ride, they strategized. Ariel was glad that she and Trey were now friends. He was a good man, and only wanted the best outcome for them both. Though they had gotten caught up, their actions had not been malicious.

Before long, they were pulling into Washington's Union Station. They gathered their belongings and headed for the taxi stand. Evening traffic was light, and fifteen minutes later, the cab was in front of the town house. Trey paid the driver, and they got out.

He looked at Ariel and noticed that the color was draining from her cheeks, turning them a pale ash. "Are you okay?" he asked as they walked toward the front door.

"My stomach is churning, my head is aching, and my palms are sweaty. Other than that, I'm just fine." She chuckled nervously. Ariel took out her keys and opened the door. The moment she stepped into the foyer, she felt a coldness. Something was different. For the first time since moving into the town house, she suddenly felt like a stranger walking into her own home. She thought that she was being paranoid, and tried to shake it off, but the feeling lingered.

"Is it always this quiet in here?" Trey asked, putting his bag on the floor and looking around.

"Most of the time it is pretty quiet. It's not like we have a bunch of kids running around the place," she said, setting her tote on the bench near the front door.

"Have you guys talked about starting a family?" Trey wanted to know. Hearing the word *kid* reminded him that Ariel didn't have any children. She was still relatively young, and he wondered how she felt about motherhood.

It was like Trey had been reading her mind. Ariel's maternal clock had begun ticking, and now she wanted a baby more than anything else. "We haven't talked about it, but I would love to have a baby. Once we get over this hurdle, maybe we can start trying."

"Well, I wish you luck."

"Thanks. Come on, let's go get this over with," she said, changing the subject. They were finally in D.C., and Ariel was ready for the dreaded confrontation.

"Michele's desk is cleaned off," Trey said, walking into the small outer office.

"Looks like Ms. Thang has gone for the day. I'm glad she's not here. I think we can handle the situation better without her adding any snide comments." Ariel went to Preston's door and knocked. When she didn't get an answer, she turned the knob and stuck her head inside. The office was empty and dark. "Maybe he's upstairs," she said, turning to Trey.

They went back to the front of the house, and Ariel offered Trey a seat in the living room, while she went upstairs to look for Preston. "He's not here," she said, once she came back downstairs.

"Maybe he's at dinner."

"Yeah, you're probably right. Speaking of dinner, are you hungry?"

"I'm getting there," he responded, rubbing his stomach.

"Why don't I go see what I can scrounge up," Ariel said, and disappeared into the kitchen. Twenty minutes later, she reemerged with a silver tray full of sliced apples, grapes, a small wedge of Brie and crackers. "This is all that I could find. Seems like Preston hasn't gone grocery shopping since I left," she said, setting the tray on the cocktail table.

Trey reached for a grape, and popped it into his mouth. "Don't worry; this is just fine."

Ariel glanced at her watch. It was eight-thirty. "Preston should be coming in soon."

"The sooner, the better. I'm ready to get this nightmare over with. The suspense is starting to get to me," he confessed.

"Yeah, me too."

They chatted and munched for another hour, and Preston still wasn't home. Ariel looked at her watch again. "I wonder what's taking him so long. I'm starting to get worried." She reached for the house phone and called his cell, but it went straight to voice mail. "His phone must be turned off."

"Maybe he's at a dinner meeting and doesn't want to be interrupted."

"I'm sure you're right."

Another hour went by, and still no Preston. Ariel tried his phone again, and again it went straight to voice mail. "Well, I guess we'll just have to wait."

"We've waited to tell him the truth for over a year, so a few more hours won't hurt," Trey reasoned.

Ariel got up and began to pace. "Of all evenings, he would be out to dinner instead of ordering take-out. This anticipation has me on pins and needles."

"Calm down; he'll be here soon. Maybe we need a drink to calm our nerves."

"That's a good idea." She went over to the liquor cabinet and was going to pour them a glass of scotch, but the bottle was practically empty. *That's odd*, she thought. Preston rarely drank more than a shot at a time. *He must have had the senator over for cigars and scotch,* she reasoned. "The Johnnie Walker is almost gone; how about some brandy?"

"That's fine."

Ariel poured the drinks, handed Trey a snifter, and sat back down. They sipped and waited anxiously, wondering when Preston would come walking through the front door. Would the revelation of the truth be the beginning of a clean slate, or the beginning of the end?

30

FOR THE first time in months, Senator Robert Oglesby had dinner without his customary extra-dry double martini. The pressure of keeping the press from finding out about his wife's and Preston's involvement in the Black Door was enough to cause him to drink—heavily. Now that Preston was confirmed and no longer an object of media attention, and he knew exactly how to please his wife, Robert put the bottle down. Tonight his mind wasn't fuzzy from overindulging. The experience with his wife and Christy had been a sobering one—in his wildest dreams he could never imagine having a threesome with Angelica and another woman—and he wanted to remain clear and conscious from here on out. He wasn't a hard-core alcoholic, but when he found out about Angelica's involvement in the Black Door, he nearly lost his mind. He was too embarrassed to discuss her cheating with anyone. The only solace he could find was in a fifth of Belvedere, so he turned to drinking to dull the pain of his wife's infidelity. Robert had no idea that Angelica detested having sex with him. She had commented on his small penis, but obviously faked orgasm to please him. Had he known that he didn't satisfy her, he would have bought a strap-on years ago. It wasn't until the night he caught her with Christy that he learned what she really liked.

When they had first met, eons ago, he knew that she was a free spirit. Back then, she had planned to backpack through Europe for the summer, and then enroll in culinary school in Paris, but her father—also a politician—had other plans for his daughter. He wanted to tame her wild ways, and persuaded her into marrying the promising young junior senator. Their life together had been like a fairy tale. Her family had clout, and so did his, which put them at the top of the A-list. They attended every major social event in Washington, from presidential inaugurations, to charity balls, to private dinners at the White House. They were childless and used their freedom to travel abroad. They would spend weeks in Capri and Monaco one summer, and the next year, charter a yacht and sail the Greek Isles with friends, or lounge on the shores of Fiji. Robert also spoiled his wife with luxury cars, designer clothes, and expensive furs. He gave Angelica everything she desired, including an extravagant, six-figure diamond necklace for their anniversary. He gave her everything except an exciting sex life. After being married for so many years, he thought that he knew everything about his wife, but apparently not.

"So . . . how long have you been into women?" Robert asked his wife, who sat across the dinner table from him.

"I had my first encounter in college and didn't indulge again until I met Christy," she answered casually, taking a bite of salmon.

"Oh, I see." He raised his eyebrow. "I had no idea that you were bisexual."

Angelica didn't think that it was a big deal being with a woman. "I wouldn't say I'm bisexual. I'm just exploring different options, that's all."

"And I take it one of your options was membership at the Black Door?" He was too stunned to ask her about the club when he had first found out. But now that the secrets were on the table, he wanted to know everything.

"The Black Door gave me fulfillment that I couldn't find at

home. At first I was an occasional member, but over time, my visits became more frequent."

"I wish you could have been up front with me. Then I would not have been blindsided when Preston's son blackmailed me. I was never so shocked as when he showed me the membership list with your name prominently at the top. You could have bought me for a penny. At that point, I had no other choice but to continue to endorse Preston, since I didn't want your business spread across the headlines."

Angelica reached her hand across the table and touched his. "Honey, I'm truly sorry for embarrassing you. I had no way of knowing that my membership would be used to extort a favor from you," she said sincerely.

"I'm sure you didn't. But remember, what's done in the dark, usually comes to light at some point in time. So, how long have you been working at the Black Door?" he asked, turning to Christy. The three of them were having dinner in the hotel suite, as if they were old friends. After two nights of nonstop sex, they were finally sitting down to talk.

"I'm new. I've only been there for two months," she said, sipping her dirty martini.

"Do you know Trey personally?" Robert asked.

"No, I don't. I only met him once, and that was during the interview process, but he seemed like a cool guy. Why do you ask?" she wanted to know.

"I'm trying to get a read on him. I met him a few times. Once in New York, at dinner with his father and Ariel. He lied then, and told me he was into real estate and the stock market, and then again at his dad's engagement party. Of course I saw him at their wedding. By then I knew the truth, but it was too late to stop the blackmail scheme. Each time we met, I got the impression that he was a stand-up guy. Boy, was I wrong! He's quite a shrewd businessman. After giving in to his demands, I was going to try and shut down his club, but it's totally legal. And besides, he has some pretty impressive people in his corner. So, shutting him down wasn't an option."

"Why would you want to shut down the Black Door?" Christy asked.

"I wanted to hit him where it hurts. I hate being bullied, and that's exactly what he did by blackmailing me."

"Well, if you want to hit him where it hurts, why don't we open a club similar to the Black Door, and really give him some competition?" Angelica said.

"That's a brilliant idea! Since I work there, I know how the theme rooms are set up, and could help you with the layout of your club," Christy said, with excitement in her voice.

"Opening an erotica club is not the answer," Robert said. "When I said hit him where it hurts, I was thinking more of closing him down. Besides, I know nothing about running an erotica club."

"What's there to know?" Angelica asked. "I think it's an excellent idea. We have the resources; besides, Christy can help since she knows the business. I've been looking for something to occupy my time, and I think that this is the perfect solution."

Robert shook his head back and forth. "No, Angelica. What if the media finds out that I own a brothel? I'd be crucified in the press, and would probably have to resign my position. No, it's just too risky."

"First of all, it's not a brothel, and secondly, we could conceal our ownership behind a few offshore corporations," Angelica said, trying to convince her husband.

"Why can't my wife pass her time entertaining and doing charity work like most politicians' wives?" He sighed.

"Because I'm not like other politicians' wives," she snapped. "I need some excitement in my life, and owning a club like the Black Door is just the type of stimulation that I need."

"I'm sorry, sweetheart, but the answer is still no," he said, adamantly. "I can't risk losing my career by being involved in such a risqué venture. Angelica, I've finally accepted the fact that you need to indulge in some extracurricular activities every now and then. Isn't that enough? I've known some husbands who have left their wives for less than that."

Angelica gave him an "I don't care about other wives" look,

turned her head away from him, and crossed her arms in front of her chest. She was pissed and didn't want to talk to him anymore. She was used to getting her way.

Robert took one look at his wife's body language and knew that she was upset. He usually gave in to her pouts, but not this time. Opening a club like the Black Door wasn't even an option. He had experienced enough grief from being semi-associated with the club, and intended to put the past behind them once and for all. "Angelica, I know when you have your mind set, it's hard to dissuade you, but this time I'm putting my foot down. There is no way we are opening an erotica club, and that's final." Though Robert had a little dick, he had finally found his balls!

31

PRESTON HELD Michele by the elbow as they made their way to the front door of the town house. She had drunk too much red wine at dinner, and didn't want to get behind the wheel. Preston took her car keys and insisted on driving her home, but Michele begged him not to. She didn't want to enter her building intoxicated. She lied and told Preston that the doormen at her complex spread rumors about the tenants, and she didn't want to be labeled a wino. He took pity on her and agreed to take her to the town house so that she could sleep it off.

Michele staggered and nearly twisted her ankle. She pretended to be inebriated but was as sober as a saint. She lured Preston out to dinner with the promise that they would drive separately, and go home separately. Well, she kept part of her promise, but had no intention of letting him go home alone. Michele needed to fuck him one more time before Ariel returned. Tonight she planned to really get buck wild. She was going to start by sucking his dick and letting him cum down her throat. Most men loved cumming in a woman's mouth, and she was sure that Preston wasn't an exception to that rule. Then she was going to let him butt-fuck her again. He seemed to really enjoy that the last time; from the way he came, she was sure that Ariel hadn't let him through the back door. And then she was going to flip the script, and eat out his asshole. She was going to stimulate his prostate with her tongue and finger so good that he wouldn't desire anybody else but her—including his wife. Yes, Michele had plans and couldn't wait to get inside the house to put them into action.

Preston opened the door. *I don't remember leaving the lights on.* He didn't think much about it, since he left them lit on occasion. Michele leaned into him with her eyes half-closed as if she were too drunk to stay awake. He put his arm around her shoulders to steady her, as they walked into the living room.

"What the *hell* is this?" Ariel shouted as Preston came into the room with Michele resting comfortably underneath his arm, like they were a couple.

At the sound of Ariel's voice, Michele's eyes popped wide open. Her worst nightmare was now reality. Not only had Ariel returned, but she had brought Trey with her. Obviously, they were there to tell Preston the truth. She would have to do some fast talking to get Preston to believe her. She started to confront Ariel, but decided to see how this was going to play out. Maybe Ariel and Trey wouldn't say anything; if that was the case, then neither would she.

Preston looked from Ariel to Trey, and back again. He was shocked. He didn't expect Ariel home for another few days, and he certainly didn't expect to see Trey. Preston released his arm from around Michele, and pointed his finger at his wife. "And what the *hell* is this?" he shouted back. "You have the audacity to bring your lover into my house again!"

"Whoa," Trey spoke up. "I'm not her lover, Dad."

"Don't sit there and lie. I know all about you and my wife!"

"Your memory is back?" Ariel and Trey said in unison. They looked at each other in amazement. It was apparent that one day Preston's memory would return, however they didn't expect him to conceal his recollection.

Preston walked closer to them. "Yes, it's back, and now I know everything, thanks to Michele."

Ariel stood up and glared at Michele. "What did she tell you?"

"The truth," Preston spat out. "She's the only one I can trust," he said, looking over at his assistant.

"Preston, don't believe anything she said. She's a liar." Ariel pointed her finger at Michele for emphasis.

"What?? And you're not! To think I trusted you and *him.*" He nodded his head at Trey, as if his son was a stranger.

"Dad, please sit down, so that we can explain," Trey pleaded.

"Don't bother. I already know the sordid details. You betrayed me. Now get the hell out of my house, you Judas!"

Trey cast his eyes to the floor in shame. It was true. He had committed the ultimate sin by sleeping with his father's woman, but was in no way a Judas. His actions were not premeditated. He hadn't set out to destroy his father. "Dad, please, please let us explain exactly what happened," he begged.

"I said don't bother. Michele has told me everything. Now if you don't leave, I'm going to call the police and have you escorted out," he said, crossing the room and picking up the phone.

"Did she tell you that she was in cahoots with us?" Ariel said.

Preston dropped the phone and turned toward his wife. "What did you say?"

"I said that Michele was part of the cover-up. She knew all about our affair and agreed to help us keep it a secret," Ariel blurted out, turning the tables.

Preston swung around to face Michele, who was standing with her back against the wall, afraid to move. "Is this true?"

Pretending like she was drunk, Michele hung her head and didn't answer. She was trying to think of a clever response, something, anything that would exonerate her, but her mind was a blank slate. The lies she had told Preston definitely wouldn't work now that Ariel and Trey were there to dispel them—so much for fast talking.

"*Michele, is this true?*!!" Preston screamed.

"She can't answer, because she's lying," Trey interjected.

Preston took one look at Michele's body language—she couldn't even look at him—and knew instantly that she had also been deceiving him. His head started spinning, and he felt faint. He had bought Michele's lies without explanation, only to find out that she was playing him for a fool. Preston slumped down in one of the living room chairs from the weight of all the deception.

"Dad, you gotta believe me; I didn't know Ariel's identity when I first met her at the Black Door. I swear to you our affair started off innocently. I would have never even looked in her direction had I known she was your woman," Trey said, speaking in a low tone.

"Preston, it's true. We both had on masks, and besides we hadn't seen each other in years. I know I was wrong for going to the club in the first place, but you had put me off so many times that I was frustrated." Ariel knelt down in front of her husband. "Preston, I'm not trying to use that as an excuse. I know I was wrong," she repeated. "I hope you can find it in your heart to forgive me," she asked, lightly touching his knee.

"Don't touch me." He moved his leg. "You slept with my son. *My son!*" he screamed. "How could you?"

"Preston, I swear I didn't know who he was. You gotta believe me."

"Okay, let's just say that's true, how can you explain the evening at your apartment? Michele told me she caught the two of you." He turned to his assistant. "Or was that a lie too?"

"No, Dad, that was the truth," Trey admitted. "That evening I had come over to Ariel's apartment to tell her that it was over. One thing led to another, and—"

Preston cut him off. "Oh, you had to tell *her* it was over? I take it she still wanted to fuck you, even after she found out you were my son?" He looked down at his wife. "Get out of my sight. You disgust me."

Ariel slowly stood up, then sat back down on the sofa. "Preston, please listen. It was all a huge mistake. I love you and only you," she said, on the verge of tears.

"Yeah, right! You love me so much, not only did you fuck my son, you lied about it, and then after I lost my memory, had the gall to walk down the aisle in a white dress and recite vows in front of God and all of our friends, knowing damn well that every word you re-cited that day was a lie!"

He spoke with such venom in his voice that Ariel was taken aback. In all the years that she had known Preston, she had never seen him this angry. His face contorted with every word that came out of his mouth, causing him to look like a different person. This wasn't the sweet man that always had her best interest at heart. No, this man was completely different—a stranger. "Preston, my vows were not a lie. I meant every word," she said, in an attempt to sway him.

"SHUT UP! JUST SHUT UP!" he screamed. "I've had enough of your lies." He then focused on his son. "I just want to know one thing. I remember getting the fax from Senator Oglesby saying that you owned the Black Door, and him telling me that I could forget about any chance of securing the nomination because of your club, but here I am a justice. How did that happen?"

"Dad, I knew that sitting on the high court was your lifelong dream, and I wasn't going to let my involvement with the Black Door stand in the way of that, so I called in a favor," Trey said, pre-ferring to leave out the details.

"Are you telling me you had to blackmail somebody, so that I could secure the nomination?" Preston asked, reading between the lines.

"Let's just say I persuaded someone to do the right thing. And you sitting on the Supreme Court *is* the right thing."

Preston couldn't believe his ears. Not only had he been betrayed by the people closest to him, he had won the nomination not by his own merit, but by unsavory methods. "Who else knows about this?"

"Only Senator Oglesby," Trey said, purposely leaving out Angel-ica's name. He wanted to spare his father further embarrassment. He didn't want him thinking that other people knew how he had won the nomination.

"I feel like such a fraud," Preston said, shaking his head.

"Please, honey, don't say that. You're a brilliant man, with a stel-lar career, and if anybody deserves to sit on the Supreme Court, you do," Ariel said, trying to redeem herself.

"Don't call me *honey*!" he snapped. Preston closed his eyes, as if trying to digest everything that had been said.

Trey, Ariel, and Michele were all quiet. They watched Preston and waited. Michele had been busted big-time and knew that she didn't have a leg to stand on. She wanted to flaunt her affair with Preston in Ariel's face, but at this point, it wouldn't do any good. Preston didn't trust her anymore.

There was no doubt that Ariel's marriage was over. The way Preston glared at her with such hate, she knew that they didn't stand a chance of reconciling. She expected the fallout to be serious, but she was completely disillusioned, thinking that Preston loved her so much, that in time he would forgive her. Obviously, she was wrong. She now understood the reason for the coldness that she had felt earlier; it was like the house was trying to forewarn her.

Trey felt lower than a snake's belly. It was etched in the "Man law" Bible that friends didn't fuck other friends' exes, let alone family dipping into another relative's cookie jar. Trey had pleaded his case, and didn't have anything else to say. He only hoped that the bloodline he and his father shared would take precedence over his ultimate act of betrayal.

Preston opened his eyes and glanced around the room at each and every one of them. "Get the hell out. I want all of you to get the hell out of my house," he said, in a low, hushed tone, almost a whisper.

Though it was her home too, Ariel didn't protest. The least she could do at this point was to give Preston his space. She wearily walked to the front door, with Trey following behind. Michele brought up the rear, as they all filed out of the town house, each feeling as guilty as sin.

The moment Preston heard the front door shut, he dropped his head in his hands and wept like a newborn. His world as he knew it was over, and now he was left with the aftermath.

32

EARLIER IN the evening, Michele had pretended to be drunk; now her sole mission was to actually get smashed. On the way home in a taxi—since her car was still parked at the restaurant—Michele told the cabdriver to stop by the liquor store. To her dismay, it was closed. She thought about going into a bar and lining up a few shots of tequila, but she didn't want to get pissy drunk in public, and then have to do the walk of shame past her doorman. She preferred to drown her pain in private—that way she could drink excessively, and pass out on the sofa without anyone knowing—so she had him take her home instead.

Upstairs in her apartment, Michele went straight into the kitchen, dropped her purse on the counter, and snatched open the refrigerator. It was practically bare, except for a container of Chinese take-out from two nights ago, a half-empty carton of orange juice, and a bottle of Prosecco. She had blown her budget on the designer evening gown for the Congressional Black Caucas affair, as well as on the expensive chemise. She couldn't afford Veuve—her favorite—so the sparkling Italian wine would have to do since that was the only liquor she had in the house. She opened the bottle and tilted it up to her mouth. Michele didn't bother getting a glass, instead guzzling straight from the bottle. She wanted a quick buzz, so that she wouldn't have to feel the sting of Preston's words still ringing in her ears, over and over.

"*Michele, is this true?*" he had screamed at her, once Ariel told him that Michele was in on the entire scheme. She was so stunned by his ranting that she was afraid to speak. Preston's demeanor was normally mild and understanding, but the way he lashed out at her was as if he were a different person. She thought that having sex with him would have softened his disposition with her, but she was dead wrong. Once Preston learned that she had also been lying to him, he really lost his temper. At that moment, all of Michele's conniving plans vanished as if they had never existed. There was nothing that she could say or do to redeem herself, so she just stood against the wall like a deaf mute and listened in horror as Preston learned the ugly truth.

"Maybe once he cools down, I'll say that I was trying to spare him the gory details of what had happened," she said aloud between gulps, still trying to find a way to wiggle back into his bed.

She was three-quarters finished with the sparkling wine when she heard a knock at the door. Michele's heart leaped into her chest. "Preston!" she whispered. Maybe he had had a change of heart, and had come by to commiserate. She put the bottle down, wiped her mouth with the back of her hand, and hurried to the front of the apartment. She pulled open the door without looking out of the peephole. "Pres—" she started to say, but stopped.

"Hello, Michele."

"Laird, what are you doing here? And how did you get past the doorman without him calling up to announce you?"

"I got clout all over this city and know what to say to get into just about anywhere I want," he said, easing past her into the apartment. "Besides, you said to stop by later in the week, so here I am. I bought champagne," he said, as if that was his entry fee into her apartment, and handed her a bottle of Dom Pérignon Rosé.

Michele took the bottle and closed the door. She stood back and watched as Laird strolled into her living room and made himself comfortable on her sofa. He took off his suit jacket and loosened his tie as if he were at home. Michele started to ask him to leave, but after the rejection she had experienced earlier, she wanted to feel desired. And though Laird wasn't the man she craved, he would do for the time being.

She went into the kitchen and came back with two flutes. Michele sat the bottle on the cocktail table, removed the foil and wire, then twisted the cork off. She poured them each a glass, and sat down.

"To special friends," he toasted, and clinked his glass with hers.

Michele nodded and took a sip. The Dom was delicious, much better than the cheap sparkling wine she was drinking before. She downed the first glass and poured herself another. She was still trying to numb her pain, and the expensive champagne slid down her throat with ease. She was on her third glass, while Laird was still on his first. The Dom Pérignon coupled with the Prosecco was giving Michele the desired buzz she sought. She laid her head back on the sofa cushions so that she could enjoy her high.

"Looks like somebody is feeling lovely," Laird commented.

"This champagne is lovely; that's what's lovely," she said, with a crooked grin.

"I'm glad you're enjoying it," he said, moving closer to her. "Now, I'd like to enjoy you." He rubbed his glass across her blouse.

Michele didn't flinch. She felt conflicted. On the one hand, Laird was the last man she wanted to be with, but on the other hand, at least *he* wanted *her*. Now that her hand had been exposed and Preston didn't trust her any longer, she needed another target, and Laird would do just fine. After all, he was a well-known politician with lofty connections. She turned to him, with a sly smile. "I think you'll get a better feel without this," she said, taking the glass out of his hand and setting it on the table.

Laird looked surprised. The other day at the town house, she had seemed anxious to get rid of him. Now she was taking the lead—not that he was complaining. "You're right. I do need both of my hands." He began unbuttoning her blouse, and then unhooked her bra. As soon as the hook popped, her breasts spilled out. "Hmm." He licked his lips. "You got the prettiest tits I ever seen."

She shook her shoulders, causing her breasts to shake slightly. She then rubbed her nipples until they hardened. Michele watched Laird enjoy her little peep show. He seemed to be mesmerized. "Are you just going to look at them, or what?"

"Oh, honey, I'm going to do more than just look at these babies." He pulled her to him so that she was straddling him. He then cupped her right breast and devoured it. He was sucking so hard and fast, that saliva was running down his chin like water, and he nearly choked.

"Slow down, baby, we got all night," she whispered in his ear.

"I can't wait." He panted. "Do you know how long I've wanted to fuck you?" Laird moved her to the side, and began frantically unbuckling his belt and unzipping his pants.

Michele wasn't ready to have sex with him just yet. She'd planned on teasing him for at least another hour, before sucking him off and sending him on his way. She knew that eventually she'd have to sleep with him, but she wanted to prolong the inevitable for as long as possible. She was still holding on to a shred of hope that Preston would forgive her and that they could build a life together, once he divorced Ariel. Michelle was caught up in a dicey game. There was no way that she could get out of fucking Laird tonight. She had led him on too many times; now it was time to pay up. "I hope you're not the kiss-and-tell type. What goes on between us is just between us. Okay?" she said, making sure that he wouldn't go blabbing their business to Preston, or anyone else.

"Whatever you say." He panted. He barely heard a word she said; he was too busy trying to get his pants off and his dick out.

"Now that that's settled, I guess you want some of my good stuff?" Michele stood up and unfastened her pants, letting them fall to the floor. She took off her panties, and started playing with herself. "Is this what you want?"

Laird was drooling like a dog in heat at the sight of her swollen clit. He couldn't take her teasing any longer; he pulled her back on the sofa, and got on top. He wedged himself between her legs, jammed his dick deep within her vagina, and started pumping wildly, without any finesse. Before he could get a good rhythm going, he ejaculated inside of her, and then slumped down on her chest.

Michele had never had a two-minute man, or in this case, a ninety-second man. He came before she could even wrap her legs around his back. Part of her was glad it was over, but part of her wanted an orgasm too. She had gotten herself turned on, only to be turned off. Michele started to say something, but what could she say without hurting his feelings and jeopardizing losing him too, so she just let him lay there on top of her, until he recovered.

"Wow! That was great! Better than I dreamed," Laird exclaimed, after about three minutes of silence.

I'm glad you think so. "Sure was." She faked a smile.

He got up and picked his pants and underwear off the floor and put them back on. "You were definitely worth the wait." He grinned.

And you were a complete disappointment. She was surprised. At the town house, he had talked so much shit, about how good his loving would be, and she had even felt him up then, and knew that he had a good enough tool to work with. The problem wasn't his equipment, but his eagerness. He was so frantic to fuck her, that he came without any consideration for her needs. She sat up. "Who knew you were such a tiger," she said, making growling sounds. She continued to stroke his ego, making sure that he thought he had rocked her world. Michele wanted Laird to think that she was completely satisfied. She had found another pawn and had to make her moves cautiously, with forethought. Michele was tired of pressing her nose against the glass, looking, but unable to touch. She was determined to live among the A-listers, and now Laird was her passport into this exclusive enclave.

"You haven't seen anything yet," he said, straightening his clothes. "Next time, it'll be longer, I promise, but I have to get home before Leona gets suspicious. She didn't have a business dinner tonight, and on those nights when she's at home, she wants me there with her," he explained, and gave her a quick peck on the lips and hurried out the door.

Michele refilled her glass and relaxed back on the sofa cushions. *Looks like I finally found my entry into the A-list,* she thought, totally disregarding the fact that he was a married man. She didn't care about his wife. Leona was old and frumpy and no competition. *Once I get him pussy-whipped, he'll put my name on any invitation list in town. After all, he did say that he could get into just about anywhere he wanted.* With that thought in mind, Michele polished off the champagne and headed to bed. The night had ended better than she could have predicted. She may have lost her chances with Preston, but at least she had another chump on the line, and Laird would do until she found another target.

33

"WHY DID you leave the town house?" Meri asked. "It's your home too."

"Legally, I know it's my house, but it sure didn't feel like home. Even before the confrontation with Preston, I felt a coldness the moment I stepped through the door," she said, still remembering the weird feeling.

"Why do you think that is?"

"Probably because Michele was fucking *my* husband in *my* house. They didn't admit anything, but the way they were all hugged up when they came in the door, I wouldn't be surprised if they were having an affair of their own." Ariel was back in New York having lunch at Meri's penthouse, giving her a recap of the final showdown with Preston.

"I'm sure you're right. The only time I felt an unexplained coldness like that was when my first husband cheated on me. He had the nerve to bring his concubine into our home, and screw her."

"How did you find that out? Did you catch them in the act?"

"You bet your sweet ass I did. I had a feeling that he was sneaking around, so I told him that I was going out of town for the weekend.

I left Friday afternoon and checked into a suite at the Peninsula, had spa treatments, a wonderful dinner, and ordered the most expensive bottle of champagne on the menu, all charged to his credit card. Saturday evening, I went back to our apartment, eased my key in the door, and slipped inside. I could hear voices coming from the kitchen. I knew it wasn't the cook, since I had given her the weekend off. I crept down the hallway, pushed open the door, and there they were, fucking on my imported marble countertop. He had her legs spread high in the air and was thrusting in between them. He was so busy dirty talking that he didn't hear me walk in, so I just stood there until they finished."

"And then what did you do?" Ariel asked. This was the first time she had heard this story.

"I started applauding. I stood there and clapped at his world-class performance. I had to give him praise for the way he was rotating his pelvis. I only wished that he had worked me over like that; most of the time he fucked me missionary style without any enthusiasm." Meri picked up a bread stick and snapped it. "That's what I wanted to do to him, break his dick in half. Instead, I took half his money." She laughed.

"That you did," Ariel said, taking a sip of her Bellini.

"Do you think that Preston made love to Michele in your bed?" Meri asked, getting right to the point.

"Probably so," she said, turning up her nose. The notion of her husband and Michele in their bed made her nauseous.

"You have to face the fact that your precious Preston may have crossed the line with his sexy assistant. You were gone for weeks, and they were in the house alone; now it doesn't take a mathematician to calculate the laws of attraction."

Ariel exhaled loudly. "I've been so preoccupied with Preston's memory loss, that I hadn't even considered the possibility of Michele seducing him. And that's exactly what would have had to happen. I've known Preston for over ten years, and there's one thing I know about him, that he's not an adulterer. If in fact he did cheat, I'll bet my year's salary that Michele initiated it," she said, with certainty.

"And, my dear, you would win that bet. Why do you think Michele came back to the house with Preston? I'm sure it wasn't to do some typing," she said, looking Ariel dead in the eyes.

"Well, it really doesn't matter now. Preston isn't speaking to me."

After he tossed everyone out, Ariel and Trey checked into a hotel—separate rooms, of course. The next day, she called the town house, but he didn't answer. She called him for two days straight, but never got a response to her messages. On day three Ariel took the Acela back to Manhattan. It had been nearly two weeks, and she hadn't heard a word from him.

"He still hasn't returned any of your calls?"

"Not a one," she said sadly.

"What are you going to do? You can't wait in limbo forever. Are you going back to D.C. or staying in New York?"

"For the time being, I'm staying here in the company's corporate apartment, since my condo is still being sublet. I told the managing partner that I'll be working out of the New York office, until further notice."

"What does Trey have to say about all of this? I'm interested to hear his take on a situation that he's partially responsible for," Meri said, sounding more like an overprotective mother than a friend.

"I've only spoken to him once since leaving Washington, and he seems to think that his dad just needs some space. He says that in time, Preston will forgive us. And honest to God, I hope he's right, but I doubt it. I saw the hatred in his eyes when he kicked us out of the house."

"Well, maybe Trey is right. After all, you guys have more than a decade under your belt, and it's hard to throw away that much history with one person," Meri said hopefully, even though she knew it was a long shot.

Ariel was no fool and knew deep down that Preston would never forgive her. She was tried of talking about something that would never happen and changed the subject. "Okay, enough about me and my sad, sad situation; it's bringing me down. Let's talk about something else. Who's your latest *beau de jour*?"

Meri wasn't ready to drop the topic at hand; she still had more questions, but she respected her friend's feelings. "Well, let's see . . . on Monday, there was Tommy, and on Tuesday I had Rory for lunch *and* dinner. Friday, Paul stopped by for a snack, and—"

"Wait a minute, what happened to Wednesday and Thursday?"

"Daarling," Meri sang out as only she could. "Rory was so delicious that I had him for three whole days!" she said, in a fit of laughter.

Ariel joined her, and laughed so hard that she began to cry. The tears were not happy tears, but tears of sadness. She tried to cover up her heartbreak with laughter, and hoped that Meri couldn't see through the charade. "You, my dear friend, are one of a kind."

"As they say, I'm the genuine article. They not only broke the mold when they made me, but smashed it to smithereens," Meri said, tooting her own horn.

For the rest of the afternoon, they ate, drank, and small-talked. Ariel needed an escape from reality, if just for a moment. Being in Meri's penthouse, eating, drinking, and joking about her many conquests was just the break Ariel needed.

"Meri, thanks for a wonderful day. I truly enjoy spending time with you." Ariel gave her friend a warm hug. "I'll call you if I hear from Preston," she said, standing at the door few hours later.

"Okay, daarling. Take care of yourself," Meri said, kissing Ariel on the cheek as she left.

The evening air was cool and crisp as Ariel strolled down Park Avenue. She needed to clear her mind, so she casually walked back to the corporate apartment instead of taking a taxi. The thought of Preston and Michele being lovers kept playing over and over in her head. If that was the case, she really couldn't blame Preston. Obviously, he had turned to Michele when his memory returned. Everything had happened so fast that Ariel didn't even get a chance to ask Preston how he had regained his memory. She was curious; however, at this point, it really didn't matter, the end result was the same. What mattered was that he knew everything, from her going to the Black Door, to her sleeping with his son, to Trey's blackmail scheme with the senator, to their cover-up.

To anyone looking at her life from the outside, it appeared to be charmed. She was a partner at a prestigious law firm, making serious money; married to a Supreme Court justice, and living in a multimillion-dollar town house; but on the inside, her life was diseased. The lies and deceit had eaten away at her core like cancer cells gone awry. Ariel took several deep breaths, hoping that the fresh air would somehow cleanse her conscience—which of course it didn't.

"Good evening, miss. This came for you while you were out," said the doorman once she returned to the building.

Ariel took the package. "Thank you." On the elevator ride up, she looked at the envelope. *It must be something from work.*

Once inside the apartment, she tossed the envelope on the table near the front door. She had had a trying day, and wasn't in the mood to deal with any work-related issues. Though it was still relatively early, she showered, put on her nightgown, and climbed into bed. The stress of the past few weeks had worn her down, and she was exhausted. Before turning off the light, she checked the messages on her voice mail, hoping that Preston would have returned her calls, but the only messages were work-related. Ariel turned off the light and slid beneath the covers.

Sleep escaped her. All she could think about was the way Preston reacted when he learned the truth. He threw her out of their house, like yesterday's trash, and that's exactly what she felt like. Ariel regretted every minute that she had spent with Trey. She had never meant to hurt Preston, and wished that she could take back the past, but what was done was done. She tossed and turned for a good portion of the night and was relieved when the sun rose. Ariel hoped that this new day would bring with it some news from Preston. She couldn't take the silent treatment much longer and was tempted to get on a train back to D.C. and confront her husband. *I'll give him another two days, and if I don't hear from him by then, I'm going home.*

She wearily got out of bed, threw on a robe, and went into the kitchen to make coffee. She ambled back into the living room ten minutes later, with a steaming cup of java, and noticed the envelope sitting on the table near the door. She had totally forgotten about it.

Ariel picked up the envelope, went over to the sofa, and sat down. She opened the seal with her pinky finger, and took out the papers.

HENDRICKS V. VAUGHN-HENDRICKS was the first thing that caught her eye. She had seen these types of documents too many times before, and knew exactly what it was. Ariel was holding divorce papers from her husband. She wasn't surprised in the least. She knew the dissolution of the marriage was a distinct possibility. Even though Preston wanted a divorce, the lawyer in her wanted to plead her case one more time. She reached for the phone to call Preston, but stopped. There was no case to plead. She didn't have a leg to stand on. She had cheated with his son, of all people. Her betrayal was unforgivable. Though she empathized with him, the fallout of her actions was hard to swallow nonetheless.

She felt a lone tear roll down her cheek, and wiped it away with the sleeve of the terry cloth robe. She had entered into matrimony with a lie. However, she had hoped against hope that Preston would have a forgiving heart, but he didn't. Her marriage was over and she had no one to blame but herself—and of course Trey. Ariel knew that this day would eventually come, and now that it was here, she fought back the tears and took the truth like a woman. She had been woman enough to go to the Black Door and fuck around, now she had to accept the consequences of her actions.

Ariel picked up the phone, called her attorney, and told him to proceed with the divorce. She wasn't going to fight Preston. She realized the sooner they dissolved their marriage, the better. She accepted the fact that he would never forgive her, and she wasn't going to ask him to anymore. Her next call was to her Realtor. She told the agent not to renew the tenant's lease. Ariel needed her condo back, since she would once again be single in the city.

34

TREY HAD been back in New York for over a month, and still hadn't heard a word from his father. He had called down to Washington a week after the dreadful altercation, to talk to Preston man-to-man, without an audience, but didn't get a response. He had e-mailed, as well as texted his dad, but still no answer. Trey didn't like the way things were left. His father threw them all out before Trey had had a chance to smooth things over. Preston had become irate, and wouldn't listen to any further explanations after he heard the entire story. Trey had hoped that his dad would have a little compassion once he learned that it was Trey who was instrumental in landing his nomination. However, he couldn't have been more wrong. Trey's only salvation now was the fact that they were related. He prayed that the old adage "blood is thicker than mud" would prove to be true. As an only child, he and his dad had always shared a special bond. Now that bond was in serious jeopardy, and it was entirely his fault. His father wasn't speaking to him, and Trey didn't know what he could do to repair the rift.

He was in the office doing paperwork, and should have been concentrating on tallying up the myriad of invoices stacked in front of

him, but his mind was focused on the scene that had taken place in
D.C. Trey had had the game plan laid out in his head. He and Ariel
were to march straight into Preston's office, and explain, without
any dramatics, how and why their affair had started. They were going to swear there was nothing between them any longer, throw
themselves on his mercy, and beg for forgiveness. However, they had
been blindsided when Preston wasn't in his office, and had walked
into the house hours later with Michele on his arm. Trey took one
look at Michele's body language—the way she was cozied up to
Preston—and knew that she'd been putting the moves on his father.
Michele was a Vixen with a capital *V*, and preyed on men like a carni-
vorous cheetah, chasing down her target and pouncing without a
moment's notice. Trey would bet all the cash in his safe that Michele
had stalked his dad, and waited until the timing was right before
making her move. Based on what Ariel had told him about Michele
threatening to expose the truth, he wouldn't be surprised if she
helped to restore Preston's memory. She was such a social climber,
and who better to climb than a powerful Supreme Court justice. Preston was a part of the world where Michele wanted to be, so she no
doubt put the moves on him. Trey thought about calling to confront
her, but didn't want to be bothered. Besides, what was the use? She
would probably lie anyway. He didn't trust her as far as he could toss
her scheming behind. She hadn't called him, so Trey decided it was
best to leave well enough alone. At least he had the satisfaction of
seeing Preston kick Michele to the curb. Trey thought about calling
his dad again, but decided against it. *When he's ready, I'm sure he'll
make the first move.*

"Knock, knock."

Trey looked up, and standing in his doorway was Lexington,
dressed in jeans and one of those red Gap T-shirts that benefited
AIDS victims in Africa. He hadn't seen or spoken to her in weeks.
"Hey there, what brings you by in broad daylight?"

"Well, it's not like I'm a vampire. I do come out during the day.
Are you busy?" she asked, looking at the mound of invoices on his
desk.

"Yeah, I am, but I can take a break." Trey was glad for the distraction. He was tired of replaying the D.C. scene over and over in his mind.

"I just came by to see how the cleanup went," she said, walking into his office and taking a seat.

"Man, your cousin is the bomb!" he exclaimed. "Not only did he pump out the basement, but he also cleaned up the sewage. You should have seen all of that sludge. It was a smelly mess. And to make sure there wasn't any bacteria lurking behind, his crew acid-washed the entire space from floor to ceiling. It's cleaner now than it was before the flood. Thanks again for the referral."

"No problem, I'm glad everything worked out. Look, I just stopped by to say hi. I'll let you get back to work." Lexi had actually popped into the club to see if Trey was going to make good on their date. He had promised to take her to dinner for hooking him up with her cousin, but he didn't mention their date, and neither did she. She wanted more than just random sex every now and then, and was hoping to turn their sex-buddy relationship into something more. However, she wasn't going to push the issue. "Well, I'll see you around," she said, getting up to leave.

"Wait a minute, didn't I promise you dinner?" he asked, remembering their deal.

Lexi's face lit up. "Yes, you did."

"Well, it's a little early for dinner, how about lunch?"

"Lunch is fine." She beamed. "There's this great sushi bar around the corner. You do like sushi, don't you?"

"I love *sushi*." He winked.

Lexi blushed at the double entendre. "How could I forget?" The last time they were together, he had eaten her out like a seasoned pro.

"Give me twenty minutes. I need to make an important call."

"Okay, I'll meet you there."

Once Lexi was gone, Trey had a change of heart, and decided to call his father again. He dialed the number, and listened as the phone rang and rang. He thought that he was going to get the answering machine again, and was ready to hang up, but his dad finally picked up.

"Hello?"

"Hey, Dad," he said, with hesitation.

"What do you want, Trey?" Preston asked, getting right to the point.

"I was hoping that we could talk. Is this a good time for you?"

"No, it's not. I have to catch a plane," he answered curtly.

"Oh, where are you going?" he asked, in an attempt at small talk.

"Out of town," Preston said vaguely, without giving up any details.

"When are you coming back? Maybe I could come to D.C. for a long weekend."

"I don't know about that. Let's talk when I get back. Look, I have to go now; my car is waiting," Preston said, ending their brief conversation.

Trey hung up, hopeful. At least his father didn't hang up the phone in his ear. This was a good sign. Now he'd just have to wait patiently for their private conversation until his dad came back. Trey gathered the papers on his desk, put them in a neat pile, placed them back in the in-box, and headed out the door.

Sushi Sake was ultrahip with over a hundred varieties of imported sake, and a four-star chef straight from the shores of Shimoda. Lexi was sitting at the sushi bar watching the chef slice, dice, and roll. His moves were precise and entertaining.

"Hey there," Trey said, sitting next to her.

"Hi. I ordered you a saketini. It's really good. Try it," she said, handing Trey the martini glass.

He took a sip. "Hmm, that is good."

"Here's the menu. The sashimi here is also good."

Trey looked over the menu, and ordered for both of them. As they were drinking their sake martinis and waiting for lunch to arrive, Mason walked up with his girlfriend Terra in tow.

"Hey, man." He looked from Trey to Lexi. He was glad to see them together. Trey needed a good woman in his life and Lexi fit the bill. "What's up?" he asked, with a pleasant smile painting his face.

"Nothing much; just having a bite to eat. Why don't you guys join us?" Trey said, extending his hand to the empty bar stools next to them.

"Trey, this is my girl, Terra," Mason said, making introductions since they had never met. "She just flew in from L.A. She was out there working on a film." He beamed proudly.

"Really? That must be exciting," Trey said.

"Yes it is." Terra extended her hand. "So you're Trey." She looked him over. "I've heard so much about you—"

"Come on, girl, let's go to the powder room," Lexi said, cutting her off. She didn't want Terra to slip and tell Trey how Lexi really felt.

Once the women had gone, Mason sat next to Trey. "So, I see things with Lexi have moved outside of the club; that's a good sign. You must be feeling her."

Trey didn't want to admit it, but he was starting to like Lexi. She had proven to be more than a fuck buddy. "You got me, man." He grinned. "She's pretty cool. I haven't had a real relationship in God knows when. I don't count being with Michele a relationship; it was more like being held captive." Trey was a free agent once again. He and Ariel had reconciled the tension between them and were friends. Michele was finally a memory, and he was now free to move on.

"So are you saying that you want to have a relationship with Lexi?" Mason asked, with an eyebrow raised.

"Not just yet, but . . . I'm open to dating." Trey smiled. He felt happy for the first time in a long while. His dad had finally accepted his call. He and Ariel had reconciled, and there was a fine, sexy woman on the horizon who didn't belong to another man. Yes, life was indeed good.

NAPA VALLEY was picturesque. The rolling hills of endless vineyards and renovated, century-old tasting rooms were straight out of a movie scene. Being in Napa was like stepping back in time. The pace was slow and unhurried, with the focus being on creating great vintages. Preston had come to northern California to drink wine, relax in mud baths, eat scrumptious meals, and think. He had to get out of Washington. Ariel, Trey, and Michele had been calling him nonstop. He had called two days after the melee and fired Michele. He had spoken to Trey briefly, but had yet to address Ariel. He had checked with the messenger service, and they confirmed that his wife had received the divorce papers. He thought that he would have heard from her the second she received the papers, but he didn't.

Preston couldn't believe that his marriage was over. More importantly, he had a hard time digesting the fact that Ariel had fucked his son. For the past year, Preston had been living a lie, unbeknownst to him. When he woke up in the hospital, after his ministroke, he had no idea what had happened. The last thing he remembered was talking to Michele and Trey on the phone. They were at the airport on their way to the Cayman Islands for a long weekend. Their trip was spur of the moment, as if Trey was trying to appease Michele for something he had done. Preston remembered asking Trey if he had gotten his hand caught in the cookie jar. Little did he know that Trey had been dipping in his private stash.

When he finally regained consciousness and saw his doctor, he was informed that he had had a ministroke, which short-circuited his short-term memory. The doctor told him not to worry, that his memory would eventually return. He wasn't alarmed. He remembered everyone closest to him, and remembered working with Robert to secure the nomination. Preston was under the impression that he knew the important details of his life. But Ariel, Trey, and Michele were hiding one very important fact, the fact that his fiancée was cheating behind his back. What really unnerved him was that Ariel had the gall to go through with the wedding after she had fucked his son. He could almost understand her going to the Black Door, since he had been putting his career before their relationship. And he could almost understand her attraction to a younger man, but he would never in a trillion years understand how she could have had sex with Trey once she learned his identity. He had known Ariel since she was a law clerk, and thought that he knew her inside and out, but he was wrong. The woman that he fell in love with would never have betrayed him in such a hideous way. Her actions were unforgivable, and he had no other choice but to file for divorce. Preston only wished that he could have also filed suit against his son, but he couldn't divorce Trey; it wasn't that simple. He had given life to the boy—well, he wasn't a boy any longer—and watched him grow into a man. But never in his wildest dreams did he think that his boy, his pride and joy, would betray him.

He swirled the wine in the handsome glass, stuck his nose in, and took a deep whiff. He then held the glass up to the sunlight, checked out the rich ruby color, and the legs slowly trailing down the side of the glass. He took a sip, and savored the fragrant liquor on his palate. This was not his first or second trip to the wine country. He had been there numerous times in the past, and was experienced at wine tasting. He knew exactly what to look for. The vintage Zinfandel was superb. It was rich and buttery, with hints of berries and chocolate, and slid down his throat with ease. Preston was standing on the small balcony of Venge vineyards enjoying the view and the wine, but he knew that he needed to make an important phone call. He took his cell out of his jeans pocket—he had abandoned his suits for more leisurely attire, since coming out west—and dialed the ten-digit number.

"Trey, it's your dad."

"Hey, how are you?" Trey was happy to hear from his father. The last time they talked, Preston had rushed him off the phone. "Are you back from your vacation?"

"No, but I thought we needed to talk."

Trey swallowed hard, trying to brace himself for the tongue-lashing that he knew he deserved. "Dad, before you start, let me say that I'm so sorry for—"

"Stop, Trey. I didn't call to hear your apologies again. I called to ask you how you convinced Senator Oglesby to support my candidacy."

Trey hadn't expected this question, but since everything had been exposed, he figured he might as well tell the entire truth. At this point, he was all out of lies. "When you were in the hospital, before you re-gained consciousness, Ariel called my cell, and left a message that you had had a stroke. Well, Michele and I cut our weekend short, and rushed back to the States. I went to the hospital, but you were still in a coma. That's when Ariel told me that you had come to her apartment with knowledge that I owned the Black Door. All I could think about was you losing the nomination because of me. After going to the hospital to check on you, I went immediately to your town house. I was looking for evidence to link me to the Black Door. The first thing I saw once I entered your office was a crumpled-up piece of paper. I picked it up, and read that the senator had found out that I owned the Black Door. At that point, I put two and two together, and realized that the senator would probably withdraw your name from the candidacy list. I didn't want's you to suffer the consequences of my actions, so I called in a favor." He then told Preston about the senator's wife's involvement with the Black Door. "You won the nomination, married Ariel, and as far as I was concerned, that was the end of the story."

"But you were sadly mistaken. The story, as you are aware, didn't end there." Preston took another sip of his wine, savoring the point.

"Dad, please forgive me. I swear on my life that if I had known who Ariel was that first night at the club, I would have never given her a second look. And as far as going to her apartment, I don't have an excuse . . ." his words trailed off.

Preston could hear the sincerity in his son's voice. Trey was as much to blame as Ariel, but his heart went out to his son. Preston knew that sometimes a man thinks with the head between his legs, and not the head on his shoulders. Obviously, Trey's hormones had gotten the better of him. He was a young man, after all, and guys his age were prone to momentary lapses of judgment. "Son, you get a pass just this one time. Do you hear me? Only one time!" Preston stressed.

"Yes, Dad, I hear you." Trey was elated that his father had forgiven him. Even though Preston didn't exactly say the word *forgiven,* Trey detected that he was off the hook. *So, blood is thicker than water,* he thought, but wouldn't dare utter that phrase. "What are you going to do about Michele?" Trey asked.

"I called her two days after I kicked everyone out of the town house and fired her. I told her that I would be out of town, and to collect her belongings before I come back, leave her key, and vanish. I don't want to ever see her again," Preston said, with disdain.

Trey wanted to ask if they had knocked boots, but since he was treading in deep water, he decided against confronting his father. And even if they had been fucking, Trey couldn't blame his dad. Michele was one hell of a sexy babe, and when she poured on the charm, what man could resist? After all, that was how he had gotten caught in her web. "Do you think Michele is still in D.C. or did she go back to New York?"

"I've read a few blogs on the Internet since I've been in Napa, and also heard from my sources that she's been seen about town with Laird Forester," Preston said matter-of-factly. He wasn't surprised that Michele had latched on to another prominent political figure. It had taken him awhile, but he had finally figured out that she was a social climber, and was using him to gain access to the upper echelon.

"Laird Forester?" Trey asked. He knew that Laird was a bit long in the tooth, and wasn't Michele's type.

"Yes, you heard me right."

"Well, God bless him. Because he's going to need all the prayers in the world to handle Michele. She might look good on the outside, but she's totally corrupt on the inside. The only person she cares about is herself," Trey said, like a man who had been scorned.

"Son, you've said a mouthful. She had me going, but I've regained my senses now, and realize that she was trying to play me for a fool," Preston confessed.

"Can I just say . . . let bygones be bygones. Dad, I love you and will never, ever, betray you again. Please forgive me," Trey said, in earnest.

"Son, remember that women are dispensable, but blood is forever. I forgive you, but make no mistake. I won't be as understanding if there is a next time," he said sternly.

"Trust me, Dad, I've learned my lesson, and there will never be a next time."

"That's good to hear." Preston looked at the prized Zinfandel that he was holding. "Son, I've got a glass of the best wine you've ever tasted waiting on me. I'll call you when I get back to Washington." With that said, Preston closed his cell phone, ending the call. He was glad that he and his son had come to a resolution, even though it had cost him his marriage.

MICHELE HAD gotten fired, but she didn't miss a beat. She should have been depressed, crying her eyes out, but she knew the inevitable was coming. Once Preston learned the truth, it was just a matter of time before she got the boot, and it didn't take long to receive the proverbial pink slip. She got the ax only two days after the confrontation. Preston instructed her to retrieve all her personal belongings from the office while he was out of town, and to drop her key in the mail slot after she left. A part of her was sad that she wouldn't be working for Preston any longer. Their affiliation had started off innocently, even though Ariel had suspected from day one that Michele had ulterior motives. However, initially she hadn't had any.

Michele tried calling Preston on several occasions, but each time she was greeted by either his voice mail or answering machine. She wanted to at least try to mend things between them, and salvage their friendship. However, Preston wouldn't accept her calls. Michele was no fool, and realized that trying to schmooze Preston was no longer an option. She truly admired his accomplishments, but admiration wasn't going to get her where she wanted to be, so she moved on to another more viable opportunity. Presently, Michele didn't have a job, but she wasn't worried about money—Laird provided her with a steady stream of cash.

Ever since that night at her apartment, when Laird loved her and then left, Michele had been working on him, hitting him up for money, and weaseling party invitations out of him. He was an easy target. All he wanted was sex, which she supplied readily. He wasn't interested in her intellect, or the way she dressed. He couldn't care less about appearances. Since they never arrived at the same function at the same time, he wasn't embarrassed by some of her scandalous-looking outfits. Now that she didn't have to impress Preston any longer, Michele had gone back to dressing like a floozy.

Laird's wife, Leona, was out of town on a business trip, and Michele used the opportunity to get into one of the biggest parties of the season. She was meeting Laird at the Four Seasons for a charity benefit, and was ecstatic. Most of Washington's heavy hitters would be there, and the event was sure to garner publicity from *Vanity Fair*, *Capitol File*, and the society pages of the daily newspapers.

Given the chance that she could be photographed, Michele wanted to look her best. She couldn't afford to buy another designer dress, so she decided to wear the Roberto Calvalli gown that she had bought for the Congressional Black Caucus affair. She wasn't concerned about wearing the dress a second time, since she hadn't gotten into that VIP reception, and no one really noticed her. She took a leisurely bath, and afterward hot-curled her hair and expertly applied her makeup. Michele then slipped into the fire-engine red dress. She tried to zip the side zipper, but was having trouble. She inhaled, sucking her stomach in and continued tugging, until the zipper slowly crawled up the side of the dress. She felt like a stuffed pepper, and looked in the mirror to make sure that the dress didn't look as tight as it felt. *I've got to go on a diet.* Michele had been lying around the apartment watching soap operas and snacking on potato chips, doughnuts, and soda since being laid off; now the pounds were starting to show. She sprayed her neck and wrists with perfume, grabbed the invitation, took the car keys off the kitchen counter, and headed out the door.

Michele couldn't have been happier and sang along to every song that played on the radio. Tonight she wouldn't be turned down at the door, as before. She had the prized invitation with *her* name on the envelope, so she didn't need to try and impersonate someone else. Yes, she was finally included amongst the A-listers.

The line of cars waiting for a valet in front of the Four Seasons Hotel was long, but moved swiftly. Michele waited patiently for her turn. She wasn't going to park in the garage and run through the building like she did at the CBC function. No, tonight she was going to arrive in style just like the rest of the important guests.

"Here's your ticket, miss," the attendant said, handing her the valet number.

"Thank you." She smiled and stepped out of her car.

The party was being held in the grand ballroom. She made her way through the lobby, and entered the majestic space. Michele marveled at the sparkling crystal prisms on the overhead chandeliers that cast a warm glow throughout the cavernous room. She suddenly felt tingly from head to toe as she scanned the room looking for famous faces. Bill and Hillary were there; so was Barack and his lovely wife, Michelle. She also spotted several secret service men *and* women, dressed in black-tie, trying not to look conspicuous. Michele wanted to pinch herself. She couldn't believe that she was in the company of such distinguished luminaries. Teetering on four-inch heels, she made her way through the room, trying to find the bar. She was feeling a bit nervous and wanted a drink to calm her nerves.

"Why haven't you returned any of my calls?" Fiona asked Michele, when she saw her approach the bar.

Michele had purposely avoided talking to her friend. Fiona could be a little self-righteous, and Michele didn't want to share her secret affair with Laird and be chastised for sleeping with yet another married man. "I'm sorry," she said, giving Fiona a hug. "I've been busy, that's all."

"Busy running around town with Laird Forester?" Fiona said, raising her eyebrow.

"How did you know?"

"Girl, this town is small and people talk."

"Fiona, it's not what you think. Laird has just been a good friend since Preston fired me."

"Oh, I see." Fiona had heard about Michele's firing from her husband. "Michele, I hate to say this, but you're in too deep. First you go after Preston, now you're hooked up with another woman's husband. I don't want to see you get hurt, but at the rate you're going it's inevitable."

"Chill out, Fiona. I've got everything under control."

As the women were talking, Laird came up and grabbed Michele by the arm. "Come here," he said, ushering her off to the side of the room.

She nearly stumbled. "Wait a minute, Laird, you're going to make me fall! I have on heels, in case you haven't noticed," Michele said, as he pulled her along.

"Leona came back in town today unexpectedly. She opened our bank statement and grilled me about why I've been making so many withdrawals," Laird whispered, once they were away from the crowd.

"What does that have to do with me?" she asked, pulling away from his grip.

"I've been taking money out of our savings account to give to you."

"Why would you take money out of your joint account? That's not too smart," she said flippantly.

"Usually, I'm the one who reviews the statements, so I didn't think it would be a problem. Besides, I'd planned on putting that money back before she ever noticed. Look, Michele, I'm not going to be able to give you any more cash for a while. Leona is starting to ask too many questions, first about my late nights, and now about what I've been doing with our money." He looked down at his shoes, and then back at her. "Listen, I think we need to cool it for the time being."

"Laird, don't be so paranoid. You can still come over during the day, when she's at work," Michele said, refusing to accept no for an answer.

"What are you two doing huddled over in the corner?" Leona asked, walking up to them.

"Uh, uh—" he stammered, "we were just talking about uh—"

Leona gave him a look like, "stop lying," and then said, "Laird, can you go and get me a Diet Coke with lime?" Once her husband was gone, Leona turned on Michele. "I know what you've been up to, girly," she hissed.

"What are you talking about?"

"I'm talking about you sleeping with my husband," she whispered, so she wouldn't be overheard. "I know all about your little affair, so don't try to deny it."

Michele was speechless. She had no idea how Leona knew. She and Laird had been extremely discreet—or so she thought. "What the hell are you talking about?" she asked, playing the dumb role.

"For starters, I know that my husband is a hound dog; therefore, I keep a private investigator on retainer, and when I think Laird is stepping out of line, I have him followed. I haven't shown him the pictures of you two yet, but when I do, trust me, he'll drop you like a bad habit. You see, my dear, I'm the one with the old, old family money, *and* the clout. My husband is accustomed to living a certain lifestyle. A lifestyle he wouldn't give up for you or anybody else."

Michele was shocked. Laird had presented himself as a well-connected heavy hitter, when in actuality, it was his wife who had the power. "Look, Leona, I don't—"

"Save it, girly! I'm not interested in hearing any more lies from you. As a matter of fact, I think that you should leave."

"I'm not going anywhere. I was invited," Michele said defiantly, putting her hands on her hips.

"Either you leave on your own, or I'll have secret service escort you out. I'm on the committee for this affair, and I'll simply tell them that you are an uninvited guest. Am I making myself clear?" she asked, staring Michele down.

Michele couldn't believe the sudden turn of events. Less than an hour ago, she was flying high; now she was crashing like a deflated helium balloon. "Whatever." She rolled her eyes. "I don't want to be at this stuffy party anyway." Michele turned on her heel, and strutted through the crowd and out the door.

By the time Michele got home, she felt sick to her stomach. It was the combination of being thrown out of the party, and the too tight dress pressing against her stomach. She quickly unzipped the gown, and crawled into bed, without taking off her makeup. She was depressed, and just wanted to sleep.

For the next two days, Michele slept on and off. She was in a serious funk. She didn't have a job, very little money in the bank, and no more sugar daddy. And to top it off, she seemed to be coming down with the flu. Michele called her doctor and made an appointment for the following week. She needed to look for another job, and couldn't afford to be laid up for weeks with a cold.

On day three, she mustered the strength to put on clothes, go outside, and pick up a newspaper. She combed through the want ads, and found some good leads, but every person she called said that the job had already been filled. By the end of the week, Michele had exhausted the daily papers and decided to consult an employment agency. The first of the month was quickly approaching and she needed a J-O-B, quick, fast, and in a hurry.

"Your résumé is impeccable, but unfortunately we don't have any positions for you," the headhunter told Michele, and then handed back her résumé.

"I have another copy," she said, returning her résumé back to the woman's desk. "Why don't you keep it on file, in case something comes in?"

"Trust me, nothing will be coming in anytime soon." The woman stood up, indicating the end of the interview. "I hate to rush you off, but I have another meeting," she said coldly.

"Thanks for your time," Michele said, and left.

That scene was repeated over and over during the course of the next few days. The doors to gainful employment were slamming in her face, one after the other. Finally it occurred to Michele that she had been blackballed. At first she thought that Ariel was behind the scheme, but Ariel had left D.C. shortly after the fallout. Then it dawned on her that Leona was the culprit. Leona had told her at the party that she was well connected. Obviously she was using those connections to keep Michele unemployed. She called Laird to enlist his help, but he didn't answer her calls, and asking Preston for her job back wasn't even an option.

Michele had no other recourse but to pack up and move back in with her parents, but before she left Washington, she decided to keep her doctor's appointment. Since it was time for her annual checkup, he not only gave her a flu shot, but a complete examination.

"You can get dressed now, and come into my office when you're done," he instructed her.

"So . . . Doctor, I've been feeling run-down lately. I'm guessing I have this new virus that's been going around. I read that this strain is from China and is hard to kill," she said, taking a seat in front of his desk.

"Yes, there is a new virus going around, but you don't have it," he said.

"Really?" she asked, with a hint of concern. "Well, if I don't have a virus, then what do I have?" she asked, praying that it wasn't anything serious.

"You're pregnant." He smiled.

"Pregnant? Did you say I'm pregnant?"

"Yes. You're about four weeks along."

Michele was dumbfounded, but shouldn't have been since she'd been having unprotected sex. She immediately thought that the baby was Laird's, but remembered that she had also fucked Preston without using a condom. Her mind began to reel. She was carrying a child, and didn't know who the father was. She started to panic, but then a sense of calm came over her. It really didn't matter who turned out to be the father, since they were both powerful men in their own right. Even though Laird's wife held the purse strings, Michele was sure Leona would be more than generous in order to keep the scandal off the front page of the paper. And as far as Preston was concerned, he was the type of man who would accept his responsibility without blinking. Michele had been looking for the ideal person to usher her into the A-list crowd, and who could be more perfect than the baby of a high-profile man?

She sat back, smiled, and rubbed her stomach. She wasn't maternal in the least, but a baby would give her the leverage she had been seeking for so long. Now it was just a matter of waiting another eight months to confirm the DNA!